I0562807

DEATH
TALES OF MIURAG

BY
A.S. ETASKI

Published by Corpus Nexus Press
ISBN: 978-1-949552-29-4

etaski.com
etaski.com/sister-seekers
miurag.etaski.com
www.patreon.com/etaski
www.goodreads.com/etaski
www.bookbub.com/authors/a-s-etaski
www.facebook.com/asetaski
mastodon.online/@etaski

Tales of Miurag - Death, Copyright © 2015, 2016, 2017, 2024, A.S. Etaski
The Deathless Rises, previously published as "Cris-ri-phon" © Etaski, March 2015
Devour the Oracle, previous published as "Ada" © Etaski, October 2015
At the Crossroads, patron request from NotSoWeird, © Etaski, August 2024
The Herald Returns, previously published as "Gavin" © Etaski, June 2017
Harrowed's Breath, previously published as "Deshi" © Etaski, April 2016

Cover Design by Eris Adderly
Book layout by DocKangey

All rights reserved. This book or any portion thereof may not be reproduced or used in any manner
whatsoever without the express written permission of the author except for the use of brief quotations in
a book review.
This book is a work of fiction and intended for adults only. Sexual activities represented in this work are
between adults and are fantasies only. Nothing in this book should be interpreted as the author advocating
any non-consensual activity.

INTRODUCTION

My main published series, *Sister Seekers,* begins underground with *No Demons But Us*, where Dark Elves live and die in darkness. A novice Red Sister, Sirana, leads us through most of the story through her eyes, but many others explore the world of Miurag with their own stories to tell.

Tales of Miurag: Death is a same-world anthology collection of novellas and short stories linked to Surface characters touched by death magic and the Greylands, also called the Nexus.

I wrote the first versions upon request by my patrons in 2015-2017 to help flesh out the world's lore beyond Sirana's POV while I finished the original epic. Now they're being rewritten and released with *Sister Seekers*.

Author's note: these "middle-epic" stories fit best between *Sister Seekers 8* and *Sister Seekers 12*. Reading earlier than Book 8 could be confusing.

First, we see **Cris-ri-phon**, Zauyrian Sorcerer of the Red Desert, and what happens upon his first and only true death.

Next, the origin of **Ada, the Ma'ab witch** who would give birth to Gavin, one of Sirana's strongest allies.

In turn, **Gavin** features in two of his own stories in this anthology.

Lastly, we see the story of **Deshi** mere weeks after the events of *Sister Seekers 10*.

Warning: This book contains mature and disturbing themes and is intended for adults. These stories contain explicit horror, sex, and violence some readers may find disturbing.

A glossary is available at World Anvil where I keep my series lore!

THE DEATHLESS RISES

A TALE OF MIURAG
BY A.S. ETASKI

Chapter 1

Dawn of the Serenity Era, Year Zero S.E.
The Red Desert

THE BLACK DAGGER HAD BEEN BURIED DEEP, BUT THIS WAS PARTLY UNINTENtional. Tombs built in the sand had a way of being lost without living souls staying behind to care for it. The grieving husband had not wished his queen's resting place to be easily found in any case, but now mortals could not access it.

Perfect.

A clandestine visitor stood in pitch blackness, peering around Innathi's tomb with his sight blade-sharp all the same. Though it lacked all color, every line and crease stood out in stark relief.

The late Queen's body had neither been incinerated nor given to the flyers to eat but preserved against rot inside a sealed sarcophagus of stone and metal imbued with magic.

Why? As if she would reclaim a decaying body as he once did?

Such a *Human* choice, grasping a foolish hope, and a further insult on top of *all* else.

Lord Indrath Rousse broke the Zauyrian's seal with ease, shoving the lid off and onto the bedrock without setting his finger upon it. Looking inside, he recoiled at the state of his granddaughter's body.

Horrid. You insisted on living among us for longer than any soul has managed as a Queen's consort and sire, yet you fail to understand the essence of she whom you worshipped.

Soul Drinker was on her belt, the dagger laughably peace-knotted, and one among many pieces of sentiment deemed important enough to be included. Indrath spared a glance for them, found nothing useful, and reclaimed the red rune blade once more.

Do cease whining, Narzeuraek. You and I are far from finished with our little game. He displayed his fangs, standing alone in the crypt. *I won again.*

Suddenly, the earth groaned far beneath him like a titan turning over in his sleep. Indrath froze, a chill spreading between his wings.

Not again, no ...

It stopped.

Drawing carefully on the vanishing air, the Ice Lord opened his aura to search beyond the stone tomb, sensing the Ley of the Desert itself.

The sand.

The infinite grains below the surface had *slowed*, ceasing to shift as they should. And at an alarming pace.

The true fallout of the war had begun.

As I feared.

The Heavens and Hells *would* have stopped the Abyss before V'Gedra fell if the Sovereign had not arrived. *She* had made it all *so* much worse, delaying the Sargt of Flame from reaching beyond his borders in time for help. Now, as usual, she had fled the wreckage she'd caused, leaving him to clean up her mess, and now these borders could not be opened at all.

Adri. I will find you. You owe the world reparation for what you have done.

The Infernal curled his lip, his fist tightening around Soul Drinker's sheath. But for now, Cris-ri-phon would answer for her sins.

As the fool sorcerer should.

EXPLORING PRETERNATURAL CHANGE JUST OUTSIDE THE TOMB WOULD HAVE trapped anyone else, but Lord Indrath used Soul Drinker to cut through the slow-compressing sand. Splitting it like a wound, he crawled up through spasming ground as if escaping the gullet of a monster trying to swallow him.

Reaching the surface, he paused, sensing the direction of a new, *fourth* center in the Red Desert. Without V'Gedra, this site existed in direct conflict with the canyons of Koorul and the Spire.

Paralysis. Indrath frowned, the vague concern of his expression belying his true disturbance. *While even a speck of primal order remains on Miurag, she will draw the warp child.*

Once each of them had settled in, *no* faction could win.

Perhaps I can do something to contain it, to slow its spread, until the Sargt finally decide what to do about it.

Although standing in sunlight was not the Ice Lord's favorite activity, preferring snow-blown, coastal days and frigid nights, the visitor to the Red Desert relaxed when he shed the cloying sand to be enveloped in hot rays and warm air instead. The full-length sarong of brown leather around his waist was a bit heavy for this climate, turning heads as often as his nakedness from the waist up, but temperature fluctuation didn't bother him in either extreme.

Hmm. Where to go next?

"Probably the battlefield," he answered himself. Flying was an option, but he didn't know who else might be here to see him and didn't mind the walk.

Taking his first steps, however, his feet sank into the sand. He frowned, reluctant to acknowledge strange sensations while watching the way the grains scrambled back onto his hem, threatening to puncture the leather, and forcing him to feel their *true* weight.

He snarled. *Uradri. Your recklessness has cost our children their home yet again.*

The Infernal exhaled to catch his breath, drawing in enough ambient power to levitate. He maintained it to stride upon the very surface of the sand without collapsing, not dissimilar to walking on water or fresh, thin ice. The magical rumble grew around him as he headed toward the newborn center. The angle of the sun in the sky suggested that this "aboveground" time may exist months *ago* ... or months *later*. Depending on how long he'd spent in that tomb.

The shock through the Ley Lines had alerted him in Vintern Hjem, and he'd come as soon as he could despite the ongoing disruptions with the other factions. Others might have crawled around to see what they could scavenge before he got there, but the Infernal cared not while two remaining stars shone on his metaphysical map.

Uradri's sorcerer and the soul blade.

Neither could wink out the way Mazdel had. Even amid the chaos, a point of everlasting time lay in the vast dunes far from his home. Ever since he'd given Soul Drinker as a wedding gift, Indrath could choose his moments to check on both in one place.

So I've come again.

The final battlefield lay far out from the Davrin's buried capital city, a crushing bruise left upon the world's veins. Among the dead were Naulor Elves and their Srann, Dwarves and their allies, Davrin and their wild shifter refugees, and many, *so many* Humans — Zauyrian sorcerers, Kurgan tribesman, and a few whose mothers had clearly been raped by the Untamed.

They were all still here, frozen in mid-ripple, just below or above the surface of the sand, a layer of unchanging life forming a giant circle around a foreign, pitted black stone.

Rot had been rejected, either naturally or warped, simply disallowed to set in. Neither harbinger nor psychopomp of death or transience could enter this massive ring. No function of nature could reclaim its resources. The sand truly did not exist to be like rock or water. The five or six would-be looters stubborn enough to force their way into the circle had joined the armies in their ultimate petrification.

Indrath redoubled his effort to step into the circle and continue his walk.

CHAPTER 2
THE PILLAR OF SERENITY

THE WIND HAD NOT BLOWN FOR SOME TIME — HOW LONG, HE COULDN'T KNOW — yet sand bit into his back as if the weight of each grain had multiplied while he clung to the shattered Archway.

Movement which had been chaotic before seemed to slow *beyond* mere stillness. Perhaps his spell had lost momentum and would never finish what he had begun? Or could it be his perception had slowed as he crossed over a coalescing boundary into …

Whatever death waits for me.

The sun didn't move anymore. Night never approached.

This can't be the Greylands, can it?

Change had exploded after the summoning. Dunes swelled, rising above others as molten stone burst upon the surface of the desert, bright red tinged with green, forming a gate.

The Archway.

His muse of inspiration had assured this final effort would stop Queen Yivon for good. Her army and encroaching allies would *never* try this again.

We can defend the Zauyrian Kingdoms, even if we failed to defend your wife and her Queendom from those who had already betrayed her.

Pain lanced through his chest. Not just her.

Our children … Leuren'qo, Matalai, Phaere … Shunraeki.

All gone.

The Sorcerer-General of V'Gedra was alone. He had known many of his own army would die with him, but the lack of confidence in Ishuna's ability to respond to the crisis had placed the responsibility wholly upon his own back. He had made his decision.

Those still believing in his strength as sorcerer and General had come with him here, had died here. Those too afraid of facing more loss had stayed behind. They had fled. Cris-ri-phon still denied that any here *or* there had faced more loss than he.

The General had been wearing enchanted armor which reacted badly to the essence of the rift. Unlike everyone else sinking upon the expanse below, he was in the nude, clinging to a black column of frozen lava; the red sand beneath him had begun consuming his feet, leading up his ankles to his calves. He could not push it away with his hands; he had tried. The Sun remained hot on his head and his back, but he could not tell if his feet were cold. His skin did not burn.

At least the invading Naulor would never leave the Desert to attack again. The Pale Queen would not recover this loss quickly. The spell had *worked*.

Beyond my fiercest prayers.

"The Sun God offers free rein these days," said a familiar voice from above, his shadow offering some respite from the bright glare.

Cris looked up. "You … ?"

"Not a cloud in the sky to cover what you've done," Indrath continued, assuring the spent mage had enough shade to make out his face. "Have we time to talk, Cris-ri-phon?"

He must know we are truly alone.

The Fey Lord's skin appeared like a brown-skinned Wilder Elf suffering the chapped redness of a scalding sun while his back bore the leathery likeness of the wings of the Red Dragon. A majestic crown of ivory horns rose from a proud forehead framed by perfect, Elven ears. His eyes lacked any pupil or iris, his distant gaze crystalline white, somewhere between sun-lit quartz and a glacier.

Rarely did the Ice Lord display this form in Innathi's Queendom.

That meant everyone was dead except for him.

Cris chortled bitterly. "Stay long enough, 'gift giver,' and we shall have an eternity, you and I."

"Ah, but we already do, in part thanks to the same man-eater with an alluring face."

The Zauyrian curled his nostril. "Do *not* talk about my wife that way."

His visitor sneered. "I speak not of Innathi, though the description may fit. I speak of the *other* seducer to whom you pledged yourself."

"When?"

"Prior to wedding the mother of your children."

Before Innathi … ?

Indrath grinned. "You and I met soon after. How I got your invitation to present the ceremony."

Fingers tightened on the black stone. "There was *no one* before her," he said. "You speak lies."

The Infernal tilted his head back and laughed. Cruelty and contempt burned the rims of Cris's round ears before the solidifying air swallowed the sound. A pregnant pause, then the Ice Lord lifted Soul Drinker in its sheath.

Sickening heat rose in his chest.

"How did you find that?!" Cris demanded.

Indrath eyed him as though he was an adorably fussy child. "One must be on familiar terms with bodiless hunger before it can be given form. I was its midwife, and I *always* find my children. Something you worked for but never perfected."

"Put it back," the sorcerer croaked, testing his legs. Still trapped. "You *gifted* it to me, and I gave it to her for all time!"

"I'm afraid 'all time' has come." Indrath sighed with a tight smirk. "I would have burned her body properly had there been enough air in that pit you created for her. Alas, I had to leave her as *you* left her. Quite distasteful."

"Less so than looting her grave, *Lord*."

The winged Elf tilted his head curiously then lowered himself to one knee, both to speak quietly and to put the sun back into his eyes. "Are you *certain* your Queen did not lose control handling the dagger? I *did* warn you."

"She was the wielder for *centuries*." Cris-ri-phon just refrained from rolling his eyes. "Her will was stronger than mine!"

"Mm-hm. Yet I've heard *many* stories of parents not acting themselves while holding a too-familiar weapon above their children. Such regret *could* be enough to give up everything. Even a Queendom."

Cris growled and struck out with his fist; he missed Indrath as the sand held him fast. "I don't ... *believe* you."

The Ice Lord chuckled, caressing the red runes on the sheath as he stood up straight. This time, he did not share his shadow against the sun as he mused, "A pity Innathi never used it on you. Although she might have destroyed a great deal in the process, she *could* have undone you before you fully realized this curse of yours. Now ..." A subtle growl entered the Lord's ethereal, smooth tone. "*You* shall finally learn what your hubris has bought you, and *I* shall be left to mitigate the damage left behind. As always."

An incomprehensible ring of truth, like nothing he had ever heard from this ruler before. It left Cris-ri-phon cold. He kept his eyes closed against the glare but sensed Indrath peering at him. Trying to probe his mind; he could feel it. He hated it, he always had but had become much better defending against it.

"Do you truly not remember her?" the Fey Lord crooned.

He heard the smile in that voice, imagined the tilt of his head.

"I saw you lying beneath her in this very Desert. Broken, old, and filled with regret. She fled when I discovered her but, by then, she had her hooks so deep, you couldn't know what she'd changed. You were too late to save your soul, Second Son of Begir-al-thon. Long before you married your first love."

Stop.

Cris's personal wall held; his memories were not breached. "I *do not* know of what you speak."

The Lord lifted the torment of his mental needle. "Hm. I can see why you'd deny it. So few souls seek to remake their essence in this world. Do you know why?"

Panicked eyes darted behind his eyelids as Indrath continued.

"Not only because the process is difficult to begin with, but because it is far too *easy* to lose bonds to the natural pathways and become lost. To become *Cursed*."

Cris cracked an eye as an elegant, clawed hand gestured to the sinking igneous column to which he clung.

"Even before this, sorcerer, *you* could never follow your Deathwalker tutors to the Greylands, though you were born to. You've lost your way. Have you realized that yet?"

"You want another deal," Cris-ri-phon said.

Indrath chuckled again, levitating above the creeping pull of the sand and brushing the grains from his sarong. "No deal we could make can free you from your fate. Why I cannot kill you, or I would have already." A shrug of naked shoulders. "At best, I can help you die."

The man's face twisted in confusion. "You said you can't kill me."

"But I can aid a transition. These are two very different things, Sorcerer-General." Fangs flashed. "Or have you forgotten your first lessons among your precious Deathwalkers?"

A reflexive shake of his head. "No more deals. I will remain here where my Queen lies."

The Ice Lord shrugged, offering him shade once again, letting him see the diabolical smile. "As you wish."

No further words, yet the Lord did not leave.

Cris clenched a trembling fist against the stone. "What do you wait for?"

"For either the Sargt or another fragment of the Broken One to come deal with you."

Broken ... ?

The fading man shook his head the thought from his mind, repeating aloud, "Sargt. I know that word, I think."

Indrath's smile turned malevolent. "Of course you do. Part of Ishuna's ramblings recently, wasn't it?"

Cris swallowed, his stomach sinking faster than the rest of him. "Dragons …"

"*The* Dragon, rather, who'll not be pleased with your threat to his Desert. You've lost all control. Anything you might have hoped for in staying is beyond you reach, and what lies within your reach is worse than the Hells."

Cris ground his teeth. Within the Circle of Serenity, a molar cracked, splitting in two and bringing tears to his eyes. He tasted no blood. "Y-you try to frighten me into another deal."

The Infernal huffed. "That you are *not* afraid proves my point. You haven't the barest comprehension what you set in motion. Either you take *my* way out, Cris-ri-phon, or you become unknowable. If the latter, you shall meet — briefly — the guardians who *flay* the unknowable." A smirk. "I see it much like your varied Human tribes occupying the same territory, except these creatures *know* you are not one of them."

"So … they will kill me where you cannot."

Again, that *laugh.*

"Worse," he said. "Much worse. Unlike Innathi, they won't pretend so they can suck down your unearned magic to enhance their own. Nor will they let you convince yourself you have the wisdom to wield that power in their realm. Unmaking you will probably kill one of them or injure many more. The survivors will use your remains as a cautionary tale, and I do *not* mean V'Gedra. The city is gone, already to be forgotten, along with all your sacrifices for the harm you've done. All you must do is wait here."

The Ice Lord may as well have pierced his heart with that black dagger, though it remained in its sheath. Gripping the stone, Cris-ri-phon tried to wrench himself out of the sands; he bellowed agony as one of his ankles broke.

Indrath chuckled softly.

"Wh-what is your 'way out'?" he asked quietly, hearing his own weakness in even *asking.*

The Ice Lord sighed softly, turning his head to peer at the horizon as if watching for something. The concern seemed unnaturally genuine the moment before he turned back.

"I will make a path for you to the Greylands," he offered. "I can do this once, but one time only. I will send agents capable of helping you keep your Vis strong until you find your direction. Attempt to meet your sun god if you dare, or embrace another way, I care not. Either way, you are out of reach of those bound to this world."

"A-and what do you get out of it?"

"What is in my best interests."

"And those are?"

"Not your concern."

"I could make it so. As part of the deal, you tell me your 'best interest' before you open that path."

"*Hmph.*" Indrath crossed his arms, pretending to consider.

During that pause, the ground vibrated, a rumble echoing in the earth, reaching depths beyond comprehension. The Infernal's wings might have quivered, or it might have been a trick of the ever-stranger light around him.

"If that is all," said his visitor, "have we a deal?"

Cris-ri-phon tried to lift his hand from the shattered archway. He could not.

"You haven't much time, General," Indrath pushed. "Shall I help you die?"

"Yes," Cris-ri-phon said, voice straining now. "A deal. Tell me … what you get out of it."

The briefest exhale, "*Yes.*"

"Tell me … what *you* get out of it, Indrath."

"What I get …" The Infernal drew Soul Drinker, his aura intensifying as he brandished it above his head. Two runes lit up, glacial eyes shifting to match.

Cris panicked. "No, wait — !"

"Is you and this column as *separate* beings!"

Darkness rushed in behind his eyes.

CHAPTER 3

THE GREYLANDS

ALL AROUND HIM FELL QUIET, YET UNFETTERED RAGE LEFT HIM SPINNING.

Stick-faced, goat-fucking dandruff on a camel's ball sack! May his asshole become his ears and shit on his shoulders!

Indrath *killed* him, using his beloved wife's dagger to do it! Such *agony* when the material had been undone, dragging him from one plane and partway into another. Escape from the hungry maw of the Elsewhere had not been easy, but Indrath had somehow snatched him back and catapulted the human soul *out*.

Far out.

Tossed into the ethers without the ease or guide of ritual, the Zauyrian's essence broke through barrier after barrier by force. He should have been scoured into nothingness but landed hard against a silent, barren ground even *his* grief couldn't shake.

He recovered his name as soon as he could and held it close.

Cris-ri-phon, son of Begir-al-phon.

A few moments more, he heard the last voice before his death.

Watch for my agents, the devil had said, gripping the man bare-handed by his parched throat, sinking in claws. *They shall seek you, but you must come together quickly. Use your pain and anger as focus. Avoid anything which looks like black glass. Keep away from crevasses and dark shadows into which you cannot peer.*

We will find you.

Cris lay on his back in grey dust and huffed, his breath chilling the moment it escaped his lips. *You enjoyed that, didn't you? You bastard. Use my pain and anger, huh? Those two are all I've known ...*

An unmoving, unforgiving sun no longer shone above him, no stars or moons, no celestial bodies at all. Puffs and swells of clouds drifted in his view, charcoal-dark to pale white. The ground beneath him was all manner of ash and hard mineral and speckles of flint.

Sitting upright, he surveyed a flat valley with sharp, rising rocks running parallel on either side. They held numerous dark crevasses framed by glinting, polished stone.

Avoid anything which looks like black glass ...

Only two directions allowed him to avoid it — forward and back toward identical horizons — and he would be fully exposed without cover.

We will find you.

Would they? What then?

What direction?

Tilting as dizziness touched him, Cris-ri-phon recognized that he possessed hands as he raised them before him. His palms were dry despite the rush of primal emotions which filled him. Bare feet, legs, arms, back and front, he even had his cock and balls and the familiar, dark patches of hair on his body. He could run his fingers through a length of black hair which fell into his eyes with no tie to hold it back. His skin color had not changed but, in this diffused grey light, it seemed all his veins were drained of blood, a sickly pallor reminding him of their Court Deathwalkers.

Yet I am not a corpse. What am I?

Cris peered closer.

... There.

Individual threads of multicolored light, the essence of spirit. It raced around and through him, hastily crafting a fabric to contain his form and hold him together. Vis and Vitas.

I am an eidolon.

As his tutor Houda once described in his boyhood lessons about the

Grey. His appearance was a close match to his memory, but his heart and lungs held an immediate strangeness in this familiar body. The former thudded within his chest yet it gave him no living warmth. Meanwhile, he drew on his lungs as a matter of habit, but he did not smell scents which should be there, nor did he really *feel* air rushing in and out as it should.

The two would not combine — his heart and his blood married to his lungs — to offer that unique state of *life* to which he'd been so accustomed.

I am an eidolon …

His magic, however, remained part of him.

Vitas. The raw motion of life. He could draw upon this like a Ley Line for a spell and focus it on the tips of his fingers. He did this without effort, as the sorcerer had for centuries upon his birth world, and considered a small test he might conduct but decided against it.

Do not draw attention too soon or waste the strength I might need later.

Cris scanned the valley for Indrath's agents. They would be colorful against this grey backdrop, and he should determine ally from enemy fairly easily. He wanted to *walk* in some direction, to *act* upon his situation, but the same as his homeland the Desert, aimless wandering could be deadly here, especially when others sought him out, and the Ice Lord had never said to seek in return.

Watch for them after coming together quickly.

He had done this. The Zauyrian had lived far too long — on his own and with his Queen — to make the same predictable mistakes as a man a fraction his age.

Cris-ri-phon stayed exposed in the valley where he'd coalesced. He sat cross-legged, his back straight and wrists resting on his knees, his hands relaxed as he focused on the Vis flowing through him. He might have focused on his breath as well but … that wasn't quite the same.

Hold together. Stay away from those dark places and that dark stone.

Indrath manipulated his bargains to hide his motives, Cris-ri-phon knew, but the horned Elf never outright lied in his instructions or warnings. Once a deal was made, his next words would be guidance for fulfilling a bargain; to stray from them was a common Human error.

A demon, in contrast, would likely set him up for failure despite any agreement; it was its nature. Indrath could not do the same; that was what separated him from his eternal adversaries.

Man-eater ... The other seducer you've pledged yourself to.

Cris shook his head.

Do you truly not remember her ... ?

Of course, he remembered Innathi.

His powerful, beautiful wife might overcome a challenge from the Abyss, finding the loophole where the rewards for success were three-fold above what had been promised. Cris-ri-phon admired her and her unblinking acceptance of this side of the world. Musanlo and the Grey Maiden both had always demanded a much more rigid service from Humans.

That was why she was the ruler and I was her Consort and General.

This was what made them so strong together, as long as they lived to serve the sun-drenched land and the God who had wanted them to have children together. Ishuna had never been comfortable with it, but she had accepted it.

It was Musanlo's Calling, his proof that their two peoples could become one. *It had to be.*

Cris-ri-phon opened his eyes, the multicolored threads shining a little brighter in his introspection. Far in his periphery, something impossibly black moved outside of a deep crevasse to his right. He jerked his head to look.

The shadow formed itself tighter, stepping out of the crevasse and entering the valley. Glowing, ice-blue eyes appeared with sharp, illuminated teeth as dotted patterns like constellations covered a body too long and thin to be man or woman. A pale, expressionless mask and a bright metal dagger glowed, attached to its impossibly thin waist.

Shaegoth.

Only a few times had any Deathwalker described seeing one. The last had been Oskar not long before V'Gedra fell. Cris had never seen one, but he recognized it here.

In its home.

By a knotted sidewinder ...

Not what he had hoped would find him first in the Nexus. Whatever

20

the shadow-born intended by coming here, it was most certainly *not* a known guide for any eidolon in the Greylands.

"Go away," he whispered, standing up, glad no shadows existed too close out of which the masked creature could spring.

Focusing on his Vitas, he created a brighter glow, widening the shadow-free area around him. The Shaegoth stopped its approach and watched. It did not get nearer but turned to look behind into the crevasse as if it considered returning to it. Indrath's advice paying off.

Now if only his agents would find me as he promised.

Cris was not sure how long he could hold it off, or how many more might join the first.

The Shaegoth held unnaturally still in the valley, and Cris kept his Vitas flowing until his penis swelled, along with the urge to pull on it. Beyond his youth, after meeting Innathi, he had rarely indulged alone, and it had always been worth that extra discipline. With her, the Zauyrian sorcerer had perfected a transcendent climax that not only brought them children more often than any had presumed possible, but the experience could not be matched with any common humper, male or female.

I didn't want anyone else. They invariably took more than they could give. They were not worthy.

Cris caressed himself, aiding a common focus of life magic as he faced off with the Shaegoth. The keen edge of loss entwined with warm memories. *I will always miss her.*

The shadow assassin tilted its head suddenly and pointed a black, knife-like finger high in his direction. The Zauyrian stared, eventually deducing that the Shaegoth pointed to the overcast sky behind him.

Such a simple trick.

I won't fall for it.

Then he heard the droning buzz.

Coming closer.

CHAPTER 4

Flanked.

Eyes locked on the Shaegoth, Cris drew power down to his right fist, preparing a concussive blast to release at the right moment. Flying things didn't have much room to react once within a certain distance to the ground. He waited.

The Shaegoth moved, circling around his ring of light, giving it a wide berth. It had broken the flank. Perhaps it wasn't here to assassinate him?

Cris took the risk, turning to keep the shadow in view while gauging incoming forms in his periphery. *Six to eight giant insects.* He glanced up for one good look as the Shaegoth stayed in the corner of his eye.

Seven in loose formation, black and white, fitting the environment, with a touch of red on the chitinous armor. Venomous, deadly pinchers and big, black eyes clearly drawn to his light.

Bane Wasps.

No riders, but he was still in trouble.

Where are your agents, goat-fucker?

He could not wait long before spinning to launch his blast from his fist, his arm extended straight at the Bane Wasp in front. The power was white-hot, shooting like a star across the grey sky, blasting into the lead insect and severing a wing. It faltered, fell with a warped, vibrating call he

22

had never known any insect to make.

The others scattered in six directions.

Thank God —

Sudden waves of exhaustion overtook him, intense dread rippling in just behind. One magical attack, and he felt it might take him a day to recover …

Shit. Cris-ri-phon sought the Shaegoth but couldn't find it. *Gone.*

He needed the light to keep such things at bay, but what if it drew more Bane Wasps or drained him further? Perhaps the display had dissuaded the others but the sucking fatigue in his veins worried him that the next display would be limited. *Unconvincing.*

The drone arose too soon and from a different direction. He swirled around, six insects appeared in loose formation from much higher up. Probably the same ones, diving down.

Cris drew on his Vitas, his vision dimming as he let loose with another blast to the one in front as they came at him. This time they split into packs of three, and he missed entirely while they flanked him. If he ran, he may stumble right into the black glass. If he stayed, he would be ripped apart and consumed by the wasps.

Troll offal …

The Zauyrian doubted he *could* run now. The second strike hadn't been as powerful as the first, and he had not recovered enough even for a dribbling third.

"There you are!"

Wha — ? He twisted to look upward as a husky, braying voice barreled down upon him.

"Drop and roll, pisshead!"

The soldier in him dropped and rolled, landing on his back and out of the path of imminent impact. A pair of blood-red, feathered wings flashed above him as a second voice shrieked in battle lust.

"Yeeeeeaaaah!"

Two brilliant bodies smacked hard against the exoskeleton of their target, cracking and wrenching off limbs and wings before moving to the next. Cris-ri-phon rolled as a wasp leg landed beside him, leaking something putrid.

About time.

Golden fur with dark spots bristled as the first agent leaped from one Wasp to the back of the next without touching the ground. She barked and laughed at once, her joy unhinged while battering the antennae and eyes of the next with the crackling wings of the first.

Cris cringed, seeking out Indrath's second agent.

She was hairless and mostly naked, her pale blue skin covered with only enough armor to make him imagine her breasts and crotch. Her feet were that of a vulture, crimson red like her wings and hair, with black talons tearing into the massive thorax of the third Wasp in the pack, just evading hook arms and pinches in a midair twist. Looping up and banking into a dive, she drove her shimmering spear through one glossy eye. Lightning zapped out of the bug's back orifice.

What … ?

"Oi, sweets! Catch me!"

The harpy yanked back her spear and darted away, snatching the she-beast from her joyous fall.

Impossible.

The flyer did not appear strong enough to lift the muscular warrior, much less carry her to the next trio of Bane Wasps, yet he witnessed it.

"Wooo, yesss!"

Against these brutal acrobatics, the Infernal fighters turned all six Bane Wasps into broken, leaking shells. Heads, wings, and insect parts plopped onto the ground as Cris scrambled to his feet, craning his neck to watch another flawless catch. Gliding down, they landed nearby without injury.

What … are they?

The inhuman females shook off the battle with an ecstatic shudder and moved to stand on either side of him.

He backed up to avoid being flanked, holding out his hand. "Stop."

The bristling brute snorted out of a muzzle that Cris couldn't decide was canine or feline. Small brown eyes stared with a feral glint. "We're here to *guard* you, ground nut," she snarled.

"The Lord of Winter Home sent us," interjected the white-horned harpy. Her voice was smooth, matching the pleasured, attractive smile on red-violet lips. "You *are* Cris-ri-phon the Zauyrian, right?"

He swallowed, noting how her eyes were blank, like Indrath. "I am. And your name?"

"Jessel." The vibrant spear warrior waved her arm gracefully to her spotted-fur companion. "This is Ranzi."

The beast-woman was sniffing him. "*Pff.* He smells like a servant."

"Most Humans are," Jessel replied coolly.

"*You* talk?" Ranzi jested with a fiercely playful glint in her eye. "I watch you kiss his hem on all fours while the corkscrew of his choice drills your shitter."

"And that is *my* choice," said the voluptuous, winged woman, folding arms beneath chain-mailed breasts and thrusting out one hip adorned by a thick metal ring holding her loincloth in place. "Plenty of Furies are free. I have vowed to be with my Master."

"Yeah, but *his* servants can't protect *other* servants very well without someone like me, can they?"

Cris held his tongue as they bantered over him, reluctant to let his eyes drift over the lovely, winged creature lest he ignore the one with jaws to crush bones.

Furies.

Where had he heard that word?

"Battle's over. Turn around, Jessel."

He jolted as Ranzi crowded past him.

"Drop down, knees wide."

The Fury lifted her eyes skyward in a dramatic sigh yet hardly resisted as she turned her back to them and lowered herself to her knees, laying her spear in the grey dust. The dominant female chuckled, glancing at him to check his position. Cris-ri-phon didn't move, despite his nose filling with her musk.

The hairy giantess stood taller than him, was likely stronger, with a short, bristly tail. She wore no clothing at all, and one set of large, dun-colored, dark-nipple breasts sat exactly where he expected them to. Two smaller sets below the first proved her capable of feeding a litter of young if she wished.

Ranzi stroked herself as Cris had seen women do before, as Innathi had done, the pads of her fingers moving down vertically over her mound, around in circles and back up.

He stared, mouth falling slack.

The spotted female had the largest, longest clitoris he had ever seen. He'd mistaken it for a penis at first but confirmed she had no testes at all. An enormous, dark-skinned clit swelled into a bobbing erection while her hood stretched back to show him exactly where her true sex drooled, making her thighs glisten.

Pungent. Cannot imagine the world upon where Indrath had found this animal.

"Jealous, thrall?" she said.

"If she is a Fury," Cris asked, "what are you?"

"I'm a Hiyena." Ranzi chortled, staring with bottomless eyes as he didn't react, then licked her muzzle, turning toward the Fury peering demurely over her shoulder. "C'mon, little pie. Convince me."

Dark red hair sliding off her bare, pale shoulders, Jessel reached to pull the silky loincloth aside, lifting her thin, blue tail up and arching the barbed end above her back. Where he'd expected — *anticipated* — seeing soft flesh and folds were instead covered by metal links, form-fitting and obscuring her secrets.

"Unlock me, Ranzi, please," the fury murmured, waving her hips. "You have the key. Master gave it to you to keep us all strong."

Cris raised an eyebrow. ★ ... All?★

Ranzi accepted the invitation at once, kneeling behind the fury and pressing her thumb against a smooth ruby resting at the top of Jessel's buttocks. Somehow, this unlocked the chastity belt, allowing her to lift the small swath of chainmail like a curtain from the submissive female's sex. Red-feathered wings fluffed and ruffled as Jessel sighed in anticipation.

"Like whatcha see, sorcerer?" Ranzi invited, rubbing the hard nub of her long clit along the damp slit.

The Fury's crotch, from red-haired mound to tight asshole, was a flushed, reddish-purple, a shade reminding him of his Davrin queen. His view was quickly blocked as the golden-furred female pressed her hips up against the flyer's backside. Barely a second of flexing muscle as she penetrated, and the Fury tensed, tail lashing as a squeal of delight escaped her. Ranzi slapped her ass cheek hard, making her do it again.

"*Ah!*" Jessel gasped before growling, "*Yes!*"

"That's it, *squeeze*," the growling creature commanded, gripping her bird-footed plaything, rutting roughly. It only took moments for him to realize the orifice Jessel had yielded was her asshole.

Cris-ri-phon glanced around them at the Bane Wasp corpses, frowning. Why were they doing this, here and now, if not for shameless exhibition in front of him? Then he sniffed the air, ever aware of the only scent present since he'd arrived.

Earthy, gagging; the scent of aggression and lust, like a breeding Desert stallion preparing to do battle with another over the mares.

Why did he *smell* this?

His cock didn't care, it had already responded regardless of the reason. Like Ranzi, he wore no clothes, and his erection stood up firm, heavy, and aching, especially when the Fury cooed, reaching between her thighs to finger her own clitoris as the she-beast humped her, quick and hard. She looked back over her shoulder, folding down a wing to see him.

"L-let me … pleasure you, too, sorcerer," she whispered, opening full, deeply colorful lips, flicking her pink tongue his way to make certain he understood her.

She had fangs like her Master. His cock pulsed in answer at the same time his mind rebelled, as Indrath's promise sounded in his memory.

I will send agents capable of helping you keep your Vis strong until you find your direction.

No, not like that.

Not with them.

He hadn't been with anyone since Innathi's death, and Ranzi had already teased the Fury about being a regular receptacle for guests at Indrath's whim.

The Hiyena woman growled in pleasure, yipping, then *howling* as she finished with three hard thrusts before withdrawing her massive clit. The Fury groaned in disappointment, a thick and gooey lubricant stretching between the two women in a clear thread from the black tip to the wet, winking hole just beneath the fury's arched tail.

"Ranzi, don't *stop!*" pleaded the Fury as Ranzi stood up.

Her warrior companion ignored her, grinning at Cris-ri-phon with wet protrusion dangling. "There, she's just warmed up. Well-greased, too. Should be able to dive right in. Go on, sorcerer."

Cris stared coldly in spite of the roaring urge to do just that. "Why would I want slippery seconds after a crude barker like you?"

Laying back her fuzzy, round ears, Ranzi brayed that horrid laugh again, shrill, eerie, and dangerous. "Wallow in her cooch, then. *I* don't care." Eyes scraped him up and down. "Didn't think a Sovereign's slave would be picky, though."

He snarled. "I'm not *anyone's* slave."

The looming Hiyena took a step closer, her wet clit nearly brushing against his cock; it took all his self-control not to step back as she sniffed him again.

"You have no idea. Gotcha." She puffed air into his face, and he felt the movement of his hair. "Let's try this. You're not *alive* anymore, boy. We're in the Greylands."

"I *know* that," he bit back.

"Then know *none* of us make magic just from *breathing* like you do back home. How tired you are after, what, two blasts and one downed bug?"

Cris scowled, schooled enough to follow where she led. "You are suggesting a mere rut will rejuvenate me."

"You should know. You've been a toy before."

He tightened his fist. "We're in the land of the dead."

Ranzi snickered. "So? They breed here, too, you know. Lay eggs. Squeeze out a litter. All of it."

Cris shook his head. "I use *life* magic."

"Yet *death* magic works just fine back home," the she-beast said with a shrug, rough, tan palms turned open. "Why not swap it around here?"

The sorcerer shook his head. "You are oddly knowledgeable for a hairy beast."

She snapped at him, clicking her teeth right in front of his nose. He didn't flinch.

"And you aren't hairy *enough*," she rumbled. "Unlike you, this isn't my first time running errands in the Nexus, twit. You want help or not? That was the deal you made with Lord Rousse, right?" She barked in humor. "We passed three Malok bands on our way here. We are supposed to make sure you get moving, but you ain't making it if you can't pull your weight. You get pouched by a soul trap, we can't help you. You can enjoy your time as a jewel in some Greylord's crown until you turn to dust."

"So this is it?" Cris replied. "I must fuck Indrath's sex slave to recharge my Vitas in the Greylands."

"That's it, yep!"

"You could be lying for your own amusement."

"She speaks truth, my lord," the Fury said softly, giving her hips a shake and drawing their attention despite themselves. "Mate me however you want, really. Ranzi thought you might not like my teeth first thing, and my Master thought you wouldn't risk getting me with child, but any hole is yours." She reached with one clawed hand to spread her buttocks wider, again displaying how flushed and wet she was. "It's not your first time, is it?"

"Of course not," the Zauyrian bit out, insulted and aroused and confused.

The Hiyena laughed at his resistance.

"Why here out in the open?" he asked, delaying.

Ranzi shrugged. "Minimal pneuma flint and shadows. Bane Wasp battle emissions stink to other scavengers, keeps 'em away for a while. We're safer here than twenty paces from here. Against your instincts, Human, taking cover won't help. Come on. Jessel's knees will wear out waiting for you."

The Fury giggled and arched her back, moving her wings and arms in a languid stretch before she resettled into position. "Fuck me, my lord. I like your size, I'll be nice and tight. Pound hard as you like, I'll love it. Leave me gaping after, your spunk oozing down my legs."

Her voice, hypnotic and seductive, called forth images that made him shiver.

Yet … Was *this* to be his first time after his wife's death?

Mounting a performance addict using a musky beast's cunt drool to ease the passage.

Ranzi stepped on heavy feet to his side, leaning her muzzle to his ear. "Listen, rube, there was a yes involved in your deal, wasn't there? You wanted something bad enough to say it. There's a lot worse trades out there than fucking Jessel."

Cris looked between them, speaking slowly. "I will regain my magic? You both swear this is part of the deal."

The two females nodded, and Ranzi spoke. "Yes, part of the deal. As you use light and magic and drain out, you'll have to fuck again."

"For how long? How far can I go in between?"

"Pointless." Ranzi grinned. "You won't be able to tell. All you need to know is to 'live' here, we have to fuck. We fight Bane Wasps or Malok or worse? We keep our skin and then fuck again. *You* keep us charged, *we* keep you charged. Understand?"

Cris expelled a breath, but it didn't ruffle Ranzi's long, blonde-streaked hair as her breath had done his. *A deal within a deal … Why am I not surprised?*

Indrath had said he did not care about Cris's direction, only that he did not stay in that circle. Refusing these agents wouldn't hurt the Ice Lord. Cris-ri-phon the Zauyrian would be the one to disappear eventually, wouldn't he?

Die a true death in the Greylands, ceasing to remember anything about myself.

To become empty. Perhaps simply ceasing to *be* before discovering what these Infernals were talking about.

Man-eater. Sovereign's slave.

What did this mean? If it was real, who had bested Indrath such that he would offer his sex slaves to a failed Queen's General instead of a deal of eternal servitude?

He said he would have killed me already, if he could.

"Very well," Cris-ri-phon croaked, taking his stiff cock in his right hand. "Let's do this."

For Innathi. She would do the same.

Chapter 5

Cris-ri-phon knelt behind Jessel and took hold of her hips. Her tail wrapped lightly around his torso in welcome, her heat somehow seeping through into his hands.

"You're not alive anymore, boy ..."

The Fury's skin was smooth like his Queen's and he could make out her personal perfume as well.

How was this possible?

"You're thinking too much," Ranzi chuckled.

He was. And Jessel was *very* excited, trembling, pushing back gently against him. "Please, lord ..."

He aimed the blunt head of his erection, nudging it up against her slick netherhole. She squeezed, giving it a kiss before relaxing, yielding ...

Waiting.

Warmed up, indeed.

The Zauyrian's cock sank into the Fury's backside almost immediately; her orifice gulping him down and gripping him snugly. Vivid, welcome heat surrounded his cock, and he only needed one explosively pleasurable stroke to understand what these two were talking about.

As if a blacksmith stoked a dying ember, him, into a blaze hot enough to shape any metal into a weapon.

Pure Vitas.

"God … !" he gasped.

Jessel's wings stretched out before him and she mewled in encouragement he thrust harder, pounding sooner and with more force than he had ever performed on his wife without her command.

"That's it!" Ranzi cheered. "Make her feel it!"

His thighs slapped against the Fury' buttocks and his fingers reached to stroke her feathers before he gripped the base of her wing by her shoulder blade for better leverage, rutting faster. Jessel made not one peep of complaint as she took his new tempo in stride.

A multi-colored aura shimmered around them, and power flooded him, flowing not from the sodomized Fury but it was as if a gem within himself had been unearthed with a whirlwind stirred up by the energy of his rut. Soon his form filled to the brim, whipping his surge into a frenzy until familiar life magic leaked out of his member buried deep within her bowels.

"Ahhhh, yesss!" Jessel moaned as though she could feel it.

Like Innathi, shortly before they conceived together.

Cris looked down to watch his thrust and a lovely purple, well-abused ring clutching him so eagerly.

I'm in her ass.

Indrath's creature wouldn't catch a half-blood from him, and the Fury could handle more. He *wanted* to give her more, harder until she was limp with exhaustion …

"Yes, my lord, yes! Fuck!" Jessel echoed, her tail squeezing him hard around his chest.

The man cried out, abruptly overtaken with a rush encompassing his entire soul, spurting magic in flux to fill every part of them to *live* in the land of the dead!

"Fuck, yes," Ranzi rumbled behind him.

Before his peak had quite finished, rows of turgid, rubbery nipples dragged along his spine before the beast pressed all six breasts along his back, weighing him down with her extraordinarily dense body. He couldn't withdraw from Jessel if he tried.

"Stop … !" he commanded weakly through a compressed chest and afterglow. "Know what you're about to …"

"Sorry, sorsh, I need some of what you got."

The Hiyena rubbed her slimy clitoris along his backside crevice, smearing his skin with the same long-lasting slickness which coated the friction-hot anus trembling around his spent cock.

Cris channeled his newly gained Vitas into his fists. "Stop at once or I kill Jessel!"

"Whatever," Ranzi growled, drooling onto the back of his neck just before she nipped it, which hurt.

"We *must* share, my lord," Jessel cooed, unafraid as though she did not feel the scalding heat of his magic in his hands. "You agreed. *Relax*."

The urge to fight shrank.

What is happening?

Why couldn't he release the magic which filled him to bursting?

Jessel braced herself underneath them; astonishing that she did not collapse beneath the mass of dominant bodies. Ranzi reached around Cris with long arms, taking hold of the Fury's armored breasts and assuring he could not withdraw his cock from out of Jessel's raw netherhole.

Jessel's tail squirmed happily between Ranzi's breasts and Cris's back as her anus squeezed and rippled in ways he had not thought possible. As if a small, soft hand manipulated him *inside* that very passage …

His prick became hard again as Ranzi humped at him, the prodding doing well in keeping him so while Jessel's cooing soothed his ears. This was not a *foreign* feeling, exactly, as no part of his body was untouched by his Queen. He had just never been prepared for being mounted like a beast *by* a beast.

"Ever had multiple ejacs, General?" Ranzi taunted, angling her hips and aiming precisely.

"*Ungh!*" he grunted.

"*Relax*," Jessel crooned again.

And he did.

The Hiyena's protrusion was not as blunt as his to require hard pressure to stretch him out. No, she had an arrow-tip capable of penetrating the bull's eye of his dark star then easing him open, teasing with the smoothest, easiest stroke possible. Her goo coating him all the way in, smearing over the backside of his scrotum as she went in deep, much deeper than Innathi had ever played.

No amount of resistance would prevent Ranzi from fucking him now, even if he could at this point.

The she-beast gave him a hard first hump.

"Oh God, *argh*," he groaned.

"You and the Sun parted ways, didn't you?" Ranzi grunted.

The Zauyrian squirmed as the long, curved clitoris rubbed incessantly along his nut gland deep inside his pelvis, causing his balls to draw up. His normal rebound time had shortened to a fraction of the wait. She was long, going deeper than anyone; on some level he was just grateful that she wasn't thick as well.

"Oh, you're so hard, my lord!" Jessel cried, her body fluttering around him again. "Cum inside me! Please!"

Ranzi responded as if *she* were inside the Fury, thrusting faster to send him over the edge.

Cris roared as he spurted a second time into Jessel's ass, filling her to the point one shift on her part sent substance oozing out around his prick and down onto her puffy lips and her thighs. Above him, Ranzi yipped in pleasure as she ground herself against his buttocks, pressing hard before pulling out and getting off his back.

The Zauyrian scrambled backward while he could, rising on rubbery knees. His buttocks seemed both hot and cold as the air of the Greylands drifted over them. He didn't figure his own ass gaped as much as the Fury's, but it was just as sloppy.

Ranzi clapped him on the back, twisting a few of her own nipples and licking her lips with contentment. "Good work! We're ready to take on that first wave."

"First wave?" he asked numbly then blinked as she pointed to the horizon on his left.

"Malok. Hunting for eidolons. Like you."

Cris stared, making out tall, long-armed bodies covered by thick, grey skin and topped with black mohawks. Rough, piecemeal armor, painted in yellow and red, completed the image of hunters with rustic weapons and nets in hand.

"Ahh, very nice!" Jessel stood up with a happy wiggle of her bottom before she replaced her chastity belt without even wiping down.

"You can't blast either of us per your contract," Ranzi rumbled, watching as he touched wetness on his ass. "So point it toward those fuckers where it does the most good."

The Zauyrian ground his teeth. "Where I drain out just so you have the excuse to mount me again?"

The Hiyena gave him a look of contempt. "You really need to recall what it was you said, bozo, or keep it simple and do what you're told. I'm here to get you out of *no*where and on a path to *some*where. That's worth a piece of your ass, isn't it?"

Jessel studied his face as he bared teeth. "Do not fight *us*, Zauyrian. Fight *them*."

"That's where we'll be," said her warrior sister with a snide shrug, "when you wanna catch up."

No time for a parting shot as Indrath's agents charged forward to defend his soul against the Malok poachers. Ranzi was right in that whenever he pointed his blast at her, it always struck the Malok nearest to her. The Hiyena kept saluting him whenever he took down an enemy trying to flank her.

Fucking infuriating!

Cris-ri-phon tried to conserve his Vitas but the fight lasted too long; too many Malok, while some used magical objects — shielding and scorching — which Jessel and Ranzi targeted with prejudice.

"Soul traps!" the brute shouted more than once. "Keep away!"

"Then take them down!" he shouted back.

"Working on it!"

The Malok numbers surged as either reserves or a competing hunting party appeared to surround the three. Cris used up all the Vitas which he had gained and more, abruptly unable to cast again.

That was when one of the smaller Malok sprinted forward, setting down what appeared to be a thurible made in a potter's oven.

Then it opened the trap.

"Come ... come," it whispered.

Cris stared into that endless black stone, becoming colder and colder, what little color existed in the grey land fading around him. Lights he'd seen streaking through him earlier were breaking down into fragmented pieces, flushed into a stream of mist falling into darkness. The pull called him home, drawing him toward the underneath, where all souls could lay and rest beneath the weight of their regrets ...

"NO!" Jessel screamed, diving white-hot lightning.

"Fuckers!" Ranzi bellowed.

Beasts roaring.

Snapping, crunching, gutting ...

"Get it closed! Shut it, shut it!"

"I'm *trying!*"

A gate slammed shut.

Silence.

Stillness.

He saw *her,* in her tomb below the sand, her body wrapped in white silk, crown still atop her head.

Innathi ...

He drifted, settled; he was nowhere. Supposedly, he was to find a path, but where would his path be without her? Without their children?

I can't move.

A rasping, panting voice trembled above him.

"Only missing a finger? *Hm.* Not bad."

"Hurry, get this off me!" another shrieked, claws scratching metal. "Ranzi, please!"

"Hang on, hang on," she muttered.

He heard a *click-clack.*

"There!"

Shuffling.

"Zauyrian, look!" She puffed her breath. "Cris!"

His mouth moved without sound. "I ... can't see."

36

"Fine!" Feminine folds pressed to his mouth, soft thighs framing his face. "Start licking!" She mashed down, swiveling her hips. "Please, my lord, *taste* me!"

Innathi …

He stirred. Extending his tongue out, passing it across her valleys, he found her neither dry nor numb. Delectable signs of life spread around his mouth, draining down his throat and flowing through his head and chest.

"Good girl, Jessel."

The Fury laid down along his belly and reached for his flaccid penis, slipping it between unbelievably soft lips, lightly scraping him with her fangs as she tongued him with centuries of practice.

Oh, God …

No answer. Wherever Musanlo was, it wasn't here in the Nexus.

He would be found at the end of a long path.

If the sorcerer chose it.

Cris flicked his trembling tongue out greedily, tasting her as she sucked on him, rousing him. She was glorious; she smelled better than any flower, her scent and moisture making his lungs worthwhile at last. In time, he sensed the world through his fingers again, the one clipped off by the Malok's trap slowly reforming.

I can feel her.

He could *hear* her feathers vibrating on that ultra-sensual level. He understood her signals on a primal level and remembered how he had pleased his Queen.

He wanted to give Jessel the same.

"Ohhh … yes!" the Fury called, her back arched, her cunt rocking along his mouth and tongue and nose. "Oh, my lord!"

A shadow fell, and he opened his eyes.

Above him, Jessel accepted the giant Hiyena's long clit between her netherlips, right next to his nose. Black and glossy and curved. Ranzi pressed in then withdrew, and as it came out coated in Jessel's fragrance he flicked his tongue on impulse to taste the heady mixture of his female guardians — the only scents stronger than black blood and Bane venom.

He much preferred it; such was the promise that he could live here, not be trapped here.

"*Rrrr?*" Ranzi rumbled as he licked her sensitive protrusion. She paused in her outstroke before dipping in once again, pulling out a little farther.

He licked her. Salty and sweaty and frosted in his own semen from before the battle. Nothing else tasted more like *life*; chasing away the sucking black feeling of the soul trap.

Pushing in then drawing out entirely, Ranzi alternated between Jessel's slit and his own mouth where he would simply close his lips around her clit and let her draw it out, sucking off Jessel's juices.

"Nice, sorcerer," the warrior woman purred. "*Very* nice. Suck him harder, Jessie, make him strong."

"Mmm!" she answered with enthusiasm, taking his full length down her throat.

Sweet glory ... .!

"HA! Think he's learning. Good practice for his second life. You hear that?" she asked as she pushed her clitoris past his lips again. "It ain't going to be so easy the second time around. The rules won't be the same."

Cris grunted, keeping his eyes closed. If the rules weren't the same, then neither were the choices.

When the three had finished, each of them orgasming from the mouths of the others, he regained the strength to get to his feet. Malok bodies and insect parts surrounded them, yet Jessel noticed something missing.

"Where's the soul trap?" she asked.

Ranzi spun around, looking on her own. Cris still felt too numb to speak.

"Fuck," she growled. "Um. Well ... the finger's growing back. Maybe don't tell the Ice Lord."

The Fury eyes grew large. "I can't keep that from him! H-he'll find out eventually, and I'd like to *keep* my wings, thank you very much!"

The Hiyena curled her lip. "Fine, fine. *Grrr*, but ... It *is* gone, though, isn't it? Just gone."

The two looked him up and down. Cris-ri-phon ignored their expressions and scanned the far shadows with apprehension. The only possible thief that might have snatched the soul trap was the Shaegoth, but of course there was no sign now.

"Should we look for it?" Jessel asked.

"Nah., we can't go walking into *those* canyons," Ranzi replied. "Besides, he seems fine. You feel fine?" A pause and a bump. "Hey, Zauyrian?"

He jolted and nodded. "I ... need to get out of here."

"Yes, yes, you do." She took his shoulder. "Let's go."

Chapter 6

The trio continued in one direction. How they chose it, Cris wasn't sure, but they kept their trail dead center in between two black flint mountain ridges. They would fight Malok twice more, this time without him losing body parts to a trap, and they fucked right after, just as Ranzi had said must happen.

Thus, he kept "living" in the land of the dead.

"What's your name?" the Hiyena would ask with irritating regularity.

"Cris-ri-phon," he growled, "son of Begir-al-phon."

"Who and where was he?"

Sigh. "The Third Sorcerer-King of the Five Zauyrian Realms."

"Good job!" Ranzi chewed her lip, eyes tracing their surroundings. "Not sure those 'realms' exist anymore."

"Don't speak about that," he said, prompting a snicker.

"If they do, they won't for long." Cruelty gleamed in her eyes. "The major power in the region just collapsed, didn't it? Why you did the … oh, what kinda 'win' was that scorched ground thing called?"

"Pyrrhic win," Jessel answered, her voice sweet, hips waving. "A favorite among generals who don't believe they can lose."

"Right."

Cris yanked the mind sliver out before it burrowed in farther. "We still have Ishuna. She had her orders if things went badly for me."

The ladies chuckled.

"Mm-hm." Ranzi kept watch, giant, elongated paws leaving prints in the dust. "So ... you *really* couldn't see it?"

The Zauyrian glanced at her. "See what?"

"The new queen for what she was. Or before that."

His voice rose. "Enough tease. *What* do you mean?"

"Ranzi," Jessel looked over her shoulder with a disapproving frown.

"What?" The Hiyena chuffed through her nose. "How is a third-cross eidolon like *this* supposed to find a path out of the endless plain if he doesn't reflect?"

"Hmph."

The Fury turned forward, leading the way while the other two enjoyed her backside.

"What are you hinting about Ishuna?" Cris asked. "Just say it, devil's *pet*."

Ranzi displayed all her teeth but refrained from braying in his face. "Sure, you know we serve the Infernal because we told you, but you can't even sense the marks left all over *you*."

"I know who I am."

"Ha! Bull jizz. You've done deals with devils but *actually* serve the Sovereign, alongside your queen, ever since you joined."

"How do you know?"

"The fact that your kids even *existed*."

His heart broke twelve times over. Again.

"I do not *know* what the Sovereign *are*," he bit through tight lips.

"Yeah, no surprise. Constantly shifting like the Abyss, barely remember their own names." The she-beast waved that away. "You've heard of demons, right? In the Abyss. And Devils in the Hells. What about Celestials or Eladrins?"

Cris shook his head. "Wait, no. Stop. Are you ... suggesting Ishuna was ... ?"

"Serving the Abyss. Yup." Ranzi wrinkled her nose. "Oh, she *stank* of the demonic!"

"Thus said our Lord Rousse," Jessel chimed in, her stride unbroken and crimson wings relaxed. "We never met this queen."

The Hiyena blew air out of her muzzle. "But same as you, we woulda recognized the taint if we got a whiff."

A chill swept through him to imagine the Desert Queendom now in demonic powers because he had left everything in Ishuna's hands.

No.

"You couldn't see it." Ranzi shook her head. "That's where your Sovereign did you a disservice. At least Jessel and I were granted the power to *smell* when another faction is involved and track it down."

"How we found *you* so quickly," the Fury cooed.

Cris snarled, fisting his hands. "If you insist, who *is* 'my' Sovereign?"

"Got no names to go with scents, sorry." Ranzi peered down at him with those large brown eyes. "You must've fucked 'em at some point. You like fucking men?"

He hadn't finished a sputter before she shrugged him off.

"Then at some point, you fucked a woman who wasn't like you," she stated with utter confidence. "No matter what she said or what she looked like."

The Zauyrian scowled without reply as unwelcome taunts echoed in memory.

" ... the other seducer ... the same man-eater with an alluring face."

The memory, if it was there, remained dark.

Damn him.

Damn them all for interfering.

Eventually, Jessel, Cris-ri-phon, and Ranzi left the broad valley and entered an endless plain of fine dust and hollow winds, dotted with vegetated mounds jutting up from the ground like sparse teeth in an ancient reptile.

"Haven't moved," Ranzi murmured under her breath.

Cris heard her and frowned. "Why would giant hills move?"

Jessel smiled, patting his back as the Hiyena laughed.

"They're not hills." She shrugged. "They're called the Moving Groves. Been warned they might not be where you last left them."

"Or where your *grandmother* left them," the Fury added with a titter.

"Right. If we can find one unoccupied, it's a decent place to rest."

Strange footprints large and small surrounded each hill, showing its relative popularity. How crisp they were and whether Ranzi heard any sounds above determined how close they drew before changing direction to the next one.

Eventually, Ranzi climbed one of the Moving Groves, and Jessel flew, letting Cris bring up the rear as they took to the only shelter that he'd glimpsed in the Greylands thus far. Sitting among ancient twists and tangles adorning a possibly slumbering beast, Cris-ri-phon finally caught sight of the Shaegoth.

"*Hsss,*" he sucked through his teeth, tensing.

Ranzi's rough hair puffed up. "What?"

He pointed, but the masked shadow had vanished.

Perhaps it was the same one, though the mask had no features. Either way, it carried no soul trap. It watched them — had let itself be seen watching them — but the sorcerer could not interpret its intent from that brief appearance.

"Did you see it?" he asked.

"No, what was it?"

"A Shaegoth."

"Shaegoth?" Jessel blinked blank eyes with clear horror. "Fuck. Why would *she* be paying attention?"

Cris tilted his head. "She?"

Her bottom lip pouted. "The Grave Mother, Nyx."

Grave Mother …

"The Grey Maiden?" he asked.

"Same thing," Ranzi grunted, standing up as if suddenly itching to leave. "And yeah, you know who she is?"

"The Deathwalkers of my Desert worship her."

I would have, too, had I not met Innathi …

"Fuck, that's right. Forgot he mentioned those." The Hiyena exhaled. "We need to keep moving."

"But —" Jessel began.

"If Nyx wanted us apprehended, we'd have been snared by now."

"Are Moving Groves *her* realm?"

"Umm, I didn't think so …"

"Wait." Cris stood up as well. "Is it possible to find her? A place to go where the Grave Mother may be."

Indrath's servants blinked at him, apparently stunned by the suggestion.

"That *is* a path I could choose, isn't it?" he said.

Ranzi reached up, scratching her bristly mane. "Maybe not a good idea to pick such a … short path here."

Jessel nodded, drawing a circle with her finger. "Like a snake eating its tail. You're not getting out."

"Some of my people never wanted to." He looked between them. "I'm Zauyrian. She will know me, or my Deathwalkers. How do we find her?"

The two females grimaced, glancing between themselves.

"You're my escort until I find my path, yes?" he repeated in growing frustration. "And who is to say this is my final one? It only makes sense if she has sent a Shaegoth to trail us."

"Assuming she did," Ranzi muttered, wrinkling her muzzle, ears laying down in concern.

"Do you know where or not?"

Jessel wrapped her arms around herself. "She … has a Citadel. We would not find it without an eidolon granted some favor in life."

Cris-ri-phon nodded with a spark of eagerness. "She granted me favor when I was a boy. Her Deathwalker Houda taught me."

"Boyhood?" Ranzi appraised his nudity with a smirk and a sniff. "You've changed a lot."

"If it's not to be, then we won't find the Citadel. Is that what I'm hearing?"

The Fury exhaled, inspecting the dull, shadeless light around them. "If we can build power, turn it into light bright enough to *draw* some shadows …"

"Might be a shortcut," Ranzi agreed. "Something we've been avoiding so far."

Cris seized Indrath's sex slave by the arms, turning Jessel's backside to Ranzi so she could touch the lock on the chastity belt.

"Then let us try," he growled. "Now."

THEIR NERVES WERE ON EDGE AS THEY RUTTED, JESSEL SPEAKING LESS ENCOURAGEMENT and moaning without words as they used her.

"You're afraid of Shaegoth?" he grunted, buried balls deep in the Fury, wings and legs spread as he gripped her ass with both hands. Meanwhile, Ranzi lapped around and between his butt cheeks. He stepped wider to give her easier access as she prepared for a standing penetration.

"Depends … on its mission …" Jessel gasped, evading the question. She dug her claws into his shoulders, triggering a pleasure as powerful as his tingling asshole. "Ohhh, harder, my lord!"

An aura of true light surrounded them, but it didn't reach far. Hints of longer shadows stretched from the nearest old growths, but they needed more.

Harder. Fuck her harder.

Ranzi did the same, slapping her hips up against him. "Better be … *sure*. About this."

Neither Bane Wasp nor Malok interrupted to drain their hard-earned essence, though a strange yapping arose from the nearest hill, as if in response to the intensifying light.

Better stay away.

Creating light in the Greylands was easy. Expanding it, causing it to spread, was difficult. Sustaining that spread after climax was grueling.

Cris pushed himself and his escorts, changing positions to go again. Then he led another time, and another. Light grew around them, creating the deepest shadows he'd glimpsed so far, but each sought to die back after climax.

"I'm actually getting sore," Ranzi muttered, spearing Jessel's nether-hole while the Zauyrian claimed her cunt, the three of them grappling for leverage.

"Don't stop," he huffed, "and I'll squat over you next time."

Her eyes bulged, vigor renewed. "Oh! Well, in *that* case ..."

He lost sight of when the light began to linger of its own accord, self-sustaining, at least for a little while. The Zauyrian was blinded to whiteness, his naked form sticky and hot and swollen.

But it worked.

Panting, he saw at last a Shaegoth step out of the shadows they'd created. He blinked.

More than one!

"*Frenikkek*," Ranzi snarled, shoving Jessel away.

They separated and scrambled to their feet, already surrounded. The arrival happened in a blink, utterly silent, and Cris couldn't remember whether he had been approaching climax or just passed it. Not that it mattered because the urge was gone.

Tall and inhumanly gangly, the Shaegoth bodies were void-black, dotted with pale blue specks like stars though seemingly solid. Icy gazes fixed on them with cross-shaped pupils, their faces awash with sharp, shimmering grins. All possessed the same mute white mask as the first, but it was attached to the red wraps secured around corpse-thin waists. Opposite each mask was a metal dagger. The unique design of each was perhaps the only way to tell them apart.

Cris-ri-phon counted nine Shaegoth, unsure which one to speak to until the last one joined them. A mask of theatrical joy and frozen laughter covered the face of this somewhat larger one. His eyes swept in a panicked count over the Grey Maiden's newest agent, down to the shoulders and around the waist.

Nine masks.

The others depicted emotions less pleasant than mirth. He scoured his memory for tales of such lore when the shadow spoke.

"Well! Isn't this a lovely venue? Although it appears we missed the show."

The odd voice vibrated inside his ears, jangling his attention like a child batting at a string of bells. Jessel jumped, tucking her wings in to shrink and hide behind the Hiyena.

"They can *speak?!*" she blurted.

Ranzi bumped into the Fury, slower to back up. "Uhhh …"

"Now now," the Shaegoth waggled a spindly finger at them. "Anything can learn to speak, given enough time. And if I may say, what beautiful, red wings you have!"

The Fury blinked in surprise at the compliment, the hint of a playful leer coming through the mask somehow. The admiration struck Cris as distinctly male.

Shadows don't feel … attraction to the living, do they?

"Who are you," he interjected, "and who sent you?"

The Shaegoth tilted his head, body following in a slanted bow; he crossed an arm over his middle while lifting his free hand with a flourish. "I am the Archivist of Woe, representing the Maiden of Shrouds. Come along now. My Lady is waiting."

"Oh!" Jessel looked at him, then the Shaegoth, and back to him. "A new escort straight to the Citadel?"

"Guess you've chosen your path, sweet meat," Ranzi agreed, sharing a look with the Fury, shifting away from him. "I guess this is where we part ways."

"Ohhhh, no, no, *no!*" laughed the Nexus creature. "You two get to tag along! I am *certain* your lord will appreciate a thorough report."

"Uhh, that's not necessary," the Hiyena began as Jessel pulled on her arm. "He understands not trespassing on neutral ground —"

Cris watched the Archivist of Woe brush the hilt of the weapon at his side. Unlike the other Shaegoth, his was not a dagger but a sword, peace-knotted with red cord.

"Oh, Ladies," the mask still frozen in a broad smile, "that wasn't an offer. Come along."

CHAPTER 7
THE NEXUS CITADEL OF THE GREY MAIDEN

CRIS IMAGINED THE LIGHT HE'D SUMMONED ATOP THAT HILL WOULD VANISH AS soon as the three of them were swept into the crevices of shadow. Change was instantaneous; had there been a space in-between, he witnessed not a glimpse. He expected to feel sick or disoriented, as if he'd covered an incredible distance, but that seemed to be the privilege of Indrath's servants.

"*Oog*," Ranzi grunted, placing her hands on her thighs to prevent falling over while the Archivist of Woe darted past Cris to catch Jessel in his arms.

"I have you!" The jesting creature yanked her upright, spinning her around quickly for inspection. "You're fine! Perfect, even! The dizziness will pass."

The Fury stumbled into the Hiyena as soon as the Archivist lifted his spindly hands. Ranzi caught her next, awkwardly gathering her close.

"Enough," she snarled. "Back off."

"Oh, my," the Archivist flicked his wrist at her. "Infernals just *love* to spin out poor eidolons until they don't know which way is up but can't accept the same play in kind? *Hmph!* I'm dismayed but not surprised."

A low growl leaked from between her teeth, but fortunately, the Shaegoth's sword remained peace knotted. Ranzi had the sense not to insult the Greylord agent in the center of their territory.

Meanwhile, Cris stared at a massive, tiered chamber, empty but for them. Although fully enclosed in dark stone, it resembled an amphitheater in its many, shallow levels all facing the smallest arena in which they stood. Beyond them and in view of any who may sit on those wide steps to watch was an arresting view of the horizon outside, wherever they were.

Jagged, obsidian mountains broke the long expanse of plains, disturbing the grey clouds above and somehow offering a suggestion of dawn or dusk just behind them. Much closer to the odd, transparent window, he glimpsed signs of a city with roads creeping out into view, implying he stood high in a mountain, a tower, or other rising structure, natural or designed.

While the Archivist distracted his escorts, the Zauyrian noted when the other nine Shaegoth slipped away, each choosing a shadow on the perimeter from which to keep guard.

"Will the Grey Maiden see me?" he asked, interrupting the hint of sparring that might take place.

The Archivist straightened up, turning the grinning mask on him, blue crosses flashing briefly behind the eye holes. "She sees you now and ever since you were born."

"Do I speak to her through you?"

Two nightmarish hands splayed over a gaunt, speckled chest. "Little ol' me?! *Haha!* No. Ha! Yes, but, no." He waved toward the upper levels of the amphitheater. "Be patient, my fellow actor. Wait for your audience to come to you."

The Infernals said nothing, their usual bluster snuffed out by the place and proximity of the unbalanced assassin. Cris admitted it was nice seeing them farther out of their depth.

Now to make the most of this, somehow.

"Revered Mother," he said despite the Archivist's advice. "The Deathwalkers of my home speak well of you, dedicate their lives to your guidance. I listened early on and thought I might do the same, though I found a different path calling to me." He swallowed. "That path ended, and I seek guidance from the first name I heard at night after Musanlo in the day, the Grey Maiden. I beseech an audience with you."

49

"Not bad, not bad," praised the Archivist of Woe, rubbing the chin of his mask with a nod of approval. The Shaegoth peered around as if expecting a response.

Good sign.

Cris waited with every mote of patience he had left, weighing his remaining strength and checking his arms as if his "eidolon" form might fade. Peripherally, he hoped he would not have to boost his Vitas yet again with the Infernal women, especially in front of that laughing Shaegoth.

But I will if I must ...

A scrape of boot and mass caught his attention. Near the top tier and on the far end, two figures entered mundanely through a grey-wood door. He recognized neither one at this distance and couldn't explain the rush of excitement until they drew closer.

Familiar, somehow ...

His gut told him they were eidolons like himself, holding the appearance of Humans, a man and a woman. The taller man wore a simple grey robe such as the Deathwalkers of the Zauyrian Desert wore while the shorter woman wore full armor as if she had stepped off a battlefield. Cris expected to see metal at first but caught the hint of gloss came from something else.

Ceramics? Or ... He squinted, eyes passing over the sunburst sign on her shoulder. *Bane Wasp ... ?*

Like the molded chitin armor worn by the Malok. Or perhaps a mix of both. The sorcerer tried not to make assumptions about the woman's ability to guard the man, such as their positioning suggested when they closed the distance without speaking. In response, Ranzi and Jessel shifted to stand at his flanks, seemingly still under the command to protect him.

The Archivist of Woe had vanished.

"Welcome, son of the Zauyrian Realms," said the robed man, his appearance gaunt and pallid.

Cris recognized the ritual scarring on his face and hands. "You are a Deathwalker."

The man smiled a little and placed an open hand on his chest. "I was called Taib."

"I ... know that name, I believe," he murmured, touching his chin trying to recall.

Taib did not play games with his memory. "You assigned me to serve the Davrin Court during the time of your wedding to their Queen." His eyes, almost normal but with a glimmer of blue within his black pupils, flicked to the Infernals behind him. "When Lord Indrath gifted you with the soul dagger during the ceremony."

"Ah! Of course." If he had been alive, his face would have flushed hot. "Taib. Well met. I ... that was centuries ago for me, but most welcome to meet you again. You served your Lady well."

As the Deathwalker bowed his head, Cris glanced at the young woman at his shoulder. Of Zauyrian descent from her appearance and size, but she had no scars or markings but for her armor, and he could not decide whether he had seen her face before.

Too many short Human lifespans between them and me ...

Too many to name.

"And your companion?" he asked.

Taib smiled this time with a hint of wryness. "This is Houda. Among the greatest of us at the Citadel."

At once, Cris-ri-phon burned with the memory of fevers which had plagued his childhood, through which this woman had nursed him. His first Deathwalker tutor had never been beautiful, but he had also never seen her this young nor bearing any hints of a warrior. Unlike the Davrin women, the Zauyrian rarely grew of a size to be effective in battle against men.

"H-Houda?" he repeated. "You've changed."

"Cris-ri-phon," she said, chin dipping. "So have you."

Her expression remained stoic and placid, and the warmth of recognition fell hollow into himself as a chill of fear spread. He looked around the chamber. "Is my brother here as well?"

Houda shook her head. "Leur-en-phon took his path out of the Nexus."

"To where?"

"I cannot tell you. That is disgrace among souls."

He smirked. "Probably Musanlo."

Neither Deathwalker reacted; not one tick. They may as well have been statues of memory.

"Have you set sights upon yours?" Houda asked. "Or do you seek to remain here?"

"No," he blurted before he could think.

"What do you want, then?"

His mouth tightened. "What are you still doing here? Why haven't you moved on?"

Houda smiled, peaceful and cool. "Among other reasons, my *lewens-bluen* still lives. I would witness what becomes of her."

"Your," Cris began, "what?"

Ranzi puffed air out of her nose at the strange word, looking up at the ceiling as if not paying attention. Taib noticed.

"Do you know of what she speaks, mercenary?" he asked the Hiyena.

"Maybe." A shrug, then Ranzi pointed her muzzle at Cris, then the two Deathwalkers. "The Ice Lord mentioned something weird about death magic where you're from."

Taib nodded. "What did he tell you?"

"Ohhh, let's see." The beast-woman scratched her chin, glancing at her companion. "How Humans pledging to the Grey Maiden can usurp the purpose of 'life' magic in odd ways, especially with those who live centuries." Ranzi lifted her brow at Cris. "He warned us something about not knowing who was *really* backing who."

"Yes," Jessel spoke up. "The Greylord isn't confined to the realm of death, so she always changes sides."

"I can see how that may be confusing," Taib replied, "phrased like that."

Houda chuckled softly. "Only pawns in the Eternal War would see her as changing sides."

"You wanna fight, little knight?" Ranzi began.

Shadows moved.

The Archivist of Woe whispered, *"Oh, please, oh please, do …"*

Hackles dropped at once, and Houda's expression saddened as she looked at Cris-ri-phon.

"What do you want?" she asked again.

The sorcerer, now that he stood here, could only think of one thing. "I want to remember the Sovereign I once met."

The Deathwalkers' faces shifted from morose observance to eyes-wide concern.

"How would this serve your passing?" Taib asked, trying to sound neutral.

Cris waved at Ranzi. "As she said, how can I choose a path if I don't recall a consequential choice everyone tells me I made?"

"Fuck," the Hiyena grunt as if just recognizing a grave error.

"Just couldn't help rubbing his nose in it, huh?" Jessel murmured, wings quivering as if in fear.

"Didn't think we'd end up here," she grumbled. "An' I can't *not* mention when I smell it."

"Foolish."

"Easy judge for a set of gaping holes."

Houda and Taib shared looks as well while his escorts bickered, and Cris felt his temper rise.

"Enough of these furtive glances and hints!" he shouted, his words bouncing off the ceiling. "Clearly you can do *nothing* useful! I *will* see the Grave Mother. I am finished with all of you!"

Ranzi snorted, crossing her arms, voice snide and surly. "Yet no one's leaving until *you* gather up your shit."

Cris turned his back on her, calling up the amphitheater. "Mother of Shrouds! Houda has been apart from my world too long! She can't aid me anymore, but you can! You rise above these factions, even Musanlo, for all eventually come through you! Help me! I want to be free, or at least see clearly where self-serving lies have obstructed my choice!"

"Nice." The Shaegoth's voice carried as a ghost out of sight. "You could have been extraordinary, I suppose, if you had any sense of irony."

"No one asked you, jester," Cris snarled back, swearing he heard the shrug of nonchalance.

Houda and Taib remained silent, the meaning of their observation as carefully masked as the Shaegoth.

"Have you nothing else you wish to say?"

Cris had almost asked that question himself, but the grand whisper filled the room at once, stirring the dust like early signs of an earthquake.

Houda turned smartly and dropped to one knee, fists loose at her sides with chin down. Taib lowered himself to both knees, resting on his heels and folding his hands until his sleeves hid them.

"I regret, I do not, my Lady," Houda answered. "He remains difficult to reach."

"My service remains hers, my Lady," Taib agreed, washing his hands of the moment. "And he will not listen to her."

Cris sneered, looking up. At the top tier stood a small woman wrapped in shrouds swaying in an unfelt wind. Her pale face could have been one of the Shaegoth masks, eyes empty, a crack extending from her left eye onto her cheek, a black scarab emerging to rise, clinging to fine, white hair at her temple.

He bowed at his waist. "Grey Lady, you honor us."

No one spoke to correct him, though Ranzi and Jessel sneaked a bit closer to him.

Her mask moved like a true face when she spoke. "The Infernals managed what Celestials could not at the zero hour. You are here, and now they have more time to fight amongst themselves."

Cris drew a gasp. "Yes! Indrath said he wanted me separate from the column! Why?"

"You unwittingly destroyed his world," Nyx answered, tilting her head. "By sending you here, he granted himself and others yet to be born more time before the inevitable."

The chamber fell silent, her whisper fast fading.

"I didn't ..." Cris swallowed, the ghostly weight of collapsing sand crawling up his legs. "He stopped it, didn't he?"

The Grey Maiden shook her head. "He did not. This is not within his power."

A deep tremor stole the lingering warmth from his Vitas. "Could *I* ... stop it? If I chose that path?"

Nyx stared from the distant end of the theater, unmoving but for her shrouds and the scarab. "Before you hear an answer, know this."

I could, then …

"For the first time since your birth, Cris-ri-phon, you are free of sibling rivalry. From extraordinary chance, your world and your death are behind you."

I can't just walk away.

"Your selective amnesia may count as a boon rather than a curse, the single act of mercy in an otherwise ruthless endeavor."

No. No …

"Recovering this knowledge may return the ring around your neck, never to be undone again."

"I am no one's slave!" he repeated.

"Right now, Cris-ri-phon, you are not. Only in the briefest moments of your existence can you claim that."

"It's not true," he bared teeth. "I don't accept it!"

The Grave Mother stared.

"Tell me who did this." He breathed from recollected rage. "Who made me forget to question why I lived to have children with my queen?"

"You did," she answered. "You chose this cost to receive your greatest desire."

"Whose *cost?* Who was she?!"

Houda and Taib had returned to their feet, frowning at his tone. Ranzi and Jessel fussed with their claws and talons, fur and feathers. The sense of foreboding choked the air within as grey clouds slowly tumbled without as the pestering Shaegoth drummed his fingers with a hum drained of humor.

Nyx approached, unthreatening, foot falls silent in closing the distance until she stood one step above him on the front row of the stage. She only just matched his height.

"The creature's bound name is Uradri," answered the Grey Maiden.

Cris shook his head. "I do not know it."

"You will. Though even she as its instigator cannot undo what is set into motion."

"Who was she when I knew her?"

"That no longer matters, though others exist who knew that form."

"Others," he repeated. "Some I could seek?"

"Of course," she answered. "Existence always seeks."

"I exist, thus I can seek a way to undo what I did."

The Archivist of Woe snorted. Cris looked up in annoyance.

"Don't mind me," the creature joked, popping his smiling mask and floating dreads out of darkness. "Continue!"

"Your return shall accelerate the deterioration," Nyx continued with no outward sign if she heard her playful shadow.

"But ... there *must* be a way!"

"She's *telling* you the way!" Jessel piped up behind him, beyond exasperated. "Walk somewhere else! Choose another path from the rut you've been treading on everyone else and making it worse!"

He spun around. "Silence! You can't understand what I've lost! You've never had children! Just a devil's whore meant for the morale of his troops."

"Idiot," Ranzi snarled, claws out and hackles rising as Jessel flinched back. "You deserve those chains."

Cris spat and turned away, taking advantage of their contract to make his point. "I must help fix this," he implored. "I must find Uradri. I can't just walk away with a huge hole in my soul! That's wrong! Humans seek redemption for their mistakes. By your leave, my Lady —"

Nyx tilted her head in the other direction. "You do not need leave to choose, Cris-ri-phon. You know this power."

"Then I choose my path," he said, taking three steps closer. "I choose to go back."

The Archivist groaned.

"I'll demolish the black pillar and find Uradri," he continued.

"Good luck," Ranzi muttered.

Cris tossed a look back at the Infernals. "Perhaps search for survivors of V'Gedra. Other Deathwalkers, my father's people, perhaps my children."

Taib and Houda moved away without comment, setting themselves behind the swaddled woman with a mask for a face.

"Can you help me get home?" he asked.

56

The Grey Maiden turned her head ever-so-slightly, gazing for many long moments out the broad window at the harsh landscape. She seemed to be focused on the roiling cloud cover.

"You may follow existing threads back," she said. "Though frayed and stretched taut, they are not yet broken."

Instinctively, Cris knew what she meant. *The Sovereign's threads. Indrath couldn't cut that with Soul Drinker.*

"Thank God," he sighed.

"*Arrgh*, you know what?" the Hiyena said, lifting her palms out, addressing her companion. "He found his path, right? We're good to go, we don't have to escort him *exactly* where he wasn't supposed to go."

"Yeah," Jessel agreed, wrinkling her nose to display fangs of resentment. "Find your own way. I hope you fail, stupid Human."

"Ooo, rowrrr," chuckled the Archivist, appearing on the stage with a bow. "Would you like a lift on your way, lovely ladies?"

"Um, well —" Ranzi hesitated.

"Yes, please," Jessel answered, turning with a feather-flirting warmth to which the Shaegoth responded with a small shudder. She lifted her breasts in both hands. "Get us safe to the border, and I'll let you squeeze these."

The Shaegoth's joyful dance matched the expression of his mask. "Deal! Oh, what fun!"

Several Shaegoth swept in, seizing and dragging the Infernals toward the shadows with them.

"Whoa, hey, I can walk — !" Ranzi tried to protest.

Then they were gone, the amphitheater blessedly quiet.

Cris turned to the three who remained. "Will you try to stop me?"

"No," Nyx said.

The Greylord stood still and said no more.

Houda exhaled with clear dismay. "We'll escort you to the gate."

THE ZAUYRIAN SPRINTED UPON THE PLAINS, AVOIDING VALLEYS OF PNEUMA FLINT and distant hunting parties, never feeling tired. The way back felt much shorter without the blinding Vitas from the sex with Indra's creatures obscuring subtle threads of light drifting from his naval and ahead of him into the wind.

If he'd known he could draw the force he needed from those ties to home …

But that had been the point. Indrath had been trying to *obscure* his path.

"You can still change your mind," Houda said at the gate of Nyx's Citadel. *"We'll come for you. I promise."*

"Sounds like a threat," he sneered.

"It isn't. If you hold any love for your home world, you will not go back."

"And leave whoever who tricked me into dooming it unpunished?" he asked. *"Who is your lewensbluen, keeping you tied here, hm?"*

"Ishuna," the Deathwalker answered, honest and plain, without a tick of regret upon her face. *"I shall bear witness to her fate."*

"Hmph." He scowled. *"If she was the one who caused V'Gedra to fall, if Innathi's people have fallen to the Abyss because of her, then Ishuna may very well meet her fate at my hands."*

Houda stared back without comment, her eyes and face as cold as he'd ever seen them. *"Remember, Cris. You can* always *change your mind. Always."*

Cris shook his head clear of the voice, running through the Nexus as freely as he had anywhere.

He ran.

He stopped only when he was home.

Cris knew when he had arrived, for standing in a void of starlight and mist, he was suddenly *starving*. The threads told him he needed to eat to regain a form that could walk upon the land.

Eat.

There must be something.

Soon, he found something to eat: a piece of ice from the peak of one of the tallest mountains, just rising above the mist under his feet. The eidolon reached for it, broke it off, and consumed it.

God …

Thirst and hunger both, sated and divine.

I want another …

He reached, breaking the ice.

"How *dare* you!"

The voice was familiar, furious. A clawed had reached up, caught him by the throat—

And dragged him down from those dizzying heights.

CRIS OPENED HIS EYES, ABRUPTLY AWARE OF THE PAIN AND CHILL OF HAVING A body once again.

I'd forgotten.

He lifted his arms, hearing the manacles before he saw them, tired by their weight a moment later. The Zauyrian sagged back, peering into the darkness.

Someone was in here with him.

"Cris-ri-phon." A disappointed sigh. "You were a fool to come back."

"Indrath," he rasped.

"Indeed. You think I will let you strut where you please after what you've done? You've grown too accustomed to no one daring to stop you, but now you've disdained the opportunities given you to save your own soul." He paused. "After too long borrowing on this debt, *I* shall see that you pay for them."

"I … I'm looking for the creature who made me and my children." The Zauyrian got up on his elbows. "I want to make this right. That's all."

The Infernal chuckled. "So do I."

"I know her name."

His wings stretched. "Hmm. Do you?"

"Uradri."

The Ice Lord's absolute stillness shouted his recognition.

"You know her," Cris said. "Do you know *where* she is?"

Indrath moved with all the warning of an avalanche breaking loose, seizing his throat again, claws so cold, they burned his new skin.

"Do *I* know where she is?" he repeated with menace. "No. Not right now. But until I do, I will *enjoy* making you suffer. For millennia, if need be, for you shall never die now. You've quashed that possibility yourself."

Cris's heart pounded; he struggled to breathe past the blistering cold. At last, he could make out the barest outline of the devil's face, his ivory eyes starting to glow crimson and light up the jail cell.

"Perhaps you'll make good bait for her," Indrath said. "We'll see."

Wicked fangs flashed in the dark.

"After all," the devil whispered, "I have always been left to clean up the messes my sister leaves behind."

DEVOUR THE ORACLE

A TALE OF MIURAG
BY A.S. ETASKI

CHAPTER 1

3066 S.E., THE FAR NORTH, THE SLUMS OF ENNIKAR

HER SMALL, PALE HAND REACHED OUT FOR THE PLUMP, BLACK BEETLE AND CLOSED around it. She brought it to her lips, allowing the scrabbling, slightly prickly legs to struggle against the sensitive skin, relishing the sensation, before she crushed the belly with her thumb. Satisfied with the crack and crush of a chitinous skeleton, she let the pale-yellow fluid and innards land on her tongue and lips before giving the husk a quick suck before tossing it away.

She considered hunting for another one, though that one had been pure opportunity as it wandered into her field of vision.

"Ada, Ada, Ada," Balkir sighed tolerantly with a black-lipped smile. "You no longer must scrounge for insects and worms to make your meal. You enjoyed Sokiuf's season stew not three hours ago."

The young woman's mouth remained stubbornly closed as if she meant to keep the aftertaste of the pillory bug to herself. Her classic, Ma'ab black eyes stared unblinking at him, the large-boned man who had so recently found her and taken her off the streets during one of the worst winters she could remember. Balkir had made it clear very soon what he wanted in exchange and none of it surprised her; as she felt quite neutral on the subject, she let him have it. Three times, so far.

In another few months he would get used to her presence and stop watching her so closely. She would take what she wanted and run, as she had already done many times before. Once she had struggled through childhood, something about her caused Ma'ab men to sniff her out and offer shelter and protection for a time. She accepted during the harsh winters but never stayed through the Sun Season.

She could never stay still.

Balkir made more effort than before to engage her in conversation that night but eventually acceded to her wishes to remain quiet. Soon after, as expected, he arose from his desk to take her arm gently and escort her over to his bed for the night. It was not tremendously large or rich for they remained deeply set within their own caste, but it was sturdy enough for his weight with just enough room for her.

"I worry about you being so dry," he said as he removed the warm, grey robe from her shoulders. "And you tell me I'm not hurting you?"

He began to pull her night-black shift up her thighs, exposing all her ghostly-white skin as he pulled it over her head. His enormous hand cupped her bottom and managed to give both cheeks a squeeze with that one grip.

She had more than a few scars; the result of studying various scraps of scroll and book she looked at most often in the Sun Season after she spent the winter hoarding, though most of the marks were on her arms and legs. The longest she had ever stayed in one place was to learn to read from a dying old woman who did not care about a snatch barely a dozen years old and had more interest in the dark, bright eyes that could not look away from the symbols.

Most of the Ma'ab men with a winter den of their own, the ones that took a second sniff at her, always seemed to have something to read, somewhere. She always found it, no matter how well they hid it. She always took it.

"No."

There. She answered his question, simply, and crawled onto the bed, pausing for his instruction, his preference. He would be able to see her light pink folds now. She looked back over her shoulder, parting her knees a bit more.

Balkir tilted his head, his smile supporting the cunning in his own dark eyes as he considered her naked body in the shut-up room lit only with candlelight. He nodded. "Yes, just like that. I like how you look."

He was no more handsome than she was beautiful, but they failed to notice any of that within the slum, just as they didn't use words of relative vanity so often as the Highborn. He possessed many scars of his own on muscled arms and chest, stomach and thighs and feet —and she knew for a fact he possessed more books than anyone who had come before.

"There is something I would like to try tonight, Ada," he said, reaching to pull a tiny vial out from beneath the corner of his straw-stuffed mattress.

"What is that?" she demanded, her voice cool but clearly considering defense. Or offense.

"Something to make the penetration easier on you," he said smoothly. "A bit of oil, nothing more."

He was lying, she knew it, but he had already spilled what amounted to a mere spoonful of that oil between her buttocks and quickly it oozed down. Just as she had time to flinch, he was already rubbing his thick fingers into her sex, then cupping it as if to hold her in place as he took her shoulder with his other giant hand to make it so.

Ada stared down at her hands clutching the mattress, uncertain what to do or how to feel. She was not frightened, per se, but Balkir seemed to be waiting for some effect from the oil. He had to be, or he would have tried mounting her by now. So far, he hadn't even removed his own robe.

Then she felt it: warmth, like being at a hearth fire in a tavern drinking hot cider, seeping, soaking in chilled flesh to defrost it. Balkir started tugging gently on her labia and she grunted, confused, as they seemed not just slick but plumper than usual. Typically, her netherlips were thin enough there was not much to tug upon, if that suited one's fancy.

"There we are," Balkir crooned, his voice sounding coarser and more eager. He dipped a finger just up to the first knuckle into her channel, and she squirmed. "Some swelling and slickness of one's own always makes this more pleasant for the vessel, our little chosen one."

Ada's eyes widened and she twisted instantly with a hiss, trying to gouge his eyes and dart away; Balkir held her tight and pinned her within a moment, keeping his body weight full and her helpless beneath him as he opened his robe. Meanwhile the heat between her legs only grew stronger.

"Arrgh! Roug … ten … fah!" she cried angrily. As happened so often, unable to form true words when her mind grasped onto pure survival.

She shifted her hips, trying to somehow escape not only Balkir but the maddening pulse between her legs. Somehow it was as if only that which Ma'ab men wanted most would satisfy her as well: the stretching, the filling, the pounding.

She had never felt that before. She didn't want to feel it!

"Ada, Ada," Balkir soothed in her ear, "calm yourself. You have a greater purpose, I see your potential. The Mother of Entrails has given sign she approves of my choice! You should not scrape upon the stones alone, only to die young and childless. We can help you, we have chosen you to be wife to us, we want you. You are wanted, little one!"

Small fingers clawed desperately at the mattress, tearing at it; she grunted and huffed in her pitiful attempts to thrash beneath him, her black, tangled hair falling once again into her face. She couldn't see anything when she felt it all: Balkir tilting her hips up by reaching under and pressing on her abdomen, the blunt head of his manhood nudging at that hole he so desired, and unlike all the previous times, the shiver that ran up her spine as she felt herself stretching, yielding, her hot and swollen insides clenching down on him in hunger.

She had known hunger all her life, but never this kind. She was used to shivering with cold, not because of molten heat.

The large male filled her up, humped her like two dogs in an alleyway, spewing his righteous words from his mouth long before he spewed his seed from his cock. When finally he did, Ada still gripped the mattress and would have been waiting for him to finish, glad that he finally had, except that she was not.

She did not know why she was not glad. Or why she was not finished.

He got off her, dragging his own swollen fire-poker out of her, and took her around the waist, lifting her up to cradle her in his arms. "Come with me," he gasped. "You have many more husbands who will be glad to see you receptive at last."

Indeed, they were. There were nine more of them, and they placed her on her back on a stone altar covered in sheep's hide so it wouldn't scrape her back or be too cold. They grabbed her legs and pulled them open, pulled them up, until she finally opened her eyes and looked down, able to see what they were describing with such delight.

Her entire sex was the deepest red beneath her black curls, spreading out to make her inner thighs flushed a spring pink. Balkir's semen oozed out and frosted her unfamiliarly puffy lips, and one of the other gap-toothed "husbands" dived in to lap it up. She would have been disgusted if she had been able to concentrate past the massive surge of sensation and heat which filled her belly at the touch of his tongue.

"Ah!" she cried, throwing her head back and by reflex thrusting her hips up in encouragement as the hooded man feasted further, sucking and biting and licking at her until she felt mad enough to scream.

"Another!" Balkir cried as well, ecstatic.

The feaster was yanked off her crotch and another man's erection charged into her, stretched her, pounded her. Ada struggled, both trying to get over the edge of the altar, to drop and escape even with her ankles held, as well as just try to get over *that edge* … that elusive precipice that called to her body, invited her to topple over and freefall in some grand ending to that which was building within her.

But she couldn't. She finally felt that bit afraid. What was happening to her … ?

Whichever husband pulled on her netherlips with his mouth, eating out whatever the previous husband sprayed into her did a far better job getting her close to her peak than the frantic poking and shuddering of the seeder, who only frustrated her.

At one point they turned her over, and one started poking at the place where her excrement escaped. Before it had only made her roll her eyes in derision, but now she jumped at the sensitivity, tense and waiting and frightened to feel more.

"NO!" Balkir roared, pulling the other male away and shouting in his face. "Not her mouth, and not her dump! You know this! We fill her womb until it can hold no more! Only there!"

That didn't stop their fingers from pressing in now they had access, their manhood impaling her like meat on a spit but their hands exploring and penetrating her rectum like a curious, self-squeezing toy. They enjoyed watching her react to the extreme stretching from their large fingers; even Balkir enjoyed it, and more fingers darted beneath play with her most sensitive nub at the same time as she struggled, hanging partly off the altar.

She screamed frequently, forming no actual words, primal in her flood of anger, fear, and arousal. Her normally numb nipples rubbed so pleasurably on the sheepskin as they mauled her and rutted on her. No reprieve would come of the noise, of course; she only communicated to them their success and warned away others in the dense, slum housing, to leave the men alone and wait until it was over.

Ada had lost count, but she thought it neared the time when the last hooded man would have just given her his seed. She proved herself right when it was Balkir who turned over to face him, gripping her petite hips and pulling her ass partly off the altar.

Holding her up and in his grip, Balkir sank into her a second time. She heard thick drops splatter onto the stone below, felt the spunk run down the crack of her ass, and the cult leader intentionally rubbed her flaming insides with his tool, in the way she'd responded most with the others.

For some indescribable and despicable reason, that was the moment when Ada's body — fever-pitched with frustration — finally climaxed.

ADA WAS CURLED UP IN A CORNER, SITTING ON THE COLD FLOOR RATHER THAN her cot; she wasn't the only one doing so, but she was the only one reading a book and muttering the words to herself.

"Will you shut up?!" blurted another of the cult's wives. Ada had silently dubbed her "the Shover."

"The Crier makes more noise," she commented, never looking up as she turned a page. She kept reading.

"She can't help herself, she's stuck in a state! You're just plain turned inside outside, the things you say!"

"Why did Master give her a book, anyway?" the Whiner asked.

"Because she's his special little wannabe sorceress!" the Shover spat, flailing her arms as she paced.

"If that is not your ambition," Ada murmured hoarsely, narrowing her eyes as she strained to hold onto the meaning of one symbol, "perhaps it's better to avoid annoying one who needs to practice on ... things."

"Are you threatening me, you little bitch?!"

"In more words than your mind is worth."

"Oh, yeah?! I'll show you! Give me that book!!"

Ada did not speak another intelligible word in the following conflict; instantly she became that "inside-out" creature of which she had been accused. She hissed and screeched, biting and clawing as she defended her book. She'd make the loud-mouthed shover pay, she'd make all of them pay! She had every intention to dig out the other woman's fresh eye from her skull and dry it to keep in her pouch of ingredients for later use.

"Stop! Stop! *Help! HEEELLLP!*"

"Ada! *Ada!* What is going on? Release her! Get away off her, come on, off! Come away, now! *Now!*"

It was a hard struggle to get Ada away from the other woman without an eye in her clutches, especially for one so small. Balkir trundled her out of the room as she screeched wordlessly, clawing at the air for the book, now kicked by accident several paces from her. The cult Master paused one moment to pick it up off the floor himself and carried her and it out, having no choice but to bring her back to his own quarters.

The peace had only lasted a few bitterly cold days.

"Alright! Enough! Be silent, Ada. *Silence!!*"

He'd slammed her hard down into a chair and the book onto the table; he banged his fist down onto the table to get her attention as he leaned into her face. Ada closed her mouth into a hard line but her eyes burned with pure hatred. Balkir stared at her in that blessed silence for a moment or two. Then his face softened and he started laughing.

"Oh, Ada," he said, "how I adore you. Such spirit. I've prayed to find one like you for some time now."

She tried to scrape the book toward her, but he pressed his palm on top of it to stop its progress. Slowly she withdrew her hand back to her lap; for all the world, she looked like an alley cat merely waiting for the next moment the mouse would poke its head out of the hole.

"Nothing will get in your way, isn't that so, my love?" Balkir said with pleasure. "That's what we need. That's what I like! Not the mewling whores in that room but one with ambition to chase down that magic until we can challenge the Ascended!"

Ada blinked slowly, choosing not to speak her thought on that, though it had something to do with the relative madness between them. He leaned forward until she could smell his rank breath.

"How about I teach you myself? Would you enjoy that? I would ask only three things in exchange."

She watched him wordlessly, waiting. He took it as an invitation to proceed.

"Each lesson equals one husbanding ritual on the altar, and you drink the fertility potion we give you to try and overcome your strong magic's natural resistance to life taking root in you."

Ada stared at him, pitch black eyes staring into his. "And?"

Balkir grinned. "And … you do not leave us in the spring. You stay." He guffawed at her slight change of expression. "Ohhh, don't think I haven't heard about you, little one. Only so many times a thief can use the same trick before she gets caught. But have no worry, there are lessons aplenty to take us through the next five winters! Any children that come remain with me." He studied her face. "Are you tempted?"

Ada twisted the metal strap they'd put around her wrist in circles, thinking. "A lesson lasts a day," she said.

"Of course, Ada."

"No husbanding at all without a lesson, or during. The husbanding cannot last more than once each, or two hours."

"Twice each, or four hours," he bargained.

"Then two lessons over four days between husbanding!" she snapped. "I do not heal this fast!"

"You are a clever one," the cult Master commented.

Her face screwed up in disgust. "You are a fool."

"Only wait until you see what I have to teach you. You will change your mind." He allowed a pause as he allowed his lust to show on his face. "Two lessons over four days between husbanding, for twice each, no more than four hours. Ada, our love ... will you become our new Mother of Entrails?"

She shuddered, hearing such blasphemy. "No. But we can bargain."

Balkir leaned down to kiss her, slobbering over her lips as she passively accepted.

CHAPTER 2

ADA KEPT BALKIR TO HIS BARGAIN, TO THE WORD; SHE DRANK THE NAUSEA-inducing potion before she tolerated holding her legs open every four days for twenty hooded men to mount her and run her through with their pricks, one after another. She didn't become pregnant immediately, although even if she had, she doubted the rutting would have stopped.

There was nothing many Ma'ab men seemed to like better than to share a willing woman between them. Ordinarily a woman drawing that wanting to service her spoke of her charm and receptiveness — it was even a way to gain status.

It was a holdover from the first years for the Ma'ab on this world, when they didn't have the time to wait to see if any particular male was fertile. When it came to impregnating a woman who wanted a child, men willing to work with care as a team were consistently chosen over the territorial, injurious ones. Those lessons had never really gone away in the slum though it worked somewhat differently for the upper Tiers.

Balkir eventually revealed what he was trying to do. He claimed to have been given instruction by the Mother of Entrails herself to discover the secrets of "life magic," as it was called much farther north around Vintern Hjem. This was something the Ma'ab had not brought with them in their heroic exodus from the Greylands five centuries ago.

They had brought plenty of death magic, though, and Balkir claimed hers was the most concentrated he had seen in anyone's aura within their caste.

"And I've been looking for decades, my sweet Ada."

"You try to change what I am," she said flatly.

"Transform! Transcend!" he corrected grandly, his dark eyes alight with passion. "The Ascended have done it! The most powerful necromancers from the nexus can still give birth to live young in our new home! One like you is unlikely to bear children, Ada, though you should! We will help you!"

Ada closed her eyes rather than let him see her roll them to the ceiling. At least his lessons were very interesting. At least she was allowed to practice her skill. They were worth the price. For now.

One ongoing lesson was a puzzle piece, a piece of scroll that even Balkir didn't understand, and he challenged her to figure out the trick to the encryption. Ada figured that was win-win for him — if she spent sixty lessons on it and never figured it out, that was sixty times on the altar with the hole between her legs raw and gaping, her nipples jutting out like the tips of red-hot pokers. Or if she *did* break the code to the correct pronunciation, well! It was something he hadn't been able to do.

In the end, Ada traded thirty lessons for it, and for twenty of them she didn't tell the cult Master that she'd already figured it out, had been memorizing the complex sounds forwards and backwards. She could pronounce them correctly, without even knowing what they meant. Every syllable she repeated, until it came to her in her sleep.

Usshhun'thagir ... vray gauldrun fregnoth'ka fri ...

She would never tell him. He would only ever think that she'd given up.

"Let us move on. Next lesson."

THE SOUNDS, SPOKEN IN A CIRCLE, OPENED A DOOR WHILE SHE SLEPT. THROUGH the door she would step into her dreams; she could travel them in an unnervingly lucid state. The other side was grey and featureless, the ground like fine dust sprinkled over black glass. Here there was no cold or hunger as she knew it, though she did hunger for a gaze to match her own.

Any gaze to prove she wasn't the only one to find this place. The only one to *feel* …

Happy.

"You have returned home."

Ada turned around to find what she sought a moment after it had found her. It belonged to a ghostly, swaddled maiden without eyes, about her own height. The other smiled modestly, more than Ada ever would.

"Home," the Ma'ab woman repeated, looking around at the grand nothingness. "When did you die?"

The maiden chuckled softly at first then her face became solemn. "Never."

The young woman twisted her fingers. "Where am I?"

A small bow. "You are where the Deathless led your people, far too long ago. We are glad to meet eyes with you, Ada."

When was anyone ever "glad" to see her? Ada frowned, speaking on pure instinct. "How can I understand you? No one can understand *you*."

"You have heard me your whole life. You've only just found the way to untangle the knots seizing your tongue." The maiden paused; she next question sounded merely curious. "Do you wish for a child, Ada?"

She thought of Balkir.

"No!" the young Ma'ab hissed, her teeth bearing a snarl. "Never by him! He is not right! Not right at all!"

The eyeless woman bowed her head. "We will seek another. I will search with you. … *vray gauldrun fregnoth'ka* …"

Words. Tangled …

Ada sat straight up in the cult Master's bed, her heart pounding. The mutterings in her head were knotted again … *Again!*

She returned to her corner with a book to start reading aloud, murmuring the words over and over and over.

Trying to find that temptingly clear voice amidst the insanity.

As hard as she tried, as often as she spoke the words flawless and per-fect, the same as before and over the next year, Ada could not untangle the knot inside her tongue at will.

But this was what she wanted. *This* was what she had been searching for ever since the old woman had found her, when she'd first learned to cut up rats for more than food.

"Ada. We adore you. Don't cut yourself like that. We'll keep trying."

Fool. He actually thought she cut because she of frustration that she hadn't become pregnant yet?

Fool! He isn't right! He will never be right!

Ada watched the winter melt before the wan spring, as Ennikar, the Ma'ab Capital City, remained grey from hard stone instead of ice and snow. Though eventually it grew more and more colorful as freshly washed banners and mended awnings could be seen marking the higher Tiers above them. Purple and crimson and indigo, and pale, pale yellow.

"Ada, Ada, Ada … you should have a big, strong son as smart as you! Take a look at what I found. Can you read it?"

Some of it. She was good with languages. Better than him.

She waited through the hot summer, always the best fighting season as the heat made the men extra aggressive. She watched various companies of military come to and fro through the slums but never stop, always on their way to somewhere better. A few might notice her if she got too close and they would always consider stepping out of line, trying to decide if she was worth raping or not.

"Careful, Ada. Don't look at them. Come here. Come here."

Maybe that one time it was a good suggestion.

The smaller, petite bodies of the female Ma'ab were always the male preference, even if the soldiers might be encouraged to press down some large-boned village girl of Paxian or Noiri or even Kurgan descent into the mud and mount her on a campaign. Better to spread their seed wherever they could; even though half-castes were never allowed into Ennikar, the Ma'ab had many places that needed working hands.

Worship, wealth, and politics protected the tiny Ma'ab women in the upper Tiers and the muscular man abided by their decisions. This did not so much help the women of the slum bottom caste, where size made much more of a difference. A body like hers simply had to be seized and restrained to be controlled, even as she was cherished.

"Easy, easy, wife. Let us help you off the altar. Oh! How red you are … ! Mind the puddle. Don't slip."

She'd rather slip in his entrails, if she had to slip on anything.

Ada had managed for several years to stay out of the clutches of any one male or group of males until Balkir, and occasionally she would tell herself again, and then again: "Not by him. He is all wrong. All wrong!"

And a soothing, clear whisper would answer. *We will seek another.*

She wouldn't catch here. She wouldn't!

Some of her cult husbands were killed and replaced with others over the next years — why, she did not care — and eventually when no children seemed forthcoming, more often they not only licked her and mounted her between her legs but also spread her buttocks to tongue her filth-star and eventually work their erections inside there, too. Balkir was no longer as insistent as to how they used her, where they spilled their seed. Even his efforts were flagging.

They would have used her mouth much more often if they could ever have gotten her to stop biting them. She had chipped a tooth in punishment, but Balkir had not let that go further because it would have affected her pronunciation of the texts that she was translating for him. Finally he was insistent about something again.

Her husbands left her mouth alone. They never soiled it.

The compromise was that they were free to sodomize her if they did not desire another attempt to seed her womb. Ada was mildly surprised with her body. It learned it was just as easy to pleasure her husband that way as the other; so long as they used oil, the sensation of pleasure remained.

By the time winter came again, she knew she could not leave the den but now she did not really want to. There were unread scraps of books and scrolls yet to go through, to find that untangling language again, and – baffling as it was – she had only to get on her knees and pull up her slip, to feel the tip of a husband's tongue tickle lightly at her filthy hole and her pale pink lips would start to get puffy and slick.

The predictable somatic responses were fascinating, beyond her conscious volition by this point, and this would help her, somehow.

Somehow, this would help her.

Then *They* came during the rite of spring.

Ada straddled her sixth husband, impaled on him and pressed down to his chest by the seventh husband, who slowly eased into her back passage at the same time. She couldn't move, couldn't run, when the First Tier militia stormed in; Husband Six was so startled that he spurted inside her right then.

Ada had been covered in sweat and semen; very soon after she was thrown off, she was covered in blood as well.

A purging.

The small woman fully expected to be ridden by every armored man who stepped through that door before being purged as well, but she wouldn't stay on the ground and let it happen.

Ada scrambled up naked, hissing and baring her teeth, clawing her hands, a tangled mass of black hair falling into her face. Some of the men chuckled but only blocked the exits with their swords and spears, observing her with the curiosity and threat level of a mangy dog trying to protect its trash. One in particular seemed to give her a harder stare, tracing her skin.

He shouted over his shoulder. "Mistress Vo'Traj! Come take a look at this one!"

It was the first time Ada had ever seen a true sorceress, and she was jealous in an instant. Not of the fine, warm clothing and the full, soft cheeks that spoke of enough food; not of the white skin kept so clean with fresh water and soap.

It was the density and high definition of her aura.

Ada growled. "You."

Vo'Traj laughed in delight, as if seeing something special underneath the filth and blood and man-sweat.

"Oh my, *yes*. You'll do."

Chapter 3
3067 S.E., The Blood Tier of Ennikar

Vo'Traj blew across the surface of her drink before taking a sip. She swallowed and closed her dark eyes to relish the heat and fragrance. Then she refocused on her new slave from the slums.

Balkir had given up the name of his little pet before he was killed, prattling about her gift of translating and reading — hardly an unusual "gift" outside of the slum, but Vo'Traj understood what the piece of filth had meant.

A good thing Balkir was a talker, because Ada had not said one word thus far.

"I hope you do not expect to simply continue being a breeder here," the noble said. "No man outside your caste will touch you, and any male within your caste who has access to you has been warned that he will lose both his scrotum and his fingers if he does."

The Ma'ab sorceress studied Ada for a few moments, receiving no reaction to this announcement – not relief, not dismay. The slum girl *was* paying attention; she did not stare into nothingness but showed awareness of where she was, furtively glancing about the room even as she wisely avoided looking Vo'Traj in the eyes.

Still, one would have thought after being rescued from that trouble-some Balkir and no longer being his cult's seed receptacle that the girl would show some opinion on the matter, some disappointment or gratitude to tell Vo'Traj more about her new acquirement. Unless something was wrong with her memory, or she was already crazy beyond redemption.

No matter. Crazy or not, Ada would give her all the insight needed into Balkir's recovered library, any research they had done, or any discoveries made which the Second Tier could use. Vo'Traj also had a new slave to bring her new pep when needed, while she lived, and a new soul that would feed the sorceress when that underfed body died. The Noble would not touch the slum girl unless it was necessary, though.

As two Ma'ab women, they were roughly the same, small size, both pale with dark hair and dark eyes, but there was a marked difference in their inherited beauty. The slum girl clearly hadn't had any to inherit. While they each possessed ritual scars for their magic, Vo'Traj's own scars were tiny, clean, and deliberate – also easily hidden with clothing – while Ada's were plain on her limbs and extremities, jagged having been slower to heal and no doubt made worse with infection.

"You will serve me for the rest of eternity, Ada. You obey my will in all things for the good of the Ascended; you may even catch a glimpse of one someday, being in my service."

No response.

"Hm. You have come this far up from the slum in a matter of hours. I trust you are intelligent enough to see your elevation and do not waste my time with rebellion. I will consume you and make your body into what I will regardless. It is up to you how you are treated in the afterlife. One foolish mistake can cost you dearly for all time."

Ada stared.

Vo'Traj's eyes moved over her slum foundling again, at her dirty fingernails and grimy, bruised feet. Beyond that, her aura and its colors bore a strange, icy silver and pale, pale blue. Such concentration of color and so tightly controlled, Vo'Traj couldn't wait to sample it.

The Blood Tier sorceress licked her lips. "And should the gift I see prove strong enough that I decide you will have children, those will be mine as well. For all eternity, Ada, you and yours are mine."

Mistress Vo'Traj was not nearly as indulgent as Balkir but being trapped during the summer and protected during the winter did not change for Ada, as far as she saw it.

The food was better and plentiful, and Ada was required to keep herself clean — something not in her previous routine. She frequently forgot at first, taken in by her by her work or her thinking, but a few of those core-shocking punishments — the only time that her Mistress touched her — was enough to change her habits.

Mistress Vo'Traj did not give her what she wanted most, keeping the scrolls and books under lock and key and punishing her when she was caught looking for them. Ada got used to some menial labor, although it remained limited by her small stature. Eventually it was clear in both her mind and her dreams that she had to wait for her Mistress to become curious about the books and scrolls from Balkir's library.

Ada was content with not being touched by anyone else most of the time. Occasionally she might catch a whiff of something similar but not quite the same as Balkir's quarters. Or sometimes her mind would wander into a memory of large fingers and primal tongues being their disgusting selves, penetrating and tasting her smelliest parts, and — frustratingly — her labia would swell and redden in response and remain sensitive as her thighs squeezed together.

She resolved to think of it less and less. There were no sires around her now, no husbands, and thus no purpose to imagining such things and becoming slick for no one, only to have to clean herself up.

Around the same time as when Ada stifled her curiosity and her base urges together, Mistress Vo'Traj granted her a reward in something to read.

"A children's book," she called it. "Your true education must start somewhere."

Frowning briefly, Ada had curled up in her cot among the servant quarters to page through it. There were bright, blatant illustrations but very few words to read. The book taught a child to count to seven, and in doing so to learn the names of the Ascended. The small woman went through them several times, repeating them, and repeating past words from Balkir's library, the ones that had once untangled her tongue.

Even if the children's book and the recitation didn't free her tongue now, she *could* hear someone whispered additional description to each picture, explaining words that were not there for her to read on her own.

"One," Ada mouthed without voice.

Another voice whispered back.

Vermillion Lady of Ebon Flame. The One Most Powerful who first gave birth upon this new world. The Divine Prime.

"Two," she breathed.

The General of the Undefeated Void. The Divine Warrior of Deeds: he made an unbreakable bargain with the Deathless which then broke the Ma'ab chains pf bondage.

"Three."

The Chirurgeon of Souls. The Divine Physician, the first of the Ascended to understand how to manipulate souls outside of the Greylands, to keep them for much, much longer.

"Four," she continued counting.

Enslaver of the Nine Circles. The Divine Enslaver who found the resources to strengthen the Ma'ab at their most vulnerable upon this new world.

Ada tapped with her finger, slow and deliberate, frowning in thought. "Five."

The Mother of Entrails. Divine Matron, the first midwife to the Vermillion Lady and the Ascended's initial salvation to prevent miscarriages and keep their bloodline going. The discoverer of this world's strangest "life" magic.

Balkir's voice came back, the touches and deep penetration, the *fluids* … Again Ada's hidden folds warmed and tingled.

She growled low and turned the page. "Six."

The Artisan of Blood. The Divine Artisan, the keeper of their genealogy and second midwife to the Vermillion Lady.

"And … seven?" Ada asked.

The Opener of Gates from Within, the Divine Assassin. The Ascended who knows all the ways to kill or destroy every creation they encountered.

These were the Ma'ab gods.

These were the First Tier who ruled them.

This small book was meant to fill a Noble's child with new wonder and gratitude.

The back cover of the book was blank.

Earlier in the day, Ada had plucked one small piece of charcoal from the kitchen fire to keep in her apron pocket. She was about to draw the symbol for "Eight" on the book in brittle, black permanence.

No! the voice cried. *Patience, child. Keep my name to yourself.*

Clear as the summer sky. Gone like the sun in winter.

"I don't know your name," Ada murmured, hesitating with the charcoal hovering above the off-white press of fibers. "No one can understand *you.*"

Finally, she tucked the black piece away and closed the child's book, setting aside that holy manuscript without defacing it.

CHAPTER 4

THE NEXT TWO MALE GIANTS WHO CAME NEAR ENOUGH TO TOUCH HER WERE not Ma'ab … Or at least with the first, not entirely.

Several winters later, Ada had been given the task of sterilizing and organizing many of her Mistress's tools and small, glass bottles and vials. It was a sign that the former slum-dweller was farther into Vo'Traj's confidence than she had started, this had occurred to her in a vague way, though the small female had no plans to misuse the items to which she was given access. They were ordinary, practical things anyway; other than their high quality, nothing differentiated them from the same items necessary to perform certain work in Balkir's place.

The heavy footsteps approaching the door just before it opened sent Ada's heart into a skip and she abandoned her task and scrambled beneath the worktable and behind the black tablecloth draped over it. She didn't question the instinct to hide, she just did it, lying down on her belly and putting her cheek on the cool, stone floor so she might peak out through a small gap near the forward table leg.

A Hellhound entered, huge and scarred, bald and tattooed, his black leather armor worn in many places. He did not have his spiked chain with him, but she could see clearly around which arm it normally resided and he still had plenty of blades.

His eyes, black and bottomless, echoed his expression like a silent, stone mountain. He approached the table, instantly noting the work interrupted, and stepped back from it, turning around to scan the room. She heard him sniffing for scent, using whatever other abilities he had to detect someone unseen.

Ada was dismayed how little time it took the Hellhound to lift the tablecloth and peer beneath at her. She had not dared to move so was flat on her belly like a lizard until the very moment she shuffled backward and got into a very small ball against the wall.

Trapped.

The Hellhound said nothing, only tilted his head curiously. He had a strange light about him; his aura was of someone alive but … strange. Not like any aura she had ever seen before in Ennikar.

He possessed too many colors, far too numerous to be Ma'ab. She hadn't realized those shades of green and purple and orange could exist; it was the first time she had ever seen them.

"Where is Vo'Traj?" he asked hoarsely, like he didn't speak often.

Ada shook her head; she didn't know. Much of the time, she knew not where her Mistress was or what she was doing.

Any number of First and Second Tier would have demanded that she speak her answer aloud. They would tell her what honorific to give them, would demand that she do something else to assuage their desire to be acknowledged properly, to dance for them like a puppet.

The Hellhound just stared at her a moment longer, nostrils flaring as he sniffed the air again. He dropped the tablecloth, standing back up.

He left.

"Wh-what … is he?" she whispered.

The voice in her head didn't answer.

ADA WOULD MEET THE SECOND LARGE MALE ONLY A FEW WEEKS LATER ON A dark, winter night, when her Mistress was a little too high on her own mists.

It would have been a good time to avoid Vo'Traj, if possible; if it had been a stressful day among the Nobles and the Ascended, sometimes the woman would inhale the burning incense in one of the cellar rooms, drink distilled liquid from tiny cups, and talk and shout to herself and her ancestors until the Sun arose.

Unfortunately, Ada was required to bring food and water on a tray, covered to keep her from breathing on it or touching it before it could pass the lips of her superior. She did not draw out this delivery, reluctant as she was to perform it in the first place. She moved efficiently to the door, waited to be allowed to enter, approaching to the low table in front of the lounge.

Ada dropped to her knees, set it down, bowed low and started backing up on all fours, heading straight for the exit.

"Stop."

The command was firm, even if the senses were askew. Ada managed one more shuffle before she had to stop, though it wouldn't do her any good. She was still too far from the door.

"Ada. What do you think?"

The slum necromancer kept her eyes on the floor. "Mistress."

Vo'Traj giggled, the sound enhancing her small stature. "Ada, what do you — ? Oh, come! Lift your eyes, gods damn you! Look and tell me what you think!"

Ada had avoided looking at the thing in the corner upon entering; she certainly did not want to make eye contact now. The creature unsettled her, even just sensing it. It possessed blood from some other place, an "elsewhere" only contacted by the Divine Enslaver, even as it possessed also that life magic endemic to this world. Their new home.

She lifted her eyes before she must be told again and looked, focused on as many details as quickly as she could before anything strange happened.

Male for certain, its black cock was long, and testes dwelled inside a scrotum for breeding. The tool seemed to work in the expected way from what she could see. He was required to cradle it, to display it for her Mistress, stroking slowly to stay erect but not to move toward ejaculation.

Ada noticed the piercing, the hoop hanging just below the large head; the shaft was knobby but not much uglier than Balkir's man-bit — only much darker with white hair at the base like an inverted Ma'ab.

The creature had black skin overall and a white mane flowing down the center from a bestial head and in between long, pointed ears; it extended down his neck and hunched spine to his middle back. Tall and strong, long fingered and with claws on hands and feet, he had no tail. He possessed yellow, demonic eyes and sharp teeth – his face could match what she imagined a Hellhound should look like better than the fighters themselves with their spiked chains.

The beast was chained to the wall by his left ankle, but he would still have an impressive reach. If he really tried, he would be just short of Vo'Traj on her lounge, close enough to move the air around her skin with a quick enough swipe.

"What do you think?" the Second Tier asked a third time, her voice low and sensual. Another chuckle and sip of her drink.

Ada didn't know what answer her Mistress wanted. Maybe a question. "What is this?"

"A gift from the Divine Enslaver that I've cherished for some years now," she answered smugly, slurring a little. "This gift can turn invisible. He is always very useful when we leave on a campaign. And I just got the command, Ada, we will be leaving in the spring. We shall travel South."

In the spring. Leaving? But she had not yet been able to read as much as she wanted to in the library.

The sorceress kept talking. "His name is Vesram, and he hasn't been serviced in a while. I want you to suck on his cock, draw out his seed. Give him some release." Vo'Traj shifted her hips slightly, pulling up at her dress to expose a thigh. "Stay low as you are, Ada, crawl over to him and open your mouth. He knows what to do."

Ada's face betrayed her as her lips contorted and her nose wrinkled. She had never liked anything jammed into her mouth that was not food — her mouth was reserved for someone else, that nameless other.

Her Mistress saw this resistance and hiked her dress up further, putting her bejeweled hand over her dark curls at the junction of her pale thighs.

"Do it, Ada. Crawl over there and suck on him. Lick his sack. Don't bite him and be careful of his jewelry."

Despite the tests of pain, challenges of obedience, cleanliness and attention to detail; in spite of regular draws upon and manipulations of Ada's aura that felt as intrusive as her husbands; and even with a host of small insults and daily humiliations from the Second Tier Mistress ... This particular form of entertainment had been a mercifully absent.

Until now.

With her demand made, Ada knew it wouldn't stop being an option when her Mistress was high like this.

She wouldn't be able to change it, either.

The small slum girl's fingers were cold, and she did not remember each small scrape to her knees as she made her way over to the demon. When she could see his crouching legs, his bopping erection, when she could smell that strange spice in his sweat, she lifted her chin yet could not make herself open her mouth for him to fill it.

She scowled at him.

Vesram saw her face, and he snorted in return, wrinkling his nose as she had. Clearly, he was of the same opinion about the act. Quite rapidly his black, swollen length started to deflate, granting the cock piercing an illusion of enlargement.

"Vesram!" their Mistress scolded, briefly flipping her dress down to cover herself as she straightened up, put out by the flagrant refusal. "Ada, suck it anyway, make it hard again!"

Ada didn't really know how; this she'd never been required to practice.

The small woman made a half-hearted attempt to lick the flaccid length of bejeweled flesh, but the demon had pressed back against the wall, trying to evade her. Vesram growled at her — and at Vo'Traj — pulling himself free and flopping, barely wetted.

How did he get away with defying her?

The answer was that he wouldn't, but he would rather have whatever punishment the incense-infused sorceress could concoct rather than let her grotesque, chip-toothed slave from the slums slobber all over him for her entertainment.

It was an interesting choice. A stupid one, perhaps, but interesting.

Vo'Traj went into a shrill cursing fit before she managed a proper tirade, grabbing clumsily for her whip.

"Only your mother could love *your* face, Vesram, and now you refuse my sweet, new servant?! Well, you're never going to get to mount a lovely face again, so you might as well get used to what you are offered! Thrice-damned, bat-nosed, snarling leg-humper! I'll — !"

Ada spun around and put her forehead to the floor, curled into her customary, submissive ball with her backside facing the demon. She covered her face and head with her arms and squeezed her eyes shut at the first crack of the whip.

Vesram roared with rage. Her blood rushed in response.

She had not been told to leave so would not make that mistake only to draw her Mistress's ire toward her in the middle of such a fury, but she was far too close to the whip and those teeth and claws for her survival instinct to be silent.

"Fine! Then *you* lick *her!* Ada, up! Hips up now!"

Ada lifted her hips, balancing on her knees as ordered but kept her head down and covered as Vo'Traj flipped up her rough, simple servant's dress onto her hips. As soon as Ada sensed their gazes and felt the open air on her snatch, she groaned quietly as it started tingling. No doubt her sex was changing color; with her pale skin, that was always far too obvious of a change, flushing a deep, welcoming red that any male recognized.

"My, my," Vo'Traj teased. "Hm! What do you think, Vesram? Do you know where I found her? Locked in a room with nine men taking turns, taking whatever hole they wanted. She was a *mess*, but those brothers were very, very happy."

Vesram had stopped growling; he was listening to the sorceress.

"Oh, yes. Ada may not look like much, but she is accustomed to pleasing multiple brothers at once. Her body misses it. She's just what you like, my boy. Isn't that just what you've dreamed of home? Some black slut taking brother after brother in some sort of celebration? Well! Let us celebrate! We will be leaving on campaign again soon!"

Vo'Traj taunted him with a laugh, an ugly sound, and after another pause, a small, gloved hand patted at Ada's puffy netherlips.

"Have a taste, Vesram. Don't look at her face, if you insist, but at least understand that breeding slum like her *will* be good enough for you. You will not tempt me ever again." Vo'Traj took a second to struggle with her breath and her anger. "I will *never* allow you to mount me! You can rut *her* instead, insufferable beast! Do you understand?"

The small Ma'ab grabbed his mane and brought him down lower to sniff at Ada's crotch. He hesitated, but for whatever reason chose to cooperate. He licked the slave, long and slow and wet.

It was gentle.

Ada wiggled her toes in unconscious pleasure. More licking as her breeding hole fluttered and relaxed beneath the attention. She moaned, more distressed than she wanted to be over the aching, the emptiness.

"You want him, Ada?" Vo'Traj asked with glee.

Shivering, she widened her knees, hoping that was an acceptable answer. Before the noble could decide, Vesram loomed over her and penetrated.

"Oh, gods!" their Mistress cried, drowning out Ada's grunt in that familiar stretching.

Vesram hunched forward, breathing heavily as he got fully seated inside her, holding her hips in a careful grip. He sighed.

Memories of her husbands flooded back alongside the certainty she wouldn't get with child from this one. Her body responded to both, wanting the practice, *wanting* that mind-seizing peak as she milked his essence.

Her sex clenched down on him eagerly. The demon hummed.

"Ohhh," Vo'Traj cooed. "You filthy, low-caste whore. I might have known you'd like it. Oh, keep going, Vesram. Deeper."

Ada tried not to be jounced forward; she held herself up, stable and presenting. This would help her when the time came to choose her sire.

"That's it. Rut on that little cunt. Plunder it!"

She climaxed quickly, moaning and drooling. It was obvious.

This will help.

He kept going.

"Wait. Wait … Don't seed her womb, fool. I won't risk it."

He can't …

"Get that pitch black cock in between those white-slut buttocks. Spill there!"

Ada whimpered as the demon withdrew, and Vo'Traj dribbled oil — just plain oil — from high above them so that it spattered into a mess between them. The beast was much slower than her husbands, and not any bigger.

He took his time. She relaxed.

"Ah …" she breathed.

The penetration seized all of her mind, blunt and slick and wide. He showed skill in loosening her up after so long, his long, slippery draws and thrusts, his gradually increasing tempo, playing Ada's voice for his Mistress.

Vesram performed well, and Vo'Traj was pleased.

"Ohhh …" Vo'Traj breathed, now back on her lounge with her legs splayed, throttling herself with her hand. "Filthy. Your jewel is getting so filthy! Oh! Ada … yes!"

Vesram leaned in, taking her deep. Ada's fingers tightened on the floor as he reached around, carefully sliding the rough pads of his fingers across her drooling netherlips. She peaked a second time, astonished with his deft ministration.

"*Ungh!*"

"Yes!" her Mistress cried again. "Ohh, he's ready, Ada! Take what he must give you!"

Ada pressed her forehead to the stone, nodding.

He's ready. Somewhere.

I know it.

Vesram gnashed his teeth, growling and snarling as he spurted inside her. Ada was then ordered to give proof, to reach back and part her own buttocks, squeezing it out.

Doing so guaranteed Ada would come with them when the army left.

"Marvelous!" Vo'Traj sighed, coming down from her own peak. "Ohhh, you enjoyed that. Such filth."

Ada bit her lip, listening to them panting.

We will seek him soon.

She would leave Ennikar for the first time in her life.

In the Spring.

Chapter 5

Many were preparing to leave Ennikar with the Army.

"For how long?" some asked.

However long it took them to make a giant circle and eventually come back with spoils.

When Ada next saw Vesram at First Thaw and around much higher activity than usual, he seemed just a bit protective of her. Many slaves hustled about, most of them slum caste who would occasionally make eye contact with her but not with Vo'Traj's demon slave.

Meanwhile, Vesram would move forward to cover Ada's small body from their view as she cleaned and packed the items she'd been shown. Ada was not sure why he did this, but their Mistress was never too far away from the beast and gave no signal of disapproval — assuming she even noticed as she spoke with official after official on the planning and logistics.

Vo'Traj was excited to be leaving; she had been stuck in the capital city for the last decade and was getting bored and anxious — as Vesram had explained. The sorceress's boredom was related to the night the demonblood had been required to mount Ada.

"Closse," the Sathoet had murmured. "Clossesst Mistresss came to piercing her cuunt on mme. Nevver sso closse before."

The way Vesram communicated with her seemed so clear compared to her own people. Something about his body language, the graceful way he moved his hands and his tone of voice, conveyed more than Ada had ever understood coming from others around her, or even her own thoughts.

But that night finally made sense to her now.

Vo'Traj wanted very much to "sample" her demon but could not bring herself to do it. Perhaps she could not even admit it. Ada had been tossed upon the altar once again, this time to spare her Mistress's pride, to be the surrogate for her true desires. Vo'Traj wanted to see the long, dark cock impale a small, pink, Ma'ab cunt.

And she had.

It dawned on Ada that this creature could not only speak her language but also understood the motives of his owner and other nobles better than her.

The slum servant worked extra hard to learn the new patterns of living on the road with the military. Only being efficient and competent would buy her the time she needed to get near Vesram and ask him more questions.

"What are you?" she asked one time. She had the time for exactly one question.

His answer, he was a half-Elf.

"My sssire was a demon called from the Abyss, presssent only long enough to impregnate my mother."

An Elf.

Ada tilted her head but had needed to wait for next time to follow up.

Farther South down the road as broad, frosty plains gave way to grassland and steppes, she could ask him her next question.

"What is an Elf?"

"An ancient race. Magic is our essence."

Natives to this world, far older than the Humans with which the Ma'ab could breed. A long-lived, well-hidden people. Vesram's knife-shaped ears were theirs. These creatures lived centuries and were beautiful, though dark-skinned with hair of snow white.

They called themselves Davrin. They called him Sathoet.

Ada nodded and left to return to work.

Later on, they spoke again.

"How did you get here?"

The air around him depressed, and he was silent long enough she wondered if he wouldn't answer before they ran out of time.

"Exiled," he said.

He and Mother had been captured by the Ma'ab over half a century ago. She had been a Priestess, sort of like the Divine Enslaver — at least in that she understood it was possible to call a being from outside the world to perform a task.

"Mother wasss a healer," Vesram said with reverence. "Counter to the scarring magics. My birth did not leave her barren like the others."

This was dangerous to the ruling order; this, Ada understood well. *If they cannot usurp, they will expunge …*

Their Queen had sent them away, the mother and son, to try for an impossible goal. Impossible even for a powerful Elf like her.

"What happened to your mother?"

Vesram lifted his head, peering out across the camp. Ada followed his gaze. He was staring at the Hellhounds passing by.

"Her body wassted away, but the Physsician kept her."

Ada blinked slowly. "How?"

Vesram nodded his chin again toward the elite warriors. He took care with his pronunciation. "Kreshel Divigna."

She looked again, her memory sparked by the glimpse of his aura.

That man with all the colors.

The Hellhound who had once found her hiding underneath the table but had left her alone.

He is more than just Ma'ab.

Divigna bore the lingering aura of Vesram's Elven mother as well.

ADA HAD WATCHED FOR THE HELLHOUND COMMANDER AFTER THAT, WANTING another glimpse of this Ma'ab who was not Ma'ab, now that she knew why.

Her patience was rewarded; slowly, she got her fill, studying the vibrant essence.

This is what life looks like. Elves make life.

On the heels of that thought came another voice.

Good, child, good. Remember this pattern, it will help you.

One day, the Ma'ab won a satisfying skirmish with the Kurgan on the steppes. After a raid in which even the barbarian warlocks were unable to burn or reclaim all the Kurgan dead now swelled their ranks, the Ascended's Army was in high spirits for some nighttime celebration.

To avoid drunken groups of soldiers who might not care about her caste or whom she served, Ada had curled in behind the half-Elf inside Vo'Traj's tent. Thankfully, they were not summoned that night to perform.

She asked him, "What did Vo'Traj learn about Elves in serving the Third?"

Vesram shrugged. "Little. The soundss Mother and I shared."

In response to the Elf's obstinacy and at the command of the Divine Physician, Vo'Traj had written down the phonetic sounds that she heard. The most common phrases, sentence after sentence, paragraph after paragraph until they filled a shelf full of notebooks, written in some code few could read.

"The Fourth ripped my name from her," he added, a keen pain fracturing his voice. "Once they undersstood more."

Now Ada knew what she had so carefully packed away into the trunk on the far side of the tent. *The Davrin language is in those books, if only I could learn how to pronounce it . . .*

"Why do you still live?" Ada asked Vesram.

He shrugged. "They will not let me die."

She frowned. "What else?"

Vesram arched a brow ridge. "What mean you?"

"I mean you are like me. You do not live at their pleasure. That is happenstance. Why?"

He dared not speak his reason that day.

In the middle of another day, cool and overcast, the Army turned

Southeast and closer to the Sea than they would be for many, many weeks. It occurred to Ada that she already knew a reason they had in common.

"Do you want to die?" she asked him.

His ears had turned back, his nostrils flaring, and eyes narrowed. "Nnot yyet."

Not *yet*. But at some point, yes.

Ada smiled a little.

There was a pause.

"Whaat about yyou?" he asked.

Ada shook her head as well. "Not yet. But perhaps not long. There is still something I must do."

Vesram glanced around. This time, he dared say it.

"Esscape now?"

"Shhh."

This Sathoet was able to read her better than any being except the nameless one.

He chuckled and nodded.

VESRAM KEPT WATCH OUT FOR HER THE FIRST TIME ADA PLUCKED ONE OF THE notebooks containing his mother's last words from the trunk.

"Willl not helllp you," he said, meaning that he would not translate it for her any more than he would for Vo'Traj.

"Understand," Ada muttered, flipping quickly through the pages.

Vo'Traj had used a similar encryption for Balkir's library. Ada understood how to make the sounds if she desired. However, she had no reason aside from Vesram's story and the fact that Vo'Traj kept these notebooks with her even on campaign to suggest they were anything but gibberish.

The low caste slave chose a few sentences and memorized them backwards and forwards, just as she had those in her husband's library. Front and back, muttered while she was polishing leather and armored bits and buckles, over and at the start again while she helped carry water to the tent, again — again-again, whisper, whisper it …

Until she would dream of it.

One night, she was tired and finally released from labor.

Having fallen asleep next to Vesram, she dreamed of waking up, of crawling out from his heavy arms and walking lightly through the door.

Of walking silently through the camp alone.

Vesram would be worried, but it *had* to be alone.

She crept up on the Hellhounds like a ghost, looking for their leader, their trainer. They were still awake.

She watched as she murmured the Davrin words, watched what his aura did when he finally heard them. He looked her way.

Of course, she was dreaming all of this. A testing of the theory where the maiden could give her answers.

Ada would try for real when she woke up.

She wasn't afraid when the great male she sought turned toward her. Like before, he stepped right where she was hidden beneath a mound of saddles awaiting repair. He sniffed, kneeled down into the trodden, churned soil, and lifted a single saddle to reveal her eyes within her hiding place.

Kreshel Divigna.

She smiled, waiting for him to leave.

He didn't. A huge hand grabbed her by the scruff of her thick dress. He dragged her out from under the leather.

"*Ngh!* Erg … feh!" she uttered in frustration as she tried to get the words working right.

She couldn't talk!

He held her far off the ground, and his hand reached for a dirk.

Not yet. Talk. Talk!

"*Xsa dos ulu l'rendan!*" Ada said to Divigna's face. "*Xal ussta valsharess' Litarifa tlu feithin whol dos ulu plynn quarne xuil l'oqu!*"

Divigna responded, his eyes widening, his aura flaring beautifully.

Such color! Unheard of in Ennikar!

She might wonder if he'd seen a memory but did not go that far. She was certain now the language was tied to the life aura; *this* was what she needed to know. Different words, different languages, would show her different things about this world.

I can read the very world like a book!

Ada clapped her hands and laughed, and Kreshel reconsidered drawing his dirk, confused and hesitating. After a moment, he drew her closer, carrying her like a child to her room rather than like a mongrel about to be eviscerated. Divigna entered the nearest supply tent, past a guard who only nodded to him.

"Eternal Hellhound," he said.

She frowned. *Wait. What happens ... ?*

Inside, the commander pressed her down onto the top of a crate and stood between her legs, working at his belt. Ada felt the strong life aura primed against her defense of death. She realized with a start that she was ... *not* dreaming ...

Not dreaming!

Too late, she started struggling. He held her down.

"No!" she cried, afraid at last but for a whole new reason.

This one. He was *life*.

He could *overwhelm* her; unlike Balkir and the others, he could stimulate her womb. This man had the ability to impregnate her in one climax!

Not time! Not yet! No!

If Ada conceived, Vo'Traj would know. *Immediately*, she would know! Ada would be trapped; she would never, never escape.

Not even after I die!

The Hellhound easily held her in place and freed his deep-red member, pulling up her dress while looking her in the face — he did not react to her protests one way or another.

My Lady!! Help!

"*Nau vrine'winith,*" she blurted, "*vrine'winith!*"

Recognition in his dark eyes.

"No?" he whispered in Ma'ab, displaying some mixed awareness, dead center of what his purpose and how his aura responded to her words. "Were not you commanding me, telling me it was time to breed again, little sorceress?"

Was I?

"No!" she insisted, even as he tugged her hips closer to the edge, pressing his cockhead against her dry gash, holding it there. Teasing her.

He was scalding.

"Leave me be, please," she whispered, the words falling unbidden from her lips. "Let me go, and my son will kill Vo'Traj and f-free her slaves."

Kreshel stiffened his hips, pressing his broad cock harder, forcing her partway open. She groaned and shook her head urgently as he sank farther in. It stung; she wasn't welcoming him in any respect.

"Please!" she moaned.

He leaned over her.

"Kill her," he whispered. A glimmer of emotion broke through his cold visage. "And kill me. Set me free."

"Y-yes," she agreed. "He will set you free. We swear it."

"You can't … without the Chirurgeon of Souls."

Ada nodded understanding. "The Third Ascended. We swear …"

Kreshel withdrew from her bruised sex, lifted his heavy hands and arms from her shoulders, stepping away from her. He turned to grip her around the middle and clutch her to his side, carrying her out of the supply tent with her dress still riding up, exposing part of her buttock which made the guard laugh.

Ada hid her face against the Hellhound's chest until he left the soldiers' rows. Standing on the edge of the officer's tents, he put her down and gave her a little shove toward the back of Vo'Traj's tent.

"I will wait," he said, staring at her a few instants longer.

She quivered, squinting at his face. Was that the faint hint of a smile or a frown creeping across his features?

Whichever it was, it vanished when he left, returning to his mortal Hellhounds.

Ada was never more thankful Vo'Traj was a deep sleeper as she carried water and kindling past the guards, nodding as she tried not to stumble into the front flaps.

"*Hsss …*"

Vesram was awake, sucking air through his teeth. His white mane stood up along his spine as he watched her approach, his nostrils flaring as he rumbled. "You *left?*"

"I'm unhurt," she whispered. "No talk now."

Scenting her as she collapsed in exhaustion, the half-Elf let her crawl in next to him. She curled up in the warmest place where she felt safe to get a little sleep before the next day arrived.

CHAPTER 6

3068 S.E., EAST PAXIA

"HOT DOWN HERE," VO'TRAJ COMMENTED CASUALLY, SWISHING THE RED SKIRT of her North-heavy outfit to gather a breeze underneath. She used a fan on her pale face while Ada held a dark purple parasol to protect her from the strong sun. "Appropriate for Musanlo's people to be locked down so tight in this sun-drenched place."

Ada kneeled in a slump beside the sorceress, silent and alone. She had already been listening to Vesram's cries for hours as she worked around the outside of the tent. She had not dared to go inside as their Mistress extracted another painful Davrin word from him which she could apply to many sentences within her books. He was recovering while Vo'Traj lounged outside.

"*U'lar,*" the sorceress continued, tasting the word even as she tasted her wine. "Not possible. A pre-determined failure. He was playful today, at first I thought he was in denial of my control again, but … no. He was translating the word for me. He is learning."

Only to make you wait.

The low caste sat small and forgettable, or so she hoped.

"You know what I've pieced together, Ada? When the Hellhounds and those bedraggled upstarts dragged back the black Priestess and her demon-son from the West, the creatures had been on a mission of some kind. They were far away from their home. They have a single queen, you know, and it was she who sent them."

He told me that months ago. Ada practiced quiet in thought and expression. *And they aren't "creatures," they are Elves.*

"I wonder if the queen misses her?" Vo'Traj continued. "She was quite a sexual creature. Appropriate for her unique magic."

Only by comparison, Ada thought. *And not unique. Just hidden.*

"Alas, the Third could not find a way to breed her before she began wasting away, almost of her own will. She could make hybrids, just look at Vesram! But she did not last long enough for us to try.

"Fortunately, the Chirurgeon of Souls had a brilliant theory how to preserve her essence all the same, to bind it to one of our own, and retain that powerful fertility within a relic of her own making."

Vo'Traj sighed, sipping wine from a metal cup before clearing her throat. "Placed within a male body of the right caste, it has never been so easy for the upper class to breed. Almost as easy as it is for the slum."

Contemptuous eyes looked down on her. "Except you, dear Ada. Really. Almost twenty husbands, plenty of food, and several years and not *one* seed could sprout in that belly of yours? Among slum females, that is unheard of. You should have several children by now."

Ada blinked stupidly, her mind an empty canyon as her Mistress leaned closer.

"You know what that means, don't you?" The sorceress covered her mouth as she belched softly. "Oof. *Ahem.* It means you are your own relic, of sorts. A concentration of our inherited Greylands magics which occasionally shows itself in the lower caste. Had you been born on my level, you might have been trained to become something more useful than you are: yet another servant I shall use to maintain my heritage."

The sorceress gulped down the rest of her drink, tapping the rim of the empty glass to her lips thoughtfully. "Hmm. Two relics in camp ... I wonder what you might look like together? Interesting."

The small, ugly woman felt her stomach seize and chill.

"What kind of child you would make with Kreshel, Ada?" Vo'Traj grinned. "Surely that Hellhound of any would be able to blast heat into that cold fortress in your gut and make his seed take root. I wonder ...”

This is it. I must leave.

And as soon as possible, never mind if they made it closer to Manalar or not. Now that the idea had left Vo'Traj's lips, it was only a matter of time. Ada already knew it would only take once with that specific Hellhound.

I can't. I made a promise.

VESRAM SHARED HIS INVISIBILITY WITH HER.

The Sathoet carried her to the edge of his leash, bending the light around them both. Abruptly, he stopped, whining in pain as he dropped her with her small bundle.

Not one step more.

“Thank you,” she whispered. “I will repay this aid.”

The Sathoet didn't believe her but took a moment to nuzzle her cheek. “Goodbye, Ada.”

He turned back, returning as swiftly to his sentence as she ran away from it.

The soil of the South was soft and dark; there were far fewer rocks and countless trees, so much undergrowth that Ada was scraped head to foot as she forced her way southwest. She climbed higher into the hills during the day and hid at night when the undead would be shambling about looking for her.

Her slum caste carcass was not worth sending the Hellhounds, thankfully, or they would have found her within a day or two. Vo'Traj would be immensely irritated with the loss and perhaps tempted to suggest using Divigna's men, but Vesram had reassured her.

“She will never get the other commanderss to spend their resources that way.”

Vo'Traj tattooed all her possessions so she could find them, another question she might not want other commanders asking about. Tampering with the markings was supposed to alert her, but this was one mark that couldn't overlay the Maiden's touch.

Ada had dreamed of a way to slough the magic, to shed it like old skin the day before her departure. Her former Mistress would attempt to discover why she could not sense her slave through the tattoo. Perhaps she would assume Ada had been killed somehow and try to summon her spirit.

It wouldn't work. Ada was bleeding red from so many scrapes in her travel, she *knew* she was alive. Later, she swore to cut the tattoo off properly in thanks to her patroness, an earnest show of faith to her secret Grey Lady.

She must only wait for the luxury of time to do so.

Would the Elf's son betray her despite his obvious affection? That remained to be seen. Vesram had despised Vo'Traj longer than Ada had been alive, and no matter how the Second Tier sorceress might torture him to insanity, the demonblood could not explain the nullified mark because he didn't know about it.

Ada had never told him about the Maiden in her dreams; thus far she had kept her promise never to tell. She had also left with two other promises to fulfill.

One to Kreshel. One to Vesram.

And she would try for as long as they each continued to live. Sooner or later, they must give their essence back to this world. She knew it must be; the Maiden had told her so.

Ada now sought something far more mundane, but no less precious: a well she'd glimpsed from the break in the trees upon the hill. She was hot and madly thirsty, and while it would have been wise to wait for the night, that was still hours away and she had not found a stream from which to drink in nearly three days.

The well itself was far too close to a collection of huts, sheds, and animal pens, which in themselves were just outside of an even longer spiked-log wall blocking her view of other foreign structures. However, she had no choice. Her starving, shriveled body screamed for water, her head and body hurt, her muscles spasmed and she could not swallow. Her eyes were blurry.

And so, one day in the late afternoon sunlight, Ada simply appeared to him.

THE MA'AB WOMAN ONLY JUST GOTTEN HER FILL OF DRINK BEFORE SHE WAS spotted. Like a startled deer she broke into a run, drawing the attention of many others. They called to each other in a language she did not know, all men taller than her but not so large as her Ma'ab husbands.

Like them, however, they worked as a team.

That these Paxians were smaller than the Ma'ab didn't matter at all as they could still run faster than her. They had not been starved of sufficient food as she had been every day for several weeks. Even as many insects and worms as there were in this rich forest, it had not been enough to keep her well when she did not rest.

They ran her down easily, enraged that she had invaded their territory.

"*Chitano bruja!*" one said, shoving her into another, who caught her and then immediately dropped her as if he was startled that she had solid, hot flesh.

Ada rolled and scrambled, alter enough to anticipate and evade several kicks as the men shouted for punishment, surrounding her and keeping her trapped.

One voice bellowed louder than the rest, and they calmed down a bit. She identified the man with the voice which had brought the others to heel and dove for his feet, trying to speak. She couldn't at first, grunting like an animal before she took his sandaled ankle and forced out, "Musanlo!"

He reached down and cuffed the top of her head. "*Neh'shanrileh ef gattishoor Patri!*"

Ada nodded urgently, curling up in submission. *Yes.* Punishment and words were good. She wanted that. It meant he would rather teach her what he wished to hear rather than leave her to the non-existent mercy of excess bloodlust.

"*Patri,*" she repeated, touching his foot again. "*Patri!*"

The men above her murmured amongst themselves for several long

105

minutes as she cowered in the dirt. Finally, the Manalar man pulled her up by her arms. She kept her eyes down and trembled, wanting to seem small and helpless. It wasn't difficult; she would have to tilt her chin up even to see his collar bones. He was tall. Very tall. Just not so very broad as the Ma'ab soldiers.

This man didn't fight for a living.

As the violence ebbed, the long, robed man dragged her to a cell. *The* cell. Their little keep made of stone and wood only had one.

Watching him from the inside of the bars as long as she did, Ada came to realize he had promised the others that he would watch her, that he would test her in various ways before he let her out amongst them again.

They weren't going to kill her.

Ada gazed at him. He had dark hair like hers but he wasn't so pale, and his eyes were brown and green like a stagnant, mixed pond. He had long fingers and arms and an intense stare with a constant, judging frown. He was intelligent; his mind never stopped working. Ada noticed all this in a moment, but soon after, when he first began teaching her to say his prayers, his aura drew her whole attention.

"*Nomilu sancji,*" he said firmly.

She nodded, watching him in fascination with her dark eyes. "*Nomilu sancji.*"

The Manalari showed his surprise in her perfect pronunciation. He *wasn't* aware of his aura, though; he didn't know how to use it, but … as she parroted his language, quite exact in her elocution to please him, his aura flared out, pushing back against her voice in various ways.

In various, *recognizable* ways.

He has the life pattern.

Not the same as Vesram or Kreshel, not Elven origin, but they were not the only source of the pattern she sought. This man was Human, and he was young. He could join their magic and help create her son.

He *could*, if she could teach him.

Inside her cell, Ada smiled after he left that night. In her dreams, her Lady agreed with her choice. A Manalari monk in the middle of nowhere with the life magic needed to overcome her Greylands aura.

Yes, him. Here. And Now.

CHAPTER 7

3068 S.E., CHIRTU MONASTERY, SOUTHERN PAXIA

"You have learned to speak so quickly, Ada. We can understand one another."

"Yes, Archimandrite."

"Your penitence is a rare but welcome quality among your kind."

She nodded. "My greatest wish."

Petris Alazar sat behind his desk, fiddling nervously with a quill. He thought he was hiding his desire, but Ada could see it plain as the moon outside.

"Then, at last, it is time to confess your sins to me," he said. "Your body has many marks on it, I could see it when we first inspected you. Are they self-inflicted?"

"Some."

"And the others?"

"Punishment."

"I see. For what?"

Ada shrugged. "Many a thing. Name one."

Her priest smirked a bit and lifted his shoulders in a mild shrug, waving his quill to one side and back. "Oh, I don't know ... copulating with demons?"

She nodded immediately. "Yes, Archimandrite. I have."

His eyes flew wide; he had not expected that answer. Very soon his cheeks flushed. He cleared his throat. "Mm. *Masturburito?*"

"Sorry?"

"Touching between your legs for self-gratification."

Her legs shifted, thighs tightening. "Yes, holy cleric."

Petris looked down at her bare feet as she crossed her ankles. "Hmm. *Sodomo?* Has someone taken his pleasure where you release your waste?"

Her hips shifted slightly. "Yes, cleric. With the demon, and my husbands."

He blinked. "Husbands … ?"

"Yes. The pack. They're dead. But sometimes one was already in my *cootus* and another didn't want to wait, so he would *sodomi'mae*."

"*Espito patri,*" he muttered, rubbing his temple, his earlier tension transforming into a tremor. "You have sinned indeed …"

"Yes, Archimandrite, I have, but it was to survive to meet you."

"Musanlo, ah, is patient for all who would come." Petris cleared his throat again. "What about *fellatio?*"

Ada tilted her head. "Sorry?"

Her priest sighed, irritated and excited. "Has a man put his cock into your mouth, to take his pleasure there? Have you swallowed a man's seed that way?"

She blinked at the lewd word, "cock" — he didn't normally use it, but some others did — and shook her head in the negative.

He clearly didn't believe her. "No?"

"No, Archimandrite."

"Do not lie to add to your sins, Ada."

"I am not lying to you. I bit him when any tried to put his … cock … in my mouth."

Petris flinched at her using the same word and shifted his robe. "You … allowed yourself to be rutted in all manner of ways, by all manner of creatures … but when it came to *fellatio*, that was too much?"

"Yes, holy cleric."

He scowled intensely at her. "Why?"

She looked down at her hands, folded properly for prayer. "I was waiting."

He eyed her; his excitement hadn't dampened much even after hearing how soiled she was. "Waiting for what?"

"For the Holy Sun Father's words to be placed in my mouth, on my tongue. If nothing else, as I was helpless to stop them forcing all the rest upon me, I would be virgin for Him in this. My mouth is pure. I have never swallowed a man's seed."

"God," he murmured, sounding awed and disgusted at once. "Enough, then. Um, enough confession for now. Go to your room and remain on your knees. Pray until I come to release you."

She did as he instructed, waiting expectantly. He might stroke himself to release after she'd left, or he might not. Even if he did, it would not be enough. She understood her priest by now.

Petris Alazar possessed a desire which his brothers, his Sky Father, and all that time on his knees could not fulfill.

AFTER MIDNIGHT, ADA REMAINED UPON HER KNEES, HER EYES CLOSED. HER door opened and someone stepped in, closing it again. She relaxed her aura, smiled when she felt his answer.

This was why his abstinence was never enough. When auras yearned to merge like this, it was an affront to the nature of this world to deny it forever.

It was a gift.

Her priest stepped directly in front of her, his breath uneven, a tremble in his hands. He stared down at her.

"Ada."

She lifted her chin to acknowledge him, opening her eyes but remaining silent.

"Open your mouth."

She obeyed, extending her tongue slightly.

The cleric swiftly lifted his robe and lightly touched his erection, just enough to aim it between her lips and rest it on her tongue. Instinctively she closed her lips around him and started sucking.

"*Dyos'gri!*" he whispered in hoarse exaltation, grabbing her hair, pushing himself in deeper. He quivered. His musky scent filled her nose, her mouth, her entire head as he shushed her, even as he was the one making more noise thrusting his hips. His body hair tickled her nose.

Lightly, Ada placed her hands on his thighs, bracing herself as he thrust harder, his breath and back shuddering and stiffening as he climbed up, and up. Petris made her gag several times, and Ada let the spit run down her chin and onto her rough-spun robe as he claimed her mouth in the name of the Sun God.

"*Nnngh! Dyos!*" he gasped, holding her head in both hands, spurting bitter seed across her tongue and down her throat. "Ada ... yes, oh, Ada ... take me. Ngh-*nomilu sancji esti patri incufes ...*"

Ada swallowed his seed, trying not to choke as he pressed more leisurely between her lips, again and again, slowly growing soft on her slimy tongue. Their auras sang together in her ears, and yearning slickness oozed from between her legs, though she knew he found her too dirty there.

He won't for long.

She would take him in every way until she got her son. Her cleric could have her mouth if that's where he wanted to begin. Sooner or later, he would need more, and she would encourage him in all the small ways; she would not resist or tease him.

Especially when his pain began.

Take me.

Mages like her rarely found a compatible match, and untrained mages such as him even less often. She had far more to teach him than he realized. He would be glad she'd come to him.

She had chosen him.

He is entirely right for me.

AT THE CROSSROADS

A TALE OF MIURAG
BY A.S. ETASKI

CHAPTER 1
3095 S.E., THE LONELY ONES

THE CRASH OF WATER WAS SO THUNDEROUS, MUSANLO MIGHT HAVE STRUCK THE Great Lake with his fist in rage and judgment. Brackish foam and polluted drops spattered over his face and skin, blistering his lips, melting sparse fat underneath and pitting the flesh of his limbs.

He groaned with a miserable pain too familiar, sweeping up every memory of long days and longer nights spent on a reed pallet forming new scars from his most recent lashing. The dawnless day found him lying upon sharp rocks eroded much like his flesh, every movement further shredding his skin.

Above him, a low, threatening drone. Coming closer.

Hovering.

The scavengers found me.

If he ran, they would chase him. And eat.

If he lay still, they might place their eggs inside.

How would I rather die?

He hesitated.

One landed, scuttling up to seize him with the polished hooks on four, chitinous feet, mandibles clicking and grinding in a mockery of speech. Antennae stroked his gut, testing its heat.

He wasn't dead yet.

And it did not need to eat.

NO!

Muscle deformed, tendons fraying, Gavin reclaimed his feet at a speed which turned the world black.

★★★

"Gavin! *Gavin!*"

The former monk sat up on a raised cot in a circular room. Wisps of shadows fled from his periphery. A fist pounded on his door, too large and strong to belong to the ass braying alongside it.

"Stop that wailing!"

He cringed back, fear flooding his gut as he realized he had locked the door.

If I make him wait, Father will ...

"Ah, that's better. You awake now?"

Gavin blinked. *Not* his father.

The Archimandrite was dead.

I killed him. I saw his ghost. He wetted his mouth to speak. "I am. Awake."

"Ha! Hells, boy. What's the twist in your head? Sometimes I hear your bellowing all the way down in the lab."

Heart still racing in his chest, Gavin forced his voice dead calm. "Do no shades or shadows torment you in the tower ... master?"

Sarilis paused outside his door. The old mage did not seem interested in speaking face-to-face. "Guess that's why I don't *sleep* in the tower," he chortled. "Much more space in this fortress than what can be seen from without."

Yet almost none of it well-lit, furnished, or supplied in any way. A barren, underground maze in which one could lose their way beyond Sarilis's lab. Only the aboveground tower had been reasonably kitted out for daily living when Gavin had arrived a few months ago, with odd storage rooms containing useful tools and trappings for winter collected in recent decades. He wagered even his "master" didn't delve deep into the abandoned Dwarven site.

"I could teach you a ward, I suppose," Sarilis continued. "As long as you provide the blood. Attach it across your door and the sounds within will be muffled even to one passing by."

Who else would even pass by to hear?

You will teach magic when it suits you not to be bothered?

Gavin's nostril lifted in a bitter wrinkle. "If you will teach this, then I will do this. Master."

"Use the space you want," Sarilis had said the previous year, upon grudgingly accepting Gavin's residence. "But maybe leave the high loft to the spirits of the mountains. Not my concern if you tread somewhere unwelcome."

Gavin had agreed, disinterested and without question. The old goat was suspicious.

A dismal autumn and a long, dark winter had passed since then. Demands and snide remarks had been as numerous as the snowflakes outside. Gavin slept, restlessly though consistently, on either the first or second floor, unable to deny experiencing more nightmares the higher up he went.

With yellow pollen dusting the windowsills on slow-warming days, the young monk's chores had quickly shifted from indoor maintenance and practical crafting to outdoor foraging with a cramping stomach and weakened limbs. He hadn't the time for further study as he worked to keep them both alive, but at least he had improved at sensing the presence and precise whereabouts of the spying corpses loitering about the death mage's lair and lands.

One day not even Sarilis's freshest rodents hunched dead-eyed outside his door, and Gavin delayed his pre-dawn chores to carry a torch up the stairs farther than he had yet gone. If Sarilis asked, he was exploring for further supplies in storage.

The third through sixth levels were familiar enough, the seventh level musty and mostly empty. The eighth level revealed an open room and stone stairs without railing curving up the right side, leading to an iron-banded wood door in the ceiling. The only entrance into the final space of the Dwarven tower, the high loft.

"*Maybe leave it to the spirits of the mountains.*"

Whatever that meant.

Gavin sensed no spiritual flotsam or detritus from Sarilis's messy experimentation this high aboveground, but a single step toward the open stairs sent every unearthly sense vibrating through his aura.

Stop.

He stood still, gaze seeing the slightest movement around him. A sensation like his greatest fear stepping down the steps toward him swept through the torch-lit room.

Run.

Gavin held still, drew no attention as he had in many a dream, for better or worse, until a conscious thought arose. *A ward.* One such like he had practiced for his own door, building from muteness to deterrence, but the strength of this one … *Incomprehensible.*

He resisted a bit longer on the will granted from his visions, noting at last a silver plate with red-tinged runes fixed to the base of the first step. *This* was the source of magic pressing him to back out of the room. Not even Sarilis tried to cross the threshold anymore, if he ever had.

The spell must have been here when he found the tower, and he has ignored it for decades.

The old man was not the "master" of all in this valley, but Gavin had known that knocking on his door.

Why do you stay?

Fear Incarnate formed before him. He uttered a cry, recoiling.

You were warned.

Like a beast, it leaped, drawing strength from his panic. All rational thought burned in the flame of its breath as Gavin spun and fled, barely escaping with his life,

He stumbled, falling down the hard stone steps, losing consciousness before the world could stop spinning.

He awoke with a fractured arm and Sarilis's most recent golem standing over him with a note. Eventually, Gavin reached for it with shaking, abraded fingers.

Bring breakfast early. Don't make me wait.

CHAPTER 2

"DAMNED THORNS," GAVIN MUTTERED, DRAGGING THE METAL TEETH OF HIS handsaw across the first woody vine blocking the garden door.

How do they grow so quickly every spring?

"Boy! You back there working it free?"

Gavin had been required to climb over the stone wall between the horse stalls and the full-sun garden to *reach* the back door blocked by these aggressive vines, but ...

"Yes!" he groused through the entrance, sawing harder in the hopes the deaf old goat would hear it. "Not long."

And once the doorway was free, he must begin work planting the early seeds from last harvest. Viable meals from the garden would be weeks away, but some food remained preserved in the kitchen cellar.

"Good. I will be in my lab. Bring my first meal around midday."

Thus, after the planting was the cooking. Then the cleaning.

Just like the monastery.

Choke on those sweaty socks, old man.

The young monk had weathered his third bitter winter in the old Dwarven fortress. Knowing the pattern of the seasons by now, he could not wait to spend more time outdoors away from the onerous bastard.

Fortunate that the decrepit death mage did not know the Archimandrite in charge of Gavin's upbringing, or he might try to outdo him in the random abuses and humiliations under the guise of "instructing" him in his morbid magics. The dismaying redundancy in this part of his life, however, often led the young man's thoughts to the same solution.

Kill him, too. Put something in his food. There are so many poisons in the forest. No one would know, much less care.

But then another seizure or trance would come to drain his resolve, gripping him in nightmares so much clearer *here* than any other place he'd lived.

He would hear her, sometimes see her.

"*Stand upon the crossroads,*" she whispered. "*Behold, your peregrination.*"

To anyone else, he would pretend. He would lie.

"I cannot behold," he confessed. "This place has nowhere to wander. It is a dead end."

"*Is it? Then may you seek your time to die.*"

In his unconscious state, he flinched.

Useless.

I am useless to her.

He wished he had never been born.

Putting together a secret grimoire had taken time but grew less difficult once Sarilis trusted Gavin to gather supplies by cart and mare at the nearest town once or twice per season. His dark, leather book began thin, and paper was precious. Gavin honed his book binding skills alongside his careful script to make the most of it.

Sparse words sufficed to describe Sarilis's spies and sentries after all this time. Gavin braved the stairs to the loft one more time, managing to keep his bones intact this time, and sketched an approximation of the sigils from memory afterward.

Sneaking into the goat's lab was nearly impossible. The apprentice always handed meals to the undead servant with the best memory of coordination for balancing on the stairs. Usually, the last mercenary or would-be looter Gavin had assisted in neutralizing out of sheer self-interest.

The coot *did* possess a meager library outside of his lab, consisting of six slim volumes. Stacked in a cabinet in the hearth room, their topics held to chirurgeons, disease, and dissection written within the last thirty years. Sarilis seemed to have forgotten about them even though one of them was his own journal from two decades past.

The handwriting was coarse, the spelling inconsistent, reminding Gavin of those who had learned scripts later in life. The scribblings were also poorly dated and haphazard in their timing, as if Sarilis were only inspired to transcribe his thoughts when something notable happened. He offered no context in between.

The 'laughing' rot? He turned a page. *A group of black …*

Black what?

Women. Warrior women? Father would be mortified …

Another page.

Hmm. Something interesting happened here, not long after Sarilis took over the tower.

Tucking the book beneath his robe for later, Gavin closed the cabinet and continued his midday chores. He'd spare the candlelight this evening to copy the pertinent details before trying once again to sleep.

"*Stand upon the crossroads,*" SHE INTONED YET AGAIN. "*Behold, your peregrination.*"

He *wanted* to bear witness. Wished for it with all that he was, insignificant though he seemed.

The shadows cloyed around him.

The fey circle in the tower warned him.

The drone of the wasps threatened him.

The return of dark, female warriors intrigued him.

"I begin to see, my Lady," he murmured. "But obscurity remains."

"Then may you seek your time to die."

This time, he better understood. The aphorism did not sting.

"What else passes through here?" he asked.

"Eventually?" she hushed. *"Everything."*

GAVIN'S GRIMOIRE HAD DOUBLED BY HIS FOURTH YEAR AT THE TOWER, SURPASS-
ing Sarilis's half-empty journal once he'd transferred those wrinkled, blank
pages. Less of his cypher described anything taught or stolen from his
"master." More of it detailed symbols and spoken words from his trances
to a level he had never dared explore at the monastery.

He timed his writing as the old man slept, which could be any time of
day, resisting the myopic focus which had led to being caught neglecting
his chores as a child. The harassment and punishment when he slipped was
about the same.

He prioritized chores or sometimes accomplished them the night before to hide the gap in his workday, double-checking for ink on his pale
hands or, failing to scrub it clean, always carrying work gloves.

Occasionally, Gavin carved runes into a selection of bones, mostly
birds and rodents, for Sarilis to use. One of the few mage-craft practices
which received the elder death mage's direct supervision.

"Ah, very nice. How I envy young, supple fingers," Sarilis said with a
cough, inspecting the dried talisman while flexing a stiff, gnarled hand.
"Enjoy it while it lasts. If only I could transplant them."

Pale blue eyes met black.

"Ha!" the old man barked. "I didn't mean *your* fingers! Peh, paranoid
monk. Letting those nightmares bleed into your day."

A pause.

Gavin ducked his head, scraping his picking tool with care to refine
the mark on the broad end of a twig-sized femur.

"You *are* the quietest of them, though," his loathsome teacher murmured.

The apprentice glanced up again, watching a distracted gaze slide into empty air. Wrinkled eyelids drooped as if his chin might drop to his chest at any moment.

The quietest of them?

Gavin kept the remark close, suspicious of what he might find in Sarilis's lab if he were able to look around. The old man never mentioned "the others" again, though the new wariness lasted up to the day they received the first visitor Sarilis did not plan to kill.

"Ahh, Mathias Briar! Welcome! I admit I doubted Brom's message. Huh! You've grown. How is your father?"

"Dead. Fell from his horse."

Gavin peeked around the corner.

The bearded traveler ran fingers through thick, brown hair that could use a wash. His clothes were well-made but dirty. He had been traveling quickly for some time. "It's alright, Sarilis. You don't need to pretend you care."

"Oh, but he and I had a *fulfilling* partnership, your father and I. Only my respect for a man who knows who he is! News of an untimely death saddens me."

"Well. Thank you." Mathias peered around the torch-lit entrance. "You can't be alone? What on earth drew you way out *here* to retire?"

"People *drove* me, actually," Sarilis chuckled. "I was one of sixteen children, you know! I've had my fill living around chattering ninnies. Come in, come in." He turned toward the stairwell. "*Gavin!* Food and drink in the dining hall! Now."

The monk paused, drew in a breath, and shuffled his feet before stepping around the corner as if he had just stepped out of his room. He may not be fooling either of them but continued his way to the kitchen without pause.

"Uhhh," Mathias began behind him. "You employ a Ma'ab?"

"Half. The Empire doesn't know about him. The boy never talks about his mother."

"Uh-huh. But we can guess what happened."

"Yes, we can! *Hehehe!*"

Gavin sneered to the wall, chopped vegetables roughly, and threw their lunch together in a pot.

"He can stay and eat," Mathias said after taking his first bite. "I don't mind. If he's the only other one here."

"Hmph! Well, if you can handle the face. Gavin, *sit!*"

His gut burning with rage, the apprentice sat to partake in his own efforts, serving himself generously and scowling with every bite. Mathias watched him with warm, brown eyes and warmer, tanned skin. Not a striking face but perfectly acceptable anywhere in Paxia.

Unlike him.

"This is good food," the man said, scooping up another bite of hash. "Reminds me of food carts in Manalar."

"Does it?" Sarilis cackled. "Ah. My boy learned to feed an entire monastery of sun worshippers, as I understand it. Fortunate that he did not inherit the blood cuisine of the Far North."

"Ah. Well. Maybe Paxian fare doesn't agree with him. He's really skinny for a Ma'ab."

Gavin's fist tightened around his wooden spoon.

"Hm. Does the apprentice speak?"

"Oh, he does." Sarilis popped a bone in his neck grinning at him, teeth crooked and yellow. "When he sleeps, mostly. He might forget how now and then when he's awake."

"Ah. An oath of silence?"

The old goat snorted. "I wish. But he's useful."

Gavin hurried to finish, his stomach cramping by the time he stood up. "The garden needs tending. I'll get my shovel."

"Excellent. Be off, then."

Sarilis waited until just before Gavin was out of earshot before saying casually to their guest, "We're waiting to see who tries to kill the other first. Poor lad. He knows he's not ready. Old age and vigor, you know."

Mathias laughed like he'd heard something like that before.

A KNOCK AT THE DOOR. THEN A VOICE.

"Gavin?"

Curse it all …

He wiped his fingers clean of ink and slipped his open grimoire into the covered cubby to dry. "What is it?"

"Open the door."

"Why?"

"I have a question."

"Ask through the door."

And curse me thrice for forgetting to set a ward!

Mathias cleared his throat. "Pretty sure one of those dead things is watching. Maybe listening."

Gavin sat in silence until the mercenary knocked again. Understanding he would not be allowed to concentrate tonight, he stood from his stool and went to draw back the chain on his door. Mathias threw his shoulder into it the moment he turned the handle, and the apprentice stumbled backward, his heart suddenly racing in his chest.

He scrambled to his feet, drawing his utility knife from his belt as the stronger man slipped inside and pressed the door shut by leaning against it. Mathias smiled with healthy teeth. The cold sense of isolation spread across Gavin's shoulders and down his spine.

"You won't need that, apprentice," the man said, his eyes turning dead in a too-familiar way. "I'd just kill you first."

Slowly, Gavin replaced the small blade, watching the predator in his room settle down. "What do you want?"

"Just information. You have one of those muffling spells?"

With a suffering sigh, slumped shoulders hiding his true concern over this invasion, Gavin pricked the back of his hand and wove the protective seal he used against unwelcome observance.

Too late.

"Is it truly just you two?" the traveler asked.

"And the watchers and guardians arranged for defense," Gavin replied blandly. "I'm sure you saw them."

The subtle warning did not work.

"And he is just loitering here? Not searching for something?"

"Working in his lab, mostly."

"Working on what?"

"I am not permitted to pick through his workspace to discover that."

The man smirked. "Keeping it secret, huh?"

"You're welcome to see for yourself."

"Heh. No, thank you. If he learned anything from my father, I won't leave that basement if I go uninvited."

Gavin grunted in agreement.

"So you do all the chores."

The younger mage shrugged, his face a shield of indifference.

Mathias eyed him slyly. "I, um ... heard that you aren't the only death mage to wander up this way and not come out. You sure there aren't other mages here?"

"None living," Gavin replied, crossing his arms. "Seems clear enough, especially after his remark tonight. He must have tantalized others with a death affinity to become his apprentice and 'dismissed' them once he perceived a threat."

"Yeah. Seems clear enough." The traveler shifted his weight, pondering. "How long will you stay? Knowing that he'll turn on you, I mean."

Stand upon the crossroads. Behold, your peregrination.

"Unknown," Gavin said, resisting the boast that he might turn on the bag of gut-rot first. "I only know I am not ready to leave."

"Hmph." Mathias smiled. "Don't suppose you've run into any Dwarven ghosts?"

"None. In fact, no spirits linger that Sarilis did not have a hand in anchoring."

"Been abandoned that long." The visitor looked around Gavin's room, annoying him. "Don't know what it is, but this place gives me creeps up my back." Eyes pinned him again. "Any contact with the Ma'ab at all?"

The apprentice frowned. "Why would I have such contact?"

"You *speak* Ma'ab, right?"

"I do not. I've never encountered one."

"All Manalari, huh?"

Gavin clenched his robe out of sight; he just wanted him to *leave*.

Or for Sarilis to send the message for the poison.

Fortunately, the strange man at last ran out of questions. "Well," he waved, "I'll see you in the morning."

We'll see about that.

CHAPTER 3

THE GREY MISTS COULD NOT OBSCURE THE GIANTS EVEN HAD THAT BEEN THEIR intent. He followed them both, the fog and the forest, walking around massive trunks with footfalls deadened.

Wherever he stood, the Quiet provided its respite here, too.

The Ley Lines here flowed like an underground river, anchored to a depth which prevented it from splitting like lightning or swirling like a gust of air against a mountain. When he paused and closed his eyes, he could see its weave within; he could glimpse its truth.

In a new world built entirely within the earth, a mix of decay and growth danced in continuous balance, each of them empowered by the water filtering through from above.

Here, in the dim of an ancient grove, the dead arose into the living, becoming one, inseparable. They were talking to each other as naturally as travelers visiting around a campfire. Not a fragment of Humans to be glimpsed anywhere.

What river is this? Who transitions through this path? It is too old for us. Our souls cannot be birthed here.

Nor would any person find it once they died.

Gavin kept walking, and the forest changed. The giants vanished, though their smaller cousins formed evermore twisted versions of themselves along a difficult, rocky land bridge. The groves grew thicker, more hostile, falling from merely dim to pitch black slashed with crimson and a molten fester. Not a wisp of mist nor a sliver of silver moonlight pierced the black bark.

A low rumble threatened to break the continent in half.

Gavin stopped, believing the threat, fearing to go deeper. He glanced behind him, dismayed to find his path erased. Unrecognizable.

How do I go back?

"You don't," she whispered. *"Look closer, but without trespass."*

Closer?

Gavin took another step but froze when the earth quaked, jerking and jolting like a corpse trying to break the crust.

Trespass.

He dropped down to one knee, planting both hands on the soil to ground himself. The quake stopped, the ripples in the nearby stagnant pond smoothing away. Small pockets of air released from the mud in a putrid sigh.

Closer.

Gavin watched death in the earth for a great amount of time without taking another step. After a time, he forgot about the black forest as it, too, passed. He found a new view.

The open steppes, wind swept, pockmarked with the hooves of thousands of horses, roamed by packs of massive dogs. Gavin was gripped by fascination for the bones laid within the stone outcroppings, and the spirits walking and standing guard over generations of Humans. Its history was more palpable to him than any land he'd ever been.

How far is this place from the crossroads?

"Too far for your life," she answered. *"Unless you leave your present at once."*

Solemnly, Gavin nodded. *I can't. Not yet.*

"Then?"

Then may I seek my time to die, my Lady.

GAVIN WOKE TO A MAN SCREAMING.

Boots pounded down the stairs from levels above.

Oh, dear.

The apprentice kept the chain on his door this time as he cracked it open, wanting a glimpse of the mercenary as he ran past. Mathias did not pause, did not look at the death mage's door.

White-faced, he fled down to the hearth room.

Hm. Perhaps I looked like that.

The snooping around surely grew annoying. How much longer would Sarilis tolerate him being here?

When Gavin came downstairs not long after, the old man was still laughing.

"I told you!" he wheezed. "Did I not?"

Mathias sneered. "So you aren't strong enough to deal with an unknown threat sleeping above your head?"

"It's not a threat as long as you avoid the place," Sarilis said with his usual moist grin. "It's not changed the entire time, it's a small footprint, and I wager even Brom isn't capable of breaking that plate."

"So sure?"

"Certain. He'd have come here, perhaps installed a lacky so he wouldn't have to leave his own 'crossroads.' And he'd have done it long before I laid claim if dispelling it was a trifle."

Gavin narrowed his eyes. Who was Brom? And why wouldn't an implied, powerful mage install a "lacky" if he already knew of this place thirty years ago? Unless Sarilis *was* the lacky?

Who else competed for this tower besides his Lady? Who else saw a glimpse of its future influence?

Hm. I should avoid poisoning either of them until I find out.

"YOU LET HIM LIVE," GAVIN COMMENTED THE NEXT DAY, LISTENING TO THE trotting gait of Mathias's horse leave the courtyard.

Sarilis splayed yellow teeth between thin lips. "I did! For the sake of his old man."

"Who is dead."

"In his memory, then." He waved a gnarled hand dismissively, plodding past the apprentice. "He brought intriguing news. We may do well to prepare."

Gavin turned with him. "Prepare for what?"

Sarilis paused by the golem guarding the stairs to his lab, his sagging face contorting with gruesome amusement. "The war of *your* lifetime, boy." He lifted both arms skyward, palms cupping the air. "The Ma'ab versus the Manalari!"

What ... ?

The old man cackled all the way down his steps, granting no further insight or instruction.

May I seek my time ...

For the fifth time, Gavin failed to kill himself.

He sighed. *Failed to die.*

His dreams swung like a confused plum bob in the following months, from the revelatory Quiet to the terrible moments just before death.

I still cling to this life. I still resist my transition.

Particularly when he had the *choice*.

Gavin worked and sweated for Sarilis at the tower. He experimented, studied, and wrote in his grimoire at a painfully slow rate. In his mind, his dreams, his nightmares, he'd overcome the fear of his death. He looked forward to all he would learn.

But I still don't know how to seek it. Or don't wish to.

The unknown remained the gateway itself.

Surely, the Lady meant something other than foolhardiness with one's body.

Like running and falling down the stairs. He could have snapped his neck.

One night, as pressure to "prepare" for some nebulous war had grown subtly with each successive day, Gavin dared to visit the curving staircase on the seventh level one more time.

If this ends the same, I'll not come here again while living.

Or if it ended worse, he would be dead.

At least we shall be over that *hurdle.* He frowned. *I am thankful She has marked me.*

The oppressive atmosphere struck quicker, harder than his first, igno-rant approach, though Gavin was certain there was no Vis, no presence in the room itself. All the power lay in that silver plate with red-tinged runes.

Fear is a trickster, and a teacher, showing you what you cannot yet stand against.

The mirrored image could, and would, change as the unseen turbulence in the depth of one's fears proved dynamic, different for each soul in the space of their journey.

Gavin exhaled, ceasing analysis when he must focus.

"We stand upon the Crossroads," he whispered, pressing forward. "Past, Present, and Future are as one to her."

The spell snarled at him. His heart accelerated a bit, ready to race.

"Her reality is all of Time. Life and Death. Real and Unreal."

A low drone vibrated the air around him.

"I ... I serve the Maiden of Shrouds, the Grave Mother —"

The runes upon the plate crackled crimson, a resounding pop nearly bursting his eardrums.

He clutched his head. *"Argh!!"*

Powerful wind arose, sweeping away the tower beneath his feet. He collapsed onto his knees, burnt-red sand absorbing the brunt of his fall. At once, the air sought to flay his meat from his bones; he lay flat upon the dune, gripping ground swiftly slipping through his fingers, feeling himself sink in the middle of the storm.

"My Lady!" he shouted, the words ripped to shreds the moment they left his mouth. "Where are you?!"

The wind howled and laughed, and his stomach sank, laden with a new, realized fear.

The Quiet does not exist here.

"Release me!" he demanded, climbing back atop the sand that sought to bury him too soon.

Hsssssssss ...

On the horizon, a city temple burned, its white spires sullied with soot. People fled, on foot, on horseback, appearing like ants fleeing a crushed hive with their eggs. Armies still fought in the streets, the outskirts.

Some of them could fly like eagles.

Disbelieving, Gavin realized he was surrounded by soundless forms composed of brilliant colors. He spotted a tall, lanky man in a grey robe riding a blood-bay horse. Somehow, he guided the stallion without saddle *or* tackle.

"What is this ... ?" he whispered.

When the horse galloped past at full stride, Gavin glimpsed the dark-skinned child gripped in the mage's clutches. She wore satin blue and clung to his front, the side of her face pressed to his chest. Her exposed ear was pointed like a knife. Her hair was a light blonde.

Her skin pitch black.

Gavin's throat was too dry to swallow.

Suddenly, a large pair of wings shaded him from the dusky sun. Somehow, the owner ignored the constant push of the wind.

"You have no business here, Noiri," a melodic, masculine voice declared with authority. "Speak what you search for or be destroyed."

"The Grey," Gavin answered without hesitation, truthful enough not to know if he'd been compelled or not. "I search for the Grey."

The wings stroked the air, shifting the angle of his shadow, the glare from the sun too strong for Gavin to see who hovered above him. All he could make out was a glimmering spear and feathered, golden wings.

"I meant no trespass," he continued as humbly as he could. "I ... I seek my time to die."

The figure paused as if surprised. The wind-driven sand had begun to score Gavin's flesh, drawing red blood, but the death mage kept his attention on his greatest desire.

"Go, then, Deathwalker," said the flying warrior. "I'll not stop you, but don't linger. There are hunters behind me."

"*How* do I leave?" he asked, voice tinged with desperation.

The flyer pointed his spear after the rider carrying the inhuman girl. "Follow them."

Without question, Gavin ran, heavy boots slogging through the sand, his eyes burning, and his jaw clenched hard against the wind. He tried to follow them, to leave this wailing nightmare cut off from his mistress.

Eventually, he lost them but still searched.

And searched.

Until he spotted a smudge of grey upon the horizon.

She waits at the border.

Hunters barked and shrieked somewhere behind him. None of them were Human.

None of them were dead.

Faster.

They mustn't see you.

Gavin pushed until his living body would have collapsed yet he pressed on, disturbed by the wordless threats of those who would consume him. They could *eat* him as if he had never Existed.

And he never would again.

Ahead, tendrils of mist reached out, threading their way with care through an unseen web. With no thread plucked or torn to alert the predators, the mist wrapped around his fingers then his hand, climbing quickly up his arm.

Leave, now.

He passed through.

And found …

Quiet.

GAVIN ROLLED OVER AND VOMITED.

Once his head stopped swimming, he reached to touch a throbbing bump on his forehead. He'd fallen down the stairs again, and now he couldn't take a full breath without excruciating pain in his ribs.

Worms rot their bellies ...

At least no golem stood over him with a note demanding lunch.

Using a steadfast stone wall as his only assistance, the apprentice carefully climbed to his feet. He began to sigh but stopped, his breath hitching at a bolt of pain.

Bah ...

The second visit to the top had ended the same as the first, too close for his liking.

I can take a sign.

Gavin would not return again.

Not while he was living.

THE HERALD RETURNS

A TALE OF MIURAG
BY A.S. ETASKI

Chapter 1

The Black Sea. The Nexus. Time Unknown

Spray from the waves burned his dry, grey skin when he stepped too close to the beach. Outside of shelter during a storm was no relief.

At the beginning, sometimes, to burn his skin was the aim; it would through and eventually expose the pneuma flint in his hands without his having to tear at the flesh himself, leaving the tips sharp and hypermobile joints building "callouses" of a sort as ridges built up and became harder.

With repeated use his hands could be like a small but sufficient mortar and pestle. He required time for his black blood to congeal and his skin to seal all exposure; until then he could work directly with the unusual compounds of his surroundings without barrier.

The flesh of his nose had worn away, yet that sense still worked, keenly. Tethered in tandem with the tough rope of his shriveled tongue which could no longer be used for speech, its function had changed with his need. He could detect precisely *what* he sought to piece together his new creation, and with the tempered tips of his fingers he could excavate it.

With his very hands, he could crush and grind it to dust.

The work was draining, and strong winds often tried to steal the new composition he built patiently within one of the few shelters on the island. Once ground to dust and mixed to proper ratio, part of it he compressed, tight and dense, as if it had spent a millennium beneath a hibernating

Geb'harik on a plain of borazoneous crystal. Next, he added it to a new shard extracted from his bone, gradually tempered, growing large and sharp. What remained of the powder went into his one remaining pouch.

Not much longer, his new tools would be ready. The next time his enemies returned …

I will be ready.

The vanishing time needed to finish, of course, was small only relative to how long he had already been here. This place on which he'd been imprisoned should have drained his will and decomposed his form and flesh, and the latter was well on its way.

His form was mostly a tall, black skeleton now, with just enough muscle to move and stubborn, thick veins and arteries filled with his black lifeblood clinging to him like vines on an ancient tree. What passed for circulation still shed toxins even without skin, still reclaimed his magic and fed his marrow to purify it despite the pull of the ghost-stone and the push of the caustic sea.

I dreamed of this, once. I stood on a beach upon the Great Lake without skin. Sirana did not recognize me.

Until she spoke with her mind. Then she *knew* him.

Sometimes the lack of dry, grey skin meant less raw pain from exposed nerves, and he was grateful. He'd learned to adapt without his physical eyes as they had gone to the acid storms first, even before the cartilage of his nostrils and ears.

Missing those external signs of how he navigated his birth home, however, he'd discovered that so little of the Greylands was truly masked to his soul when he paid attention. Like the Malok and the Roh'ghast, he could exist quite successfully without eyes, nose, and ears, if need be. He could sense the Nexus all around him as other senses arose soon enough, either developed by need or borrowed by wit.

The island, like most of the Greylands, existed in a perpetual twilight. He didn't count days, he counted storms; within the grip of those was when he was most tempted to let himself go and be taken up in a vortex. It would be easy and, according to his captors, the only way to ever go elsewhere than here.

You underestimate my devotion to my Lady. I have not fulfilled my purpose. I will not stay, and I will not vanish.

They always arrived on "clear days," his captors, when the Black Sea appeared hauntingly still and unnatural in its minute ripples and waves. Not a sea in those eerily calm periods, but a pond reflected in infinite mirrors. The Bane Wasps could not fly so far from the coast otherwise, assured to be slapped by wave or cloud, or ambushed from beneath by the giant serpents. The serpents of the deep hunted far less when the roiling waves did not mask their stalk of those above.

This "day" was clear and calm such that his new spearhead was almost transparent, suffused with just the thinnest black threads like tiny capillaries. He had lost his staff, and no trees grew to make something to which to attach the spear tip. He had nothing but his skeletal arm.

"*Yyyoooooo-Yi-Yi-AI!*"

Their call once again.

Time to fight for my mission.

For his ability to Walk the Nexus. Ever again.

He could not lose this time.

The Herald of Nyx had Walked thrice before.

The first time had been agony, forced upon the frail apprentice he'd been with a silver dagger punched through his heart. From the sheer abruptness in leaving his body behind, he had learned what it meant for one's aura tear like delicate cloth, no way to stitch it whole.

In hindsight, his Lady could only have anointed his soul as she had through such a wound, but he had to learn to walk first.

Just as well that it occurred during my first transition. The mortal death destined for all Humans.

Once the silver had been removed, no longer interfering in his return to his body, the crows of his patroness had closed his aura tightly behind him to prevent fester on Miurag. At the same time, she left what cherished marks and scars she would upon his soul. In some strange way, he had likened it to rolling out of a bridal bed with the uncanny understanding there was another now who was as familiar with his form than he was.

Perhaps more so.

The second Walk had perhaps not been a true crossover but a conditioning, a tempering of his dedication to help break the restraints on the gate of Io'sulta. An old sigil on his back — placed by white-hot iron held in his own father's hand — allowed him to turn their attack to the side.

Thanks to her blessing, his Vis and Vitas had remained whole. His memories of self along with the essence replenishing itself to prove his soul was alive had stood strong against the Sunfire of the Bishops of Manalar at their sacred pool. Neither his aura nor his will had torn or weakened this time, even as his body had burned.

Briefly, Gavin had stepped through to the Greylands only long enough to ensure he was seen. She had whispered through his soul.

You please me, Greyblood. Be patient. They will come for you.

That was the first time Gavin had heard this private title, and one he kept so. He could not express what he felt to hear it. He returned to his charred body once again and welcomed the cool mending of the Grey as his mother, Ada, had arrived to give him, once again, a functional body.

"*Worth every lash,*" whispered the smiling, self-mutilated oracle.

Her pride shone for her son, even as her pneuma flint eye glinted with secrets untold and knowledge of fates yet to come.

His third crossing was the first he would call a Walk, for it held the pinnacle quality of a Deathwalker from his world: he could take his body with him. The Herald had been better prepared and tutored; nothing was hurried, all deliberate.

Sirana had been anxious to see if he would return.

Many times, lewensbluen, many times yet.

So it must be. No other outcome would suffice.

CHAPTER 2

STILL, WARM AIR DRONED WITH THE HUM OF CHITINOUS WINGS, HIGH ENOUGH to avoid disturbing the water. With so little interference, Gavin could "see" the outline of four Bane Wasps carrying their riders in a loose, fluid formation. They were nevertheless direct; they never circled, and they always came from and left in the same direction.

Distance to travel and the weather determined how long they could torment him before the risk of roughening seas would be too great to return to the coast. Wisely, they did not wish to be stranded here along with him.

The riders' mounts were extraordinary; freak outliers in the Greylands allowing another creature to cling and barely retain control. Unlike the Roh'ghast, Bane Wasps could not be domesticated by "normal" means. This was well known. What was *not* well known was by what "abnormal" means one could attain tolerance from a Wasp to be carried.

Through enough time and suffering at their hands, Gavin had observed enough of this dynamic to develop a theory for how it had been accomplished. Another visit or two, and he'd detected enough evidence not only to confirm it but to contemplate a way to subvert it.

He had been preparing ever since.

Only one chance for this experiment to succeed.

Gavin had no place to hide either his spear tip or the half-filled pouch; he could but hold them, one each in his bony hands. His stillness and their over-familiarity must work in his favor.

"*Eidolonitha!*" their new leader squalled over the drone of their mounts, spitting down onto the beach the first time they passed overhead. "*Et'sheeran lit? Prau'shno edden, hurssill'et confuetrissh'un!*"

After such periods of long silence, hearing a new captor speak took effort for their prisoner to absorb and process. Gavin parsed the Greylands speech, the Dead Tongue, accented though it was. His starving intellect swiftly translated that same sentence into several languages from his birth world; he chose not to forget those permanently.

Ghostwalker. Now you await us? Surely you are hungry, submit and we will feed you and give you a good home.

Sanct'camminii. Nuncsi asputin? Certa'she avtefame, presaeti nutruc e vi diremo baniticas.

Shanbisvak. Al'ant tanzirna? Bialtaaki kunt jayiean, wataqdim wahn sawf 'iiteam lak watuetik jayidin.

The Common tongue of the Surface. Manalari. Miuragian Ma'ab … those languages returned clearly to his mind. More difficult to churn through his head was the incomplete Davrin language he'd absorbed from Sirana and the various planar dialects important only in his magic, though he did his best approximation.

Gavin had yet to offer any signs of submission regardless of which Leader showed up. What they always took as his silent refusal occurred as he translated their usual greeting through his various tongues, part of the ritual as the clones of his original captors prepared to land on the same bit of rock with him. With laughter, they renewed their collective assumption that the Eidolon was addled and confused. They thought his Vis degenerating.

Just as well. He could not speak anyway.

Gavin stood on the border between the sand and the harsh rock of the inner island, his captors between the Black Sea and him. The droning stopped, pinchers clacked, and giant, insects' legs stamped onto the grey, glassy sand in a semi-circle around him.

The Bane Wasps hissed to each other, exchanging chemical scents which he sensed simply standing near them without his skin. They were scavengers as well as hunters, as interested in his corpse as their predecessors had been the first time they had surrounded him.

Thankfully, the insect mounts held back as the lowest ranking Wasp-rider dismounted and casually placed his chemical-soaked body between the fearsome predators and the withering, skeletal prisoner. On the surface it appeared the best kind of confident control, sentient will over primal instinct, but Gavin knew otherwise.

"What is that you've got there?" the rider asked now, close enough to see the two items in his hands.

"What mean you, Cheff?" the second-rank rider asked.

"Look. In his first hand. Is that a hand-axe?"

"Where would one'a found it here?" the leader scoffed. *"Nothing ever lived here."*

The low-ranked one sounded frustrated. *"Found or made, he has it, Leader! This is strange, yi?"*

A mere shrug. *"He wants to fight. This is good with me. What trouble is chipped flint against us?"*

What indeed? Unlike him, they possessed Bane Wasp armor and very tough skin. They did not bleed readily, but they *did* bleed.

Gavin habitually translated all their words into his native tongues as they spoke easily around him, giving him the time to practice. Interrogations hadn't given them much in return for their own memories were imperfect recalling what had occurred before with their "parents" and "grandparents" for six relatively short generations.

The best he had been able to determine was that the motives lay in limbo somewhere between a torture-and-murder for fun spanning and suspected political imprisonment for random and that "big haul" every thief yearned for.

Their first encounter was simply bad luck for him as a solo traveler with some potential valuables entering the wrong area. These were a familiar type of murder-thieves seen on many worlds despite their unusual means of propagating. Through some admittedly clever and brutal means, they had learned he was a messenger of *someone,* but they hadn't determined who; therefore they could not know to which Greylord to offer him for the most profit.

Assuming they could remember from one generation to the next.

The first ones and their later incarnations had enjoyed trying to find out. It cost them very little when they had a private prison cell no competitor or mercenary could access. If Gavin waited them out and transitioned into something else over time, if they never found out who he was or whom he served, then it was not a true loss. To this sixth generation of self-proclaimed "Bane of the Wasp," their unknown Greyblood was a "side" inheritance at this point.

The Wasp riders used a hand-crafted projectile launcher not unlike Sirana's single-hand crossbow. The small, barbed stingers were fastened to resilient threads of ligament as well, and therefore retrievable without setting foot on the ground. The attacker could then hover at leisure and circle around as the diluted Bane Wasp venom incapacitated the victim but, in most cases, kept them aware.

This was how the original band had caught him by surprise, and how they had warily approached him on this island for at least the first visit of each generation since, particularly when he could still talk and cast spells. This current version of the odd coastal clan had returned to the island thrice so far and never witnessed Gavin speak the incantations of their forefathers. They observed only how he remained still and eyeless, not directly focused on their approach.

Thus, the Bane of the Wasp landed for a second time without using the paralysis stingers. They chattered, curious how much he had deteriorated, how desperate he might be, and about the primitive tool now in his hand, whether they could steal it for their own use.

Even if they did shoot him again, it would not be like the times before. His own composition had been changing, adapting to the island as well as repeated exposure to the Bane Wasp venom. The last time he'd been shot, he had been exaggerating its effectiveness.

The low-ranking rider took a step closer, snapping his three-fingered hand as if he could snap Gavin out of a wandering stare. The Greylands native's voice echoed through four languages in Gavin's mind.

"Harraanis yur, Eidolonitha?"

You awake, Ghostwalker?

Evigi svegio, Sanct'camminii?

Kun must'qiza, Shanbisvak?

While he listened, Gavin also "heard" and "felt" the visual detail around him. This one's form wasn't portrayed in muted colors but in the location and space taken up by the rider. Exquisitely precise. Extraordinary in its way, because Gavin fully understood how Sirana fought in the dark.

The Herald nodded his black skull in an affirmative and coaxed with his hand holding the spear tip, turning to take five steps away.

"Hey, hold up!" cried one of those still mounted.

He stopped again to "look" back. One rider prepared his stinger shot as the Leader chortled, leaning on his twitching mount's loop saddle.

"Eidolonitha wants to play, or negotiate?" he asked.

Gavin kneeled and scraped a rudimentary picture into the hard stone just beyond the beach, white-blue glitter lingering against charcoal black. The components of his efforts grated off the spear-tip, leaving it ragged, and with the friction had been set to light in that lingering, bluish glow. This light appeared at the fore of his mind regardless, whether he possessed eyes or not.

The ones still mounted in the air could see it best.

"An arrow ... pointing at ... hrm?"

"A crown!" the second cried. *"It's a crown!"*

"What, that mean he fin'lly wants to tell us which Greylord he serves?"

"You know, that's a right point, yi? He can't talk. We can't read those scribbles he made last time. How we gonna — ?"

"Shut up, Cru. Look."

Gavin kept drawing on the stone. He drew the impression of a blacked-out eye just above a line intended to be the horizon. Then a basic feminine form, and beside her, a thin, dark shape with glowing eyes and spots, holding a dagger. It was like a child's picture of chalk on a wall, but even rubes who passed partial memories from one copy to the next recognized certain crests and symbols, illiterate or not.

All the same, he made a couple extra marks that would mean nothing to them.

"*Herrish dung ... "* Cru muttered.

"*What is it?*"

"*The Prophetess.*"

"*Who?*"

"*The Mother of Shrouds. And her Shaegoth.*"

A satisfying round of nerves passed through his captors, but the Leader dispelled it when he laughed.

"*He says nothing for years, when he even had the choice. He keeps his secrets, and now he just* **tells** *us his Greylord? He does not even bargain?*"

"*You did say he should submit —*"

"*Pah! He is lying. Desperate not to join a swarm.*"

"*Yes, but if he say, then we go sell him, yi? Grandfathers say!*"

"*That's the prank!*" the Leader barked. "*This could be his Lord or be false claim to* **avoid** *this Lord!"*

"*The Devourer would take him,*" Cru muttered, "*if she* **is** *his Lord.*"

"*PAH!*" the Leader repeated loudly. "*And it could be a trick to take him to the Devourer, knowing we go there if he claims to serve her! Perhaps he wants most to avoid her!"*

"*But ... she's not that powerful anymore, is she?*"

"*Doesn't need big armies to tear up half the Devourer's lands in revolt,*" Cru said carefully. "*She has agents and assassins, they say, impossible to stop.*"

"*Not true, she'd have taken over by now.*"

"*Or the Devourer would have. She holding him back, yi?*"

"*Shuttit, all o' you! I'm thinking.*"

A single breeze attracted all their attention, even Gavin's, as they scanned for storm clouds on the horizon. Storms never took long to build once they began. The Bane Wasps in displeasure, ready to leave whether their riders wished it or not. The riderless Wasp would have had Cru not reached for the hook bridle.

"*Now what, Leader?"* the one on the ground asked.

Only a moment to decide.

"*We leave.*" He looked to their prisoner."*No games this time, Ghostwalker. We ask around, send message, see who pays. You still here next time, we take you off this island back to coast.*"

Fools.

Gavin nodded clearly his understanding, but he stepped forward and knelt as if to communicate one last picture with his scratching tool. More than leaned forward, expectant. He tugged open his pouch as if to sprinkle its contents across the dulled edge of his spear.

No one protested.

The Herald stood up mid-stroke, flicked his wrist holding the pouch and the end of a long, skeletal arm, coating Cheff standing on the ground in gritty, blood-infused reagents. Some of it got into his eyes and mouth. He cried out and spat.

"*Hyi!*" another rider shouted.

Gavin hadn't stopped moving. He clutched himself to the staggering Cheff and twisted him around, holding him as a shield against the Bane Wasps. He raised the magically crafted spear tip and sliced through the tough skin of his neck, nicking an artery just beneath the jaw. Red blood spurt over his hand in a stream.

Its fresh scent drove the Wasps beyond their riders' control as they beat their wings to lift off.

"*Woh-woh!*" they shouted, struggling to stay mounted.

Gavin opened his exposed teeth next to the fresh flowing blood, his dry, black tongue lapping the rough skin, drawing in enough vivid fluid along with his powder to achieve dual results: to grant a surge of healing and offer a second set of eyes through his captor-turned-prisoner.

Vitas flooded into him, drawn directly from his victim. As Cheff wailed in terror, the Bane Wasps chittered and ground their jaws in blood-lust.

Much longer and the Wasps will tear us all apart.

Gavin used his tool next to cut open the gut of his struggling victim just beneath the chest plate, aiming to release the entrails but not go so deep as to damage them. The riders attempted to surround him from above, to shoot him with their retrievable stingers. The Wasps jerked wildly, causing one to miss his aim as Gavin kept turning. The others couldn't get a clear shot with the revolting mounts buzzing in agitation.

"*What is he doing to Cheff?!*" one cried.

Not his best work. The incision was ragged and torn from the struggle and rudimentary tool, but intestines and life fluid splattered onto the barren rock. The rider ceased to fight as Gavin lowered him quickly and reached inside his body cavity, searching.

"*Kellgirohn!*" the Leader screamed in fury.

The Herald's languages sounded in his mind.

Blood clot from a diseased womb …

Ibi congreti sanguinex utepris …

Taja damu man rahim murid …

Gavin found what he sought. Though wrapped in tough membranes, his fingers were sharp enough to sever the tethers. The eviscerated rider grunted as he did so, wide-eyed and still aware but paralyzed as Gavin had often been.

There …

Swiftly, the Herald pulled out three, squirming larvae not yet ready to pupate, their growth stunted by whatever chemicals these "Bane of the Wasps" ingested day after day. Each was a pale cream color and smooth, about the size of a Human kidney. Gavin cradled them to prevent dropping one; he needed all three.

Each of these riders held the same inside his body. This was why the Bane Wasps did not attack them and even allowed some token control, though little of *that* could be seen above now with the Wasps driven mad with bloodlust and rage at the dangers to their young.

Gavin backed up, his marked tool having already claimed the soul for his Lady. The four Wasps landed upon the gutted corpse and began to consume him, the three surviving riders watching underneath them and shouting in abject helplessness.

Another gust of wind.

The next storm appeared on the horizon.

Gavin smiled for the first time in many years, beyond the default of his skeleton's grin. His tongue and mouth reformed first, stained in a mixture

149

of red blood dripping black, preparing him for his most powerful spells. He could already feel his control insidiously seeping into the Wasps as they ate the tainted flesh. Temporary only, but the next stage would begin with but a word.

He held the larvae gently in skeletal hands which would not remain bare for long; he waited, ignoring the curses of those too petrified to dismount, standing well outside the range of those stingers.

While Gavin would like to eviscerate each and steal their larvae, to leave them here as they had him, he hadn't the time. If he made it back to the coast, so would these three, but they wouldn't be the victors.

"*No more!*" the Leader bellowed, trying to yank his mount away from the fresh meal, but it did not heed his command."*We never come back! You remain and face the hungry winds of the Black Sea until End Time!*"

Gavin's body filled in quickly. His shriveled organs, barely present before, like grapeskins clinging to the vine through three seasons, now revived themselves, plump and wet. As it happened, he settled the three, moving larvae in among his own swelling guts. The cushioning closed in around the precious brood, and his grey skin continued to knit together to keep them safe. His vision was returning at last, and his mouth had repaired enough to speak.

"*Uthrishh valrenegri duhrisss,*" he intoned."*Geth'ric punfah-shek!*"

Tiny pieces of the broken rider twitched as if they might have tried to stand, to come to him, but that was not to be. Instead, the four Bane Wasps flinched as he searched from their thorax out, seizing command of the powder they'd ingested. Gavin's will seeped through the circulatory system into the nerves, trace elements speeding through their body, deadening the conscious connection between mind and body no matter how feral.

He focused on the riderless Wasp. *I carry your young. You understand. You must carry your brood to safety before the storm.*

She approached him as an individual with a hyper-focused goal rather than as one of the most feared swarms in the Greylands. Antennae sensed the truth of his commands, sniffing his form in transition from black bone to pale flesh. She clacked her pinchers while turning her side to him, urging him onto her back.

No time to waste, he climbed on, made sure of his solid balance and grip, and commanded the other Wasps through the corpse they'd eaten.

Danger is coming. Return to your nest **now**. *Beware the Sea Serpents below.*

His remaining captors shouted threats which could not be translated while he focused on his spell; it became background noise to him with the buzzing of brittle wings. Their vitriol lessened in the storm's wake, three subdued enemies carried along as the clouds blackened and the wind picked up.

The once-light grey of the sky which made a lighter ocean shifted together. Dark shadows flitted into view before vanishing beneath the surface of the water. This happened more often as the surface of the sea roughened and the tiny ripples became small waves.

Then the sea turned black, effectively hiding those gargantuan predators.

Gavin gave the Bane Wasps their head, as many a horseman back home would say, for they were experts at flying together in strong winds and using fluid formations difficult for a lunging sea creature to predict. The small swarm hovered at neither a close nor steady level above the water, even as they could not go as high as to be directly in the clouds of acid. Perhaps their exoskeleton and wings had adapted to deal with such rains, but the Wasps knew at least one of the four "walking meals" carrying their young was not.

"Do you hear, yi?! Can't! I've tried!"

"Don't use the stingers, Leader! We need him! He's controlling the Wasps!"

"GRAAGH! How is he doing it? How?"

Again, he smiled, new eyes barely open to the wind.

Whenever the Herald needed more stability and speed without suppressing those natural instincts, he dug the tip of his spear into the exoskeleton of his mount. That his tool wore through the tough armor at all was telling of his skill in creating the shard. A little life fluid from the Wasp would leak out and mingle with the dark veins inside the spear point. Like the powder itself — the real weapon ignored in favor of a prominent sharp edge — the primitive tool kept him connected to the living Wasps.

Focus on the mainland. Fly to safety.

All his observations and theories had paid off; his theories and planning had seen him off that condemned island. Would they also set him free? *Yet to be seen.*

Once they reached the coast, he must improvise more than he cared to admit.

I shall return, my Lady. I shall find you.

No matter the obstacle.

CHAPTER 3

THE BLACK SEA COAST. THE NEXUS. TIME UNKNOWN.

GAVIN HAD ONCE DESCRIBED THE GREYLANDS TO SIRANA AS A "BRIDGE" OVER which souls migrate.

Close enough at the time. One does not have to take the bridge to cross a river, but it is often the more chosen and easier path.

He had since learned, taken as a whole, the Nexus wasn't just one bridge but too many to count. More like wheel with innumerable spokes reaching out from a center hub.

The Greylands connected to realities uncounted, and because of this connection, the Nexus remained the preferred crossing method for many beings. The path of least resistance and the crossroads for a seemingly infinite choice in destination, even with the inherent difficulty in "leaping" planes of reality outside of the natural current of mortal birth or a death transition.

Some time go — how long, he did not know — Gavin had crossed over by choice from Miurag to Nexus, taking his body with him. The challenge and leaps of faith, as it were, separated Deathwalkers from the other necromancers of Miurag.

Even as time had passed, Gavin remembered how it had felt.

The incredible strain on his essence, his worldly anchors, his mage's aura, and his physical body with each step. As the borders around him blurred and shifted, he had felt as if his heels were at the edge of a continually crumbling cliff. There was no way to jump back, nothing else to grab hold of as he prepared for the next leap. To make the transition to the "land of the dead" as a Whole Being, without being splintered or sloughing off the heaviest weight of one's existence, took immense will and knowledge, focus and endurance.

To achieve this was to achieve a level of difficulty which a Dwarf had once likened to looking up to one of the Sister Moons shining in Miurag's sky and somehow building a way to fly out and step onto its very surface. Not just the force of propulsion but having also solved the problems of how to breathe and how to prevent the body's destruction in that void where Miurag's natives could not thrive.

Like a Tundar walking upon the moon, Gavin was not and never would be truly native to this otherworld of the Greylands. He possessed the will and the tools, plus the understanding of how to use them, to anchor and stabilize himself, to prevent his own self-destruction as he Walked back to where the universe began.

As proud as he imagined his Mistress had been with his rising enlightenment, he had yet to see Her this time in the Grey. He'd witnessed no evidence of Her presence, no interference in his journey. He could neither feel Her Hand guiding him nor hear Her Whispers hinting at a path.

Not so blatantly as it had been on Miurag.

Small moments of inspiration had touched him on the island, the intuitive connections of what he had studied coalescing into something complex yet practical. He might attribute those to Her influence or simply to his devotion to Her.

She had not saved him from the bandits or his imprisonment by them; neither had She punished him, pushing him into their arms. She had not comforted him or denounced his failings as he had on his own. She had not provided him any direction from the moment he began this Walk.

His test in the Nexus thus far, it seemed, was to keep his faith that She was still here for him to reach at all.

RETURNED JUST AHEAD OF THE STORM, GAVIN SAW THIS COLONY OF BANE WASP nests was a small one compared to what other travelers had talked about.

Only several score of nests.

The Wasps could number in the hundreds of thousands if the hunting was good, for that hunting triggered their breeding cycle. Colonies would split and scatter as they got too large to sustain themselves, take up or abandon stretches of the coast for a distance not yet measured.

As dangerous and feared as these creatures were in any number, those numbers opened the floodgates on hunting them. The insides of the Wasps could be decent soup when needed, but most viewed them an unlimited source of armor and weapons for the Greylords, with Malok and other armies using the strongest chitin in the Nexus.

The Bane of the Wasp, still bickering about what to do and rightfully wary of landing, had discovered a unique way to utilize a few of the aggressive insects beyond food and armor. Only a resilient, self-cloning race would bother to deliberately destroy one body after another carrying larvae and ingesting the chemicals slowing their maturation, imperfect Vis and Vitas passed on to a fast-growing "child" to do it all again.

Gavin had long figured this small colony had changed with the exposure to this native race as well, and the two groups had become linked in breeding and guided riding, almost symbiotic.

Regrettable that such an extraordinary curiosity shall have to end.

Another unlucky "side inheritance" like himself would not become an everlasting target. Sooner or later all bandits met their end upon the road on which they preyed.

"No! Wait, no!"

Bane Wasps possessed pinchers which could snip the heads off the riders, if they could but reach them. Gavin's mount achieved just that on their Leader, catching them off guard, while the other two dismounted and tried to run along the cliffs.

Follow. Take their heads. Your young will be released unharmed.

Many other Bane Wasps here flew not under Gavin's control. They observed and communicated in bewilderment as the Herald sliced open the gut of the headless Leader with his tool and again retrieved the three larvae inside. He set them carefully in a crevice sheltered from the ocean spray where the colony could reach them.

Hands slick with gore, Gavin stood on the rocks with his own passengers wriggling inside him, protecting him from the rest of the colony. Once two more heads had rolled, he pursued the others guarded jealously by a trio of confused and agitated breeders.

The Wasps allowed him to approach, and he again kneeled to conduct crude birthing rites, retrieving the final six larvae from the guts of his former captors. The three worked quickly to secure and protect their brood elsewhere while other Wasps crowded in to feed on the bodies. Gavin's personal mount hovered near him, hissing and snapping at any that might approach.

"Oi! You! Strange Man! Who are you?"

Gavin looked up.

Crawling out of a deep cave, new half-grown clones of his captors, their smaller torsos struggling to hide the burgeoning movement beneath their tough, grey skin. He sighed as Cru the Seventh spoke.

"Doesn't matter, yi? He killed our Fathers!"

"Yah! Let's get the stingers! We'll show'im!"

They did not recognize him in this newly healed body — that original memory had gone with the generations. Now, they underestimated the danger.

As the murder-thieves ran back into the cave to retrieve their weapons, Gavin looked to the "motherly" Wasp who remained beside him. His command was simple.

Protect me.

Wings buzzed as she flexed her mandibles and stalked the opening to the cave. She could have entered with wings folded, he noted, but she chose to remain outside. Anything nearby could hear the clones whooping and shouting as they ran back out, their first, clumsy shots loosed too far away to reach him. Fortunately, their target practice had not yet reached the advanced stage of their predecessors.

The Wasp who'd carried Gavin from the island followed behind them, creeping up. Three other Wasps remained to follow his commands if necessary.

This will not take long.

THE LAST CLAN CLONE DIED AN APPROXIMATE HALF-DAY SINCE GAVIN ESCAPED the island. The spell had run its course, and the four Wasps were free of his will as well as theirs.

Yet he remained on the cliffs as the window of opportunity to get inland closed.

He had been wasting away on the island too long to recover quickly after such expenditure of magical focus. Though grateful he had the capability to strengthen with rest, the fact remained that the spell had been a powerful one, and he was exhausted. He may have had it in him to kill a few Wasps obstructing his way but not the whole colony. He doubted he could take on a hundred Bane Wasps were he in top form.

The Deathwalker also couldn't simply leave in peace, though he had tried. The insect which had carried him here now prevented him from climbing up to crest the flat mesa above.

Not while he carried her young.

For three days Gavin waited for an opportunity to slip away, but she was never far away, ever ready to herd him back to the nests. She even brought him food stolen from the jaws of the drones returned from hunting inland. If he refused to eat some of it, she would try to to climb atop him, to shove the strips of flesh directly into his mouth like the most bizarre cross-species kiss, unless he acquiesced and took the food while she watched with huge, compound eyes.

Gavin had already considered that if he cut the larvae out to return them to the colony, he would *still* not be allowed to leave. Black blood or no, he was still a nutritious food source in a place of bare rock, apparent in the number of Wasps that tried to sneak close to snap at his naked feet.

The breeder queen would have to drive them off.

Three days and he still sat upon the cliffs of the Black Sea, curled tight and naked, buffeted by the increasing winds, mildly burned on his ears and shoulders, his arms and legs by the light mist. He could do nothing but consider his own pregnant state as the larvae seemed to be growing quickly, shoving his organs around as if to get more comfortable. It was anything but comfortable for him.

This will take further contemplation.

Oddly, he thought of his first year traveling with Sirana. For his mortal self, a stark change in circumstance leading to survival, renewal, and self-discovery. The difference on this day was that he had instigated this change himself rather than having it thrust upon him.

One step after another; a decision begets another, and another. The catalyst had been added, the reaction begun, and he could not stop until all possible outcomes were spent. A string of events set up out of view except in hindsight, he'd been pushed to the depths of a sentient's will to survive, reliant on no one, when Fear passed by and ceased to be an obstacle. Deliberate choice to look Fate in the face and stride toward solution and risk, come what may.

Such bits of wisdom seemed always swirling around, repeated often among allies facing their own changes, remembered by those who didn't know but saw the results. Whether it struck a nerve at any point depended on the sensitivity of that nerve at that moment in time.

Gavin decided he was quite sensitive to this wisdom now. He had the true comprehension of a long-lived race to show for it, the hands-on experience of what direction events might have taken to land Sirana at his doorstep the way she had, and why she had made all those decisions which had led him to Manalar and beyond.

He understood the many *years* the young Elf must have waited and watched in the Deepearth, much as he had on that island. Observing the rules, using her wit to survive in an extreme, hostile trap.

Then she escaped.

Carrying her own squirming young inside her gut, no less.

So much had changed in a year on Miurag — in her lifespan, more like a seasonal camp trip. On such a small world, her actions would have great impact whether she lived long or not. The point was that she had *lived*.

Gavin's experience in the Nexus, already scaled down to seven generations of bandits in a contained area, might mean only what he would take from it.

This assumed he found yet another solution before the larvae feasted on his organs and chewed their way out to be like their parents. Their increasing heat and activity concerned him as the slow-growth toxins he'd ingested from the blood of the rider must be wearing off.

The simplest solution suggested exploring the bandit clan's cave when his queen would tolerate it. Up until now, the Wasps seemed to think the place a bad location for their brood and Gavin could only get closer a small distance at a time. Now, fortunately, they crawled closer and closer to it, as if they were forgetting the generations of bandits which had crept out of it.

Gavin had to check if the cave sheltered any leftover chemicals to slow the larvae growth, and he wanted to see if he could replicate their methods to make more, to give him time carrying the stunted young as long as possible. Perhaps he could regain control of his queen and ride her as far as she would go inland, to find help. To call an ally of his Lady.

But would the chemicals be as commonplace away from the coast as to make more when he needed it? How long or how much strength would it take to find such an ally, and who would he run into in the meantime?

Or perhaps he would have no choice but to risk getting as far from here as possible, disabling his mount, and then cutting himself open to destroy the little beasts himself. Would he recover before something found him? Would he be too weakened to evade further stalking and recapture?

With these concerns filling his mind, Gavin found rare insight into what Sirana's journey might have been like.

He sighed, his limp, black hair regrown long enough to fall into his eyes. Slowly, he got to his feet, moving yet closer to the cave. He walked the last several strides, reached the entrance at last, and the shelter was a welcome relief from the spray and the rain. His "mother" Wasp somehow understood this as she watched him carefully, following him closer to the entrance but did not go in. She kept guard outside.

I wager there is no rear exit.

Detritus and evidence of past thefts from Nexus travelers lay in piles and scattered around, the only well-kept equipment being the stinging crossbows. Gavin looked around for what "payment" they might have asked of a Greylord had they the chance. What had they desired enough that they would ask ransom for it?

Unlike his birth world, metal of any sort would not enter negotiations — no Greylord negotiated for that too-limited resource — but there might have been gems. Yet, what use would gems be to these barbarians squatting on the coast, constantly impregnating their clones with Bane Wasp young and feeding them poisons to stay uneaten?

Better food if they bother to trade at all, better armor or equipment ... or perhaps something less tangible.

Cru the Third had once said, *"Time'll come the adults recognize their own."*

Perhaps a merging of fundamental essence between the two very different beings? Add to that an increase in their cloning numbers beyond four. Something only a Greylord or a scholar with mastery of the Greylands could achieve and might comply for no reason other than to witness a curious change.

Gavin had only begun his search for vials or corked bottles when a strange sensation stole up his spine and the back of his neck. A series of tiny bumps popped up and spread over his skin — a truly odd experience for he had not worn skin in quite a while and, when he last *had*, it was too dry to respond naturally in such a way.

He spun toward the source, his black eyes extending past the dim light from the mouth of the cave to trace a lean shadow even darker than those around it. Pale, shining blue eyes opened; the creature revealed a broad, sharp grin as well.

"*About time you walked in here,*" the Shaegoth whispered.

A familiar, blue light emanated from the back of the "throat" as the living shadow spoke. Gavin's eyes flicked down. The ornamental wrap draped around its "waist" possessed not just one pale mask but several — each with a different, extreme emotion molded into it. No silver dagger, but a sword was peace-knotted at its side.

"*Take me to my Lady,*" he murmured quietly so as not to warn the Bane Wasp queen.

Long, thin arms displayed themselves. "*That is the plan. Hold onto that spearhead, don't lose it.*"

Hard, unsettling limbs snapped around the Deathwalker's bare chest, pinning his arms. The shadow was behind him before Gavin had fully grasped the instruction. For how spindly and immaterial the Shaegoth seemed, its strength was uncanny. He could not inhale if he tried.

"*Oh! And congratulations, Herald,*" the Shaegoth teased. "*I hear they're triplets.*"

CHAPTER 4
OUTPOST UNKNOWN, TIME UNKNOWN

GAVIN AROSE TO CONSCIOUSNESS IN A PLACE FAR MORE FAMILIAR THAN HE HAD been willing to hope.

A room.

One inside of a strong structure of deliberate design which he would prefer to imagine was far, far away from the coast. The air was dry and blessedly quiet with a scent a little like books or scrolls, though he saw none.

Perhaps it had once contained such things.

He was in repose, unclothed and on his back. A large, stone platform elevated his frame, overlaid with some kind of absorbent, reedy mat. A ceramic tray sat near his head, chirurgeon's tools laid out neatly: scalpels, scissors, tongs, needles with thread; clean sponges, wraps, and bandages.

On a separate table were five non-porous bowls, four empty with one containing clean water, he hoped, alongside multiple glass bottles and vials containing various substances and colors.

All in fine condition.

A figure came forward then, moving neither naturally nor bipedally, no balanced steps but more gliding or slithering. From Gavin's placement on the operating table, he could not tell which was more accurate.

The chirurgeon was a tall, bird-eyed woman, staring at him with large, glossy eyes. Her features were sharp and intense, hawkish. It was a face that could either show disapproval or deep concentration but nothing else.

She bowed her head to him, gesturing to the array of tools and preparations. He took it as both an invitation and a test.

"*Very well*," he whispered hoarsely, surprised how a few words made his throat sore after decades without one. Or perhaps it was the effects of breathing in acid spray in a full-flesh body.

Gavin tried to sit up, to reach for the tools, but two Shaegoth — already in the room, it seemed — appeared on either side of him, taking him by his upper arms. They pressed him back and held him down.

"*Too dangerousss*," one Shaegoth chided.

"*Too preciousss*," the second hissed.

Neither were the multi-masked Shaegoth who had come to retrieve him in the cave, but they grinned down at him with similar, glowing, blue teeth. The ethereal chill of their grip was welcome somehow. That elite agents were to stay as mere orderlies and see his Lady's Will be done, whatever it would be, *must* mean She knew he had returned.

The Herald remained calm, though they did not release him. Given the opportunity, he memorized the unique spot patterns over their chest and arms, should he see them again, before turning his attention to the other servant in here with them.

Getting a second look at her and furthering the bird impression, he noted long black feathers threaded through her skin in places, contrasting greatly with the pale blue of her flesh, not dissimilar to Ada's gown being sewed into her skin.

Acolyte, he guessed.

A black leather apron concealed her slim form, and he finally noted the long, over-dexterous digits of her hands joining in a fluid yet unfamiliar configuration. She did not speak but reached out to choose her first tool from her selection: a bottle.

As soon as her fronds uncorked it, he could smell what it was.

"*No*," he refused, staring at her eyes, unblinking. "*Do not anesthetize me.*"

It probably wouldn't work anyway.

The chirurgeon stared down at him. She shrugged lightly, returned the bottle unused to its place, and selected her first scalpel for the appropriate size and angle with which to begin. He approved.

"*We must extract those Bane Wasp eggs from you,*" she said in the Dead Tongue, her mouth taut like skin wrapped around a beak, her voice as coarse as a crow.

"*Larvae,*" he answered, sensing another deep shift as the creatures recovered from the Shaegoth shadow trip. Hard points nudged at his abdominal wall. "*Far beyond eggs at this point.*"

She nodded, unperturbed at being corrected about such an important detail, given her task. Perhaps she was merely testing his mental clarity.

"*Our Mistress has instructed live extraction, if possible,*" she continued. "*They have drunk deeply of you, Herald. She wants them.*"

Gavin nodded and did not fight as the scalpel hovered above his bare, bulging stomach. Her steady clasper adjusted with the movement beneath his skin, ready to choose the first incision.

"*The other side,*" he said. "*And lower. Their instinct is to climb.*"

"*Are you certain you will not sip from the bottle?*" the chirurgeon asked, casually.

"*I am certain,*" he answered, sensing the tightening grip of the two Shaegoth holding him down.

"*Very well.*" The bird woman craned her neck, nodding toward a darkened corner. "*Your assistance is needed, Archivist.*"

"*Delightful.*"

A third Shaegoth slipped in to join them, the same one from the Bane Wasp cave, and this time wearing a mask. The pale, frozen smile fixed on him, eyes holes aglow and centered with cross-shaped pupils.

"*Archivist?*" Gavin asked as his stomach visibly roiled.

"*Of Woe, yes!*" The Shaegoth offered a theatrical bow. "*A pleasure to meet again, Herald!*"

The Deathwalker squinted. "*Do you ... archive anything?*"

"*I wouldn't be much of a librarian if I didn't!*"

Gavin frowned. "*May I see it?*"

"*Certainly! One of them.*"

"*One.*"

"*Indeed! But let us focus.*" The Archivist wiggled black, phantom's fingers. "*For now, I am but a spare pair of hands to catch these bundles of joy.*"

"*Hm. Be wary, then, both of you,*" the Herald replied, determined to bear witness. "*They bite.*"

GAVIN WAS CAUGHT WITH HIS NOSE TOO CLOSE TO A SCROLL TO SIMPLY BE READ-ing it unless doing so cross-eyed.

"*Ah, yes,*" said the other Deathwalker with placid amusement, carrying in a giant stack of old, fraying texts as if they weighed nothing. "*To be among familiar scents after being away in the wilderness.*" A chuckle. "*And to have a nose once again to enjoy them.*"

Gavin lifted his gaze, tempering resentment at the interruption; it was an old habit he found to be unhelpful. Bracing his elbows on the table, he threaded his fingers in front of his mouth. "*Curious, rather. These scents are less familiar to me despite the parchment and ink.*"

"*I'm not surprised. The waryx pulp here is a bit different than the wood and thread you'd be familiar with, but it takes an epoch to start looking so worn like these.*"

The ancient Deathwalker set down the mix of texts on a bone cart to be sorted. Gavin stared at the strong, greenish-grey hands with extremely thick digits with very sturdy fingernails at the end of each. They were attached to a broad and muscular body, the features of which all aligned as a birth form, not one modified or assembled from components.

Gavin had met this tusked man before. Oskar had been one of four Grey guardians, standing with Houda, Ada, and the wasp girl around the sacred pool at Manalar as they waited to see whether Willven Isboern would survive the war.

By the shadowlands, that meeting feels centuries old.

He grunted, noting the items Oskar had collected from the library shelves for repair and further preservation. Scripts identifying the topics were all embossed, resistant to the elements in ways his own lost copy of his grimoire hadn't been. His book had been too easily destroyed.

"*Can you smell the difference as well?*" Gavin asked.

Oskar nodded, his thick neck flexing, his gruff voice a mismatch to the eloquent way he spoke. "*Better than you can. I still remember Miurag. Rarer senses can be given to those devotees of Our Lady when we serve the pact well and make our final crossing, bringing our bodies with us as few can.*"

The large man faced him directly, dusting off his hands, and looked at Gavin with jade eyes, such a green almost in texture as much as color. He inhaled slowly through a prominent, cavernous nose one could well believe was highly sensitive. It was attached to a heavy-boned and hairy face, faded red hair covering most of a head attached to a massive, fighter's body a full head taller even Gavin's lanky height.

He scanned the other skeptically. "*Did you serve our Lady as a mortal upon the Kurgan Steppes, perhaps?*"

Grey-olive lips stretched back from jutting lower canines. "*I did not. I was born in the Red Desert and served the Court of Queen Innathi and her General-Consort, Cris-ri-phon.*"

"*Impossible,*" Gavin blurted.

"*Oh?*" Oskar leaned back against a bookshelf. "*How so?*"

The Herald regathered his poise. "*I retract it. I should know better. It is only that I … met someone who saw Cris-ri-phon's memories. She saw an 'Oskar,' the last Deathwalker of the court. The final one of the Davrin-Zauyrian alliance.*"

Oskar nodded. "*That was me. And?*"

"*And you look nothing like that memory.*"

"*It happens.*"

Gavin huffed. "*How did this happen?*"

The other Deathwalker exhibited teasing patience in a tusky smile. "*This body was one of the last mercenaries who came after me and the General's Daughter, by way of the Queen's sister. If I could not transition bearing my own body, I would gladly take the ruffian who was foolish enough to steal and don my amulet as my birth form lay dying.*"

Gavin drummed his fingers. "*Well. Yes, that would explain what I see. Out of curiosity, did all Kurgan 'ruffians' of the time have tusks?*"

166

"*No.*" Oskar shook his head. "*Those of Orcish descent were becoming few even in my time.*"

"*Orcish …*"

"*Not a word you hear often anymore?*"

"*Never, rather. Until the Elves crept out of hiding.*"

"*Hm. That makes sense.*" Oskar's eyes crinkled at the corners. "*Speaking of Elves, how do you find them? I'll admit being tempted to fall to the floor seeing Davrin and Naulor as allies, but the Davrin clearly favored you.*"

Gavin shrugged. "*Mm. Much yet to learn. I listen and observe.*"

The other Deathwalker kept his smile but did not pry at the deflection. "*My observation, if I may, was the Davrin seemed restless and forgetful while the Naulor seemed fearful with astonishingly distant memories. Both could hide it behind pride and ego, but if I would wager on which might be fully aware during times of strife and change, to take action and influence the outcome, it would be the Davrin. If I must wager which might build something lasting upon the lessons of what came before, it would be the Naulor.*"

"*Interesting,*" the Herald admitted. "*You met many Naulor?*"

Oskar motioned a tepid affirmative. "*During the lead up to a war, mind you. Diplomats and emissaries warning of dire things to come. Not the everyday people such as I observed in the Dark Elves and their Wilder Ones.*"

"*Wilder.*" Gavin frowned, snatching hold of that mention. "*Were they not blood of the Naulor as well?*"

"*So spoke the tales, though few I knew said so themselves. The Desert was their home, Innathi was their Queen. That was all that mattered to most, it seemed, until everyone had to flee.*"

Oskar paused, frowning in memory. Gavin waited, curious what vision he might volunteer.

"*At first,*" the Orcish Deathwalker murmured, "*I did not want the child but had been given my duty. Our bond altered as refugees, for we had no others we could trust. She prodded me to speak more, and I recall feeling true regret when our time of separation was at hand. After I took this body and entered the Grey, I speak more. I am not sure why, except … .*" A pause. "*No matter. Different bodies alter the Vis as they blend, we know this. At V'Gedra Court, I would say I was more like you, Herald. Sour and reclusive.*"

Their eyes met, and Oskar chuckled, showing wide, square teeth. *"Social indelicacy is a common trait for Deathwalkers because of our appearance and solitary rituals. We do well enough to push a few mortal allies to see past the scars and stand apart from other death mages on Miurag this way."*

The large librarian scratched his chin, noting Gavin's face screwed up in suspicious confusion. *"Ah. Did I lose you along the way?"*

"What child?" Gavin asked. *"The wasp girl who was with you at the pool?"*

Jade eyes flicked down as if he might see the new stitches in his abdomen. The mere weight of that glance made them itch. A moment later, surprise passed over Oskar's face, followed by concern as he reconsidered the direction of their conversation.

"I am perhaps speaking too much," he said, rebalancing a short stack of codices with broad hands. *"It can be challenging, Herald, keeping track of our meetings."*

Gavin made a face. *"Is this not our second meeting? Our first being inside the Manalar temple."*

Oskar grinned. *"If you and I stood at a place where you knew which child I spoke of, you wouldn't need to ask."*

"Meaning?"

"Meaning I've let my mind wander too far afield, and we should wait until our next meeting."

Gavin thought this over, letting his fingers become familiar with the unique texture of the parchment. *"Are you suggesting we've met before? At a later 'place' than the pool of Manalar but before this one?"*

"You're catching up." Oskar chuckled, motioning to his torso. *"How are the stiches?"*

"Absorbed or squeezed out," Gavin said, accepting the change of subject. *"R'rilgya does decent work."*

"Every chance she gets." Oskar flexed his own strong hands barely dexterous enough to turn a thin page. *"Better she worked on you than me. She is not from our world, of course, but with similar skills and appetites."*

"Of course."

Gavin reached for a sapphire glass bottle, taking a sip of the bitter solution his chirurgeon had provided at the end of the extraction. While his flesh had mended as he would expect normally it to, why he was already sitting upright in a library one wing away, the defensive toxins left behind by the frightened and vicious young remained potent and stubborn. The substance resisted complete eradication and would have to be neutralized each time his middle flared up as if on fire.

Eventually it will stop.

Yet the pain only sharpened his memory of the wasp girl as one of the Grey Guardians at the sacred pool. She had never spoken to him or anyone, often crouching behind Oskar's massive frame whenever anyone stared too long at her.

Anyone such as him.

Gavin lifted a nostril. *Hmph. If that is all I am to be given now, then I should leave soon.*

The Herald didn't know where he resided, only that this holding or outpost wasn't the Citadel of his Lady from his dreams. Oskar had informed him some time ago that he would not be allowed to walk elsewhere, by whatever means, until the flare-ups from his surgery had ceased.

So be it.

Gavin had spent much of that time reading what he could on the shelves and re-scribing his grimoire from memory. This haven of his Lady would work while he recovered, but he was far from finished, not yet ready to return to his birth world.

"*If I were to seek more direct source of knowledge about the Ma'ab revolt before their crossing to Miurag,*" he began, "*how far do I have to Walk?*"

Oskar rumbled in his chest, a sound like deep amusement as green eyes glinted. Standing up, he lifted one of the books of maps and brought it closer, towering over the Herald as he sought a page. He poked a misshapen area with his thick finger.

"*Not far, if you remain in Nyx's borders to start. She claimed some of them. I can offer you the best route to take, and the Umbaldes often head through there on their trails.*"

"*And where can I meet their caravan?*" Gavin asked, replacing the cork in the glass bottle after a second sip, setting it aside to study the map.

Oskar nodded. "*Just wait here. The Umbaldes passed through ten days ago.*

They will be through here again within the next ten."

"Ten 'days'? How can you tell with neither sunrises nor sunsets?"

The ancient Deathwalker's smile reached his eyes. *"I can feel it. I am stationed here because of its chrono-familiarity to Miurag, and the Archivist of Woe brought you here because he knew you would heal more predictably."*

Chrono-familiarity? Gavin nearly curled the edge of the scroll with his dry finger. He stopped himself before he could damage the parchment. He cleared his throat. "He? You mean the Archivist."

"Correct. He also said you would better orient yourself and estimate when you must Walk again. Which you just demonstrated to me."

"Hmm. *Has the Archivist visited our home world recently?"*

A shrug. *"I am not privy to where our Lady sends him, even with all these records. You might ask him but don't expect a serious answer."*

"Why not?"

"He jests."

"Jests."

Oskar chuckled. *"One of the few Shaegoth that does."* A pause. *"Although, I would be remiss not to mention one doesn't* want *the Archivist of Woe to show up on one's home world. As his title suggests, it's a bad omen for those living there."*

Gavin squinted at the unfortunately likely thought. "Hm. *I see."*

Oskar watched and had stopped talking, waiting to see if he had any further questions. Gavin would *always* have questions, but it seemed he had much to sort through to avoid going in circles.

Gavin finally nodded, partly in dismissal. *"Very well. Thank you."*

The other stood up to take the cart of ratty texts into the back to work on them. *"I shall check on you again, Herald. Best to your studies."*

CHAPTER 5

THE TRADE ROUTES OF THE NEXUS, TIME UNKNOWN.

ALMOST NO ONE BLENDED INTO AN UMBALDES CARAVAN EVEN WHEN THE MERchants stood to their peak height, which was shorter than Gavin was at his hip. Quick moving and often high-strung, the six-legged creatures had tattoos on their fleshy throats and colorful dyes permeating the fur covering their insectal abdomen. Gavin thought they might best be described as a homogeny of beetle, snake, and — going by the ears and body hair from the thorax down — some kind of capra goat.

An Umbaldes scurried around Gavin's long legs now, peering up at him and curling the sensitive tendrils on its upper lip like a sentient mustache. "*Good suppression-sneak, Happenly-Sir, keep it much! But stretched high you are! Keep look-out with useful high-eyes, yes, yes. Do this, Neverwilt never forget!*"

Gavin replied formally, striding with his new staff alongside the string of lightweight brill carts. "*That is the payment, Yilkin Neverwilt don' Meticulous Accountancy of the Terrorized,*"

"*Exceliness!*" Yilkin clapped tiny hands at the end of stalk-like arms. "*We lead, you follow! You warn!*"

Gavin nodded, staring at the grey carts in which he could not ride. Each would be pulled by something resembling an extremely hairy bovine if one ignored the number of limbs and eyes. Neither beasts nor cart reached the Deathwalker's shoulders.

The tallest creature here besides himself was the young Malok, Luhk. Taller than Gavin by a head or so, as eyeless as any of the grey warriors he'd witnessed crossing over to raid souls at Manalar, this one didn't serve a Greylord at all. Rather, the freeborn warrior owed loyalty only to this small collection of grey merchants in a lifelong pledge.

"*Yelcom,*" he greeted, raising the giant hand of a pugilist. "*See far, before I smell, ya?*"

"*Yes,*" Gavin agreed, thinking oddly of the Naulor Druid's falcon. *I suppose I shall fulfill a similar role.*

Luhk interacted with his environment as well as any species which had traded large eyes for other heightened senses. If a threat encroached, he could fight and defend his employer-family blind, for his nose and ears were keen as any wolf, perhaps alongside less tangible senses.

The Umbaldes, in contrast, possessed extraordinary color vision for a race traveling a place called the Greylands. Their fleshy whiskers picked up subtle flows of energy difficult to describe in his grimoire.

Not unlike the Dark Elves seeing in pitch black, in a reversal of spectrum.

The Grey Merchants described it as sensing "the blooming," especially those particles in the current which responded to qualities that catalyzed germination, like a seed on Miurag landing in moist, nutrient-rich earth warmed with sunlight. This ability led the Umbaldes almost flawlessly to the next source of food or water in what appeared to be a barren land of grey dust.

Often it led them to the Geb'harik, the massive "Moving Grove" of the dusty Greylands Plains. The tiny merchants frequently climbed these living hills to find the potent, hypnotic fungi dyes which enhanced their visible tattoos. These additions were invisible to anyone else until their body reacted to some threat, creating its own strange sort of magical Vitas. By then, it was too late for the unwary or uneducated.

Threats and beggars alike could be lulled to docility, working for the Umbaldes for free until they could be dropped off where they couldn't follow. Gavin had not yet read or heard of the Umbaldes killing anyone, though the Malok among them might in defense of their tribe.

Despite these advantages, the Umbaldes generally welcomed working with knowledgeable souls with far-seeing eyes, even if most eidolons were blind to the spore trails and vapors that could feed the natives.

This curiously persuasive symbiosis allowed easier bartering for Gavin and his kind, if one knew about this lack among the Grey Merchants. One could strike a good bargain, if not a risk-free one. The harsh consequences for "sleeping" on watch held stakes which included extended servitude. Not all the leverage lay on the eidolon or Deathwalker's side, no matter the desirable qualities of their eyes.

"*A mountain rises at kelsin degree*," Gavin said in one of frequent reports to the scurrying Yilkin.

"*Posh-gep*," the merchant acknowledged. "*Highs-eyes spot any Roh'ghast?*"

"*Not yet.*"

The furry, long-necked beetle chittered, inhaling as whiskers curled and waved. "*Maybe get close-nigh. Shortcut if not nesting to wild breed, the Meticulancy will be ah-Right.*"

The caravan navigated through a long spine of grey cliffs with only a few curious creatures noting their passing. This sliced off a few "days" of travel to get to the former Ma'ab territory Oskar had indicated — though his suggested route was longer and perhaps too cautious.

Early warnings like his made the Grey Merchants bold, Gavin noticed, as over the next length of time — four or five days though there was no night or day to measure — Gavin closed his eyes only for brief spells requested by the Umbaldes and Luhk, with proper defenses set up.

The Herald remained cooperative, benefiting from the depth of knowledge kept by the tiny, nomadic creatures. While traveling in the canyons and cliffs, he learned more of their skill in artistic crafts beyond tattoos and dying their fur.

The insides of their enclosed carts were joyfully colored, forming mosaics of flint and shale of concentrated color possibly found nowhere else in the Nexus. Less-permanent murals of mud paint implied refined dexterity in those many little limbs. Included with the color were small ovals of black glass, their deliberate imperfections creating a startling illusion of depth and an appearance such as the stars Gavin had not seen since leaving Miurag.

He felt inspired.

"Would you consider a contract on behalf of the Grey Maiden?" he asked Yilkin one night while Luhk stood guard.

The merchant waved his tiny hand. *"Tell-tell, always consider, Herald High-eyes."*

"It would not be in the Nexus, but a shrine built in Her Name upon my birth world. I have means to pay, including metal."

They were excited to hear this, surprisingly so.

"Would need the Prophetess Permission in sigils," Yilkin said, stroking a somewhat open spot on his throat, space enough for another tattooed rune to be added.

"Ah, well. Noted."

Gavin could provide no such thing on Her behalf, not until he stood in Her presence once again. A very long time since he had heard the whispers of Her voice or felt the euphoric pain of Her proximity. Oskar's easy speech and recent actions backed by Her Will reassured him that he was not forgotten and should not doubt his purpose here, even including the time lost on the island.

Much as he missed the riddles of his muse and the contorted revelations sometimes dropped into his pale hands, Gavin forced nothing from his mistress and never forgot that.

I will build a shrine worthy of Her Gaze on Miurag regardless, and it would be profound.

"You shall receive the permissive sigils in time," Gavin said with more surety than he had ever conveyed in Her absence before, *"and we will negotiate the particulars."*

"Posh-gep!" Yilkin said, raising his stein the size of a teacup to Gavin and then his fellows.

"Posh-gep!" answered his merchant clan.

As one, their body fur puffed up as they drank, their ears swiveling in all directions as voices yipped and precious, clear water spilled down long, gulping throats.

GAVIN WOULD SPEND, HE APPROXIMATED, FIVE YEARS ROAMING AND SURVEYING lands now held by his Grey Lady but which had once sheltered the Ma'ab at the height of their revolt against the Devourer.

Although he knew those who would become the Ma'ab gods had reached Miurag roughly five centuries prior to his birth, the precise timing of the exodus in this part of the Nexus was uncertain. Most locations yielded very little in artifacts or records, and any stories once held by inhabitants were vague or entirely forgotten.

It might as well be the same distance from V'Gedra falling to Sirana's birth as far as they remembered anything useful about those meant to become the Ascended.

The Umbaldes wandered with him, finding greater opportunity in his focus and determination. At one point they insisted on turning a profit far into a long, narrow valley, at a town straddling the known territories of Abalok, the Devourer of Conflict, and Nyx, the Seer of Shrouds and Prophecy.

The quietest traders — mostly the Umbaldes but not only — slipped in and slipped back out, smuggling small, portable rarities across the ever-contested borders of these two Greylords. Patrols were light since the town was difficult to reach and of little strategic value to either army, its resources not currently in demand and unlikely to sustain the smallest metropolis.

As soon as Gavin arrived, however, his very bones began to tremor, and his interest grew.

This valley may yield research value at last.

The Herald had never felt the need to leave his guides, as often as he pressed for more time in any one place as they wandered up and down the long stretches, meeting and trading with others. The pneuma flint of the valley, however, had been exposed through erosion, not by quake or mining. On the edge of his senses laid many, many "death impressions" — the last sights or thoughts during a transference or transition of Vis, which had occurred close enough to the obsidian rock to be absorbed into it.

Conflict occurred here. A large one.

But so had many smaller ones.

So many deaths.

They called to his bones laced with the same flint, though sorting the essence from the large event from the smaller ones proved difficult. He could not harvest *all* the pneuma flint which contained some short vision or set of impressions any more than he could carry a whole mountain out of here.

Gavin tended to stand out in the Greylands, no matter his drab robes and hood covering his or how well he suppressed his aura. He often stood next to the Malok when other traders were present, leaning on the unspoken suggestion that he held a similar function to the clan of the Meticulous Accountancy of the Terrorized. Yilkin and the others never countered otherwise, even if Gavin hadn't needed to prove it yet.

During these first negotiations, he contemplated three different veins of pneuma flint, imagining he would have to chip parts out of each and meditate on them to know which to focus on. This trio was only one of a score of similar sites on this one hillside. The Umbaldes would not stay that long, regardless that it held the greatest potential of Ma'ab record Gavin had found so far.

"A veritable ocean of memory," he muttered aloud as he realized the full extent of the task. "And I carry a bucket."

"*What say, Walker?*" Luhk rumbled.

"*Nothing,*" he replied in the Dead Tongue.

"*Not nothing, tell trouble,*" the Malok insisted. "*You mining like Ma'ab fathers, but missing age scents?*"

Gavin held utterly still in his surprise. *Ma'ab fathers ... ?* How could he know that? He had never mentioned anything of the sort among the caravan.

He narrowed eyes at the sizeable pugilist. "*Luhk. Please explain that.*"

The freeborn kneeled by the three veins which had held Gavin's interest, sniffed the air deeply, blew it out again in a startling burst. A colorless vapor from the wide nostrils mixed with the grey dust stirred up and overlaid the pneuma flint veins.

While Gavin senses a change in the flint, he wasn't sure how to interpret it. Luhk, however, opened his mouth a few times, lightly chattering his teeth and clicking his tongue as if he sampled the air like a delicacy, and pointed to the vein on the left.

"*Ma'ab Vis*," he said. "*Age, second eldest.*"

The Deathwalker grimaced skeptically but coaxed a fragment of shard from this vein and gave it an abbreviated pulse with his aura, willing his bones to extract what impressions they would.

The veil behind his eyes parted black smoke, and the Herald did indeed "see" the Ma'ab army in this very valley. Recognizable in their uniform black hair and white faces, the males were huge and strong while the females were petite but formidable mage and endlessly motivating to their men.

The view began to dim around the edges as the rebel slave laying dying in the past, yet the unnamed fighter kept his dark eyes fixed on his leader.

A massive Ma'ab fighter with metal armor.

Metal. Incredibly rare in the Greylands.

Fast and agile, he reminded Gavin of the Hellhounds and the chains they carried as weapons. He led a group of supporting guerrilla fighters, devastating the Devourer's forces in their coordination within the chaos.

I have seen this one.

The General of the Undefeated Void.

The Second Ascended.

Moments later, they regrouped. Coming up to the enormous leader was another figure with darker bronze skin.

Gavin recognized this one as well. *The Deathless …*

Someone called out in that battle long ago.

"*Long fight the General and the Unrelenting Void!*"

The memory went black, the pneuma flint empty as it absorbed into his skeleton.

Gavin opened his eyes and stared at Luhk, truly stunned. "*You are very young.*"

"*Yes?*" Luhk answered, confused.

"*You have never met a Ma'ab.*"

The Malok confirmed, shaking his head in the negative, and Gavin added, "*They have all left the Devourer. They are all gone.*"

A nod. "*Yes.*"

Gavin grunted. *Interesting.*

Luhk had asked about mining. The slave revolt would have included pneuma flint miners, and the Devourer would have had Malok fighters aplenty facing them in skirmishes and battle. Freeborn or not, the adopted Malok had unexpectedly suggested a type of hereditary memory in his kind if he were able to tell the Herald was not only was of their bloodline but could gauge their death-scent in the flint.

Perhaps something in my own actions or aura triggered the recall.

"*Can you do this for other places here,*" Gavin asked, "*if I were to show you?*"

"*Hrrrnng,*" Luhk considered, lacking the devious glee of the Grey Merchants whenever trade options opened up but demonstrating he had learned the basics. "*Give extra metal to clan in craft deal with Maiden? My weight.*"

"*You are too large for several days of sniffing. Half your weight.*"

Luhk nodded without fighting that. "*Silver.*"

Gavin shook his head in denial. "*Not silver, or gold. Too rare. I could get your hand's weight, perhaps?*"

The Malok clicked his throat in thought, shook his head. "*Half my weight, iron?*"

A firm nod. "*That I could do. But you must identify all pneuma flint from the same age in each location I ask for until we leave, no refusals. Deal, Luhk?*"

The Malok was happy with this and nodded his blind head. "*Deal, Herald.*"

Luhk's service was an invaluable benefit easily worth a lot of iron. Once he learned the "scent" which interested Gavin the most, the Malok was possibly the best bloodhound to be had sorting out the different ages of things, be it veins of pneuma flint on eroding cliffs or grey-dusted armor and bone in old settlements.

An unexpected skill in an egg-laying race mostly trained to be fighters, Gavin thought. *No wonder the Malok Queens are so valued as to nearly all be enslaved.*

He worked diligently to collect the most telling bits of evidence in the clearest pneuma flint he could find. He "preserved" them from unnecessary exposure in a thin film of his own blood before wrapping each piece in a scrap of cloth, tucking it in his pack.

Sirana might have compared this to finding a natural deposit of blood-stone "spying" on the world at large. A mage was not necessary to "record" these exchanges. Gavin must meditate on each before he truly knew what they contained, however, and record his discoveries in his grimoire. He was also unsure how easily, if at all, these moments may be "recalled" a second or third time if he emptied the pneuma flint of its natural energies into himself.

Will contemplate this later.

Gavin spent each outing with Luhk filling his belt pouches to brimming with specific, single-event shards and chips before rearranging them carefully inside his pack during each rest period.

The Deathwalker's actions seemed a mere hobby to the Umbaldes, yet Gavin possessed the most precious pack of black glass he could imagine for himself. He was all too aware that time would work against him the longer these pieces remained in close proximity to each other and to him.

The motivation to Walk has begun to fade at last.

Now Gavin felt a strong need to hurry back.

CHAPTER 6
THE GREY PLAINS OF THE NEXUS, TIME UNKNOWN

THE HERALD TRADED OFF WITH A DIFFERENT UMBALDES CARAVAN WHEN SEVERAL clans met up on the same Geb'harik. This goods his meticulous partners with which had come into possession on the same trek as him, would press them in a different direction that he wished to go.

"*Message-open through Lady-Welcome point,*" Yilkin invited, which Gavin took to mean they would remain interested in a crafting contract for a shrine in the future.

Luhk confirmed, growling, "*Half weight of iron for mining service.*"

"*Of course,*" Gavin replied. "*As agreed.*"

Yilkin the Neverwilt hopped a bit like a flea in excitement and patted the Malok's heavy grappling bracer, red-dyed fur puffed up with pride. His tendril-whiskers were highly mobile as he watched Gavin expectantly.

The Herald said. "*I shall have the iron as payment ready prior to sending a message to bargain further. Whether we agree upon a price for the shrine or not, you take the iron for Luhk's service.*"

Wilken's small, dexterous front hands fluttered in pleasure as he bowed his small head and long neck in agreement and gratitude, expounding on a flowery reply that Gavin struggled to translate fully. In essence, the Meticulous Accountancy of the Terrorized were grateful to be considered for such an opportunity.

"*Now!*" Yilkin yipped, one of four arms pulling out a small needle from a sling sack, another a small bottle of ink — Gavin bet he knew which kind — and a third held out a muted, grey hand for his own."*Puncture-dot, we three. A reminder up, dismiss once parlay come circled-round with High-Eyes.*"

Gavin frowned a bit. "*I am not sure my skin will take a tattoo, temporary or otherwise, unless it is blessed by my Lady. And I doubt you would want my blood on your needle should it transfer to your kin. This is not a refusal, din'Accountous, I would be transparent with those of great value like yourselves. Is there another way to hold a promise between the Herald and the Meticulancy?*"

Fortunately, Yilkin did not look insulted as he paused, using his fourth free hand to scratch his bearded chin. He glanced up at Luhk. The Malok only waited patiently as if he hadn't been listening to all the words spoken, breathing a bit like the millipede-rugs pulling the carts.

After a few moments, the short creature put away his needle and ink and instead pulled out a short string of polished, multicolored beads.

"*Trade shard, Herald's choice,*" Yilkin said, offering the beads to him. "*Equal value, but each prefer private use, yes? No profit, we trade back to meet again.*"

"*If you say they are equal, what value are those beads to you?*"

Yilkin grinned, his teeth tiny but distinctly pointy. "*What High-Eyes Seer gain in soul-glass? Quest clear, yes, but secret-Lady-hush. Never ask, did we?*"

Gavin sighed inwardly. Neither knew if the trade was equal. He'd have to give up one of the shards he'd collected, hopefully temporarily, not knowing the memory that was on it, and safeguard this trinket instead.

He supposed neither of them truly had much use for the other's precious item; it was a good idea. And motivating. Somehow, he was reminded of Sirana trading away her sapphire pendant to Mathias at Kurn's insistence in order to be able to come along on their travel with them.

"*Very well,*" Gavin said, shrugging off his pack to choose a shard, truly having no idea which one to select.

He chose, but the pneuma flint he offered Yilkin may as well have been spilled at random.

An Umbaldes clan could vanish almost in the blink of an eye, though the little dust clouds and tiny footprints at least argued against space-bending or portals.

Gavin stood alone with the mercenaries to defend the carts and cargo, as agreed. *This is oddly familiar …*

"*Soul Pouchers*," barked one large, three-tusked merc, drawing a maquahuitl made of dense bone and sharpened stone, similar to those carried by the attackers along with nets and man-catchers.

"*What the back-hole are these twiggy-sherps carrying in those carts?!*" another of the elephantine bulls bellowed. "*We ain't escorting no eidolons!*"

No, they weren't. Not technically. But this pack of Malok smelled something of interest, Gavin knew, be it himself or the pack he carried.

Or both.

"*You!*" the merc leader called over the spine-tingling calls of those rushing toward them. "*They said you were a necromancer! Can you hold off the Harvesters if we take the Blood Runners?*"

"*I can,*" Gavin replied, disliking that it would reveal his presence to enemy eyes but having no choice if he wished to protect his own body and other treasures beyond value. Not to mention his oath to the caravan.

"*Then do it!*"

The Herald would do much more than that, but he was not required to explain.

Gavin set his pack and staff down on the ground out of necessity, to free his hands and minimize the interaction with the flint shards yet to be recorded. Out came the scalpel from his belt pouch, which he'd learned to keep handy and sharp. He cut his own arm as deeply as he could, pressing in harder until the metal tool touched bone. A surge of power flooded his body.

"*Rrewshaffusa kaul ushenfi,*" Gavin whispered, his blood clinging to the bottom of his arm, collecting there without dripping to the ground. His words taking on an eerie, echoing quality that saw the Harvesters trailing behind their Blood Runner, already slowing down as if a chill had gone up their spines.

"*Look out!*"

The hunters struck, weapons thumping, snatcher poles clacking hard against fighters turning them with similar weapons. The opponents were about the same size, though the Malok poachers had tired themselves running the distance. Gavin waited until they were close, turning his palm up and holding it open, scalpel still buried deep, linking the pneuma flint and preventing the wound from closing.

"*Juruthah grashnag'et frohn,*" the Deathwalker intoned, drawing every drop of black blood along his white skin to his hand on willpower alone.

He watched the blood slither in tiny, black threads from his arm to pool on his palm, the transfer so complete that his skin was left clean. From there, a perfect, black sphere formed in his grip, as endlessly deep as his void-black eyes while he concentrated.

Far out and away, a swarm of hungry ghosts heard his call. Their trajectory changed, darkening the pale grey horizon like innumerous locusts. The Malok in the rear sensed it at once. They began to yip and call to the others in melee with the caravan mercenaries.

The cry to retreat went unheeded as Gavin stepped closer, holding his arm ahead of him with blood-sphere at the ready. The moment a Malok cut down a caravan merc, Gavin's power pulsed and spit a fine spray of the Herald's blood over them both. As the three-tusked mercenary lay dying, so, too, was the Vis and Vitas of the Malok drawn out as they were linked.

Gavin wove them together, holding the treat like chum to encourage the incoming cloud to speed up.

"*Swarm!*" one Malok skidding partway down the hill cried."*Swarm!*"

"*Must take something!*"

"*No time!*"

A caravan guard managed an injury on a Malok, not incapacitating but it was enough. Gavin's aura arched in a powerful sweep, widening in the skirmish, carrying blood and essence with it force entanglement with the blood of the wounded Malok. Gaining a hold like the strongest webbing, the Herald began draining the essence of all three at once, two Malok and the three-tusk merc, feeding his blood-sphere for his next action.

The process was stronger and faster than any Harvester's soul trap, suggestive of the powers of a Greylord.

"*Run!*" one Blood Runner shrieked, breaking off its attack as others finally listened.

"You may try," Gavin murmured as the swarm of hungry ghosts arrived.

The Herald released the potent charge, turning the mass of madness like he was guiding an ocean wave. It flowed up the hill, black flames erupting around those overtaken. The screams as the swarm plucked flesh and soul in countless tiny bites were, in their own way, musical.

Soon enough Gavin felt his donated strength return to him sevenfold, husk after husk of poachers dropping into the grey dust as he stole the Vitas from of the swarms' hungry mouths but letting them have the rest. His eyes burning icy blue, Gavin used a portion of it to push the swarm to continue on.

Leave. There's nothing here.

The speed and trajectory of the swarm would not change until they were far from the caravan, well beyond the scent of blood and fear. All was quiet now, and four mercenaries remained with him, shaking as they stared.

"*B-Back my hole ...* " one whispered."*You. They ... you ...* "

"*This ain't good,*" another said. "*Didn't sign up fer this. Look, ah, we can't travel with you, whoever you are.*"

"*We know who he is!*" blurted another. "*They'll devour us fer giving a Greyblood passage!*"

"*How would they know?*" Gavin challenged him. "*Unless you tell them yourself.*"

The merc lead shook his head, genuinely scared even as he tried to sound the toughest of the four. "*No. We've been through here before. There's a weather house not far from here.*"

A weather house.

Gavin cursed to himself as his face scowled. *What is one of those doing out here?*

Such a structure was not unique to any territory; Nyx surely had some in her realm. Their construction seemed to be partly a watchtower for the Greylord's holding but also the source of a powerful signal cancelling out the surges not only from powerful magics in the unpredictable weather but also in planar travel in the region.

One of many tactics used to prevented those in the Eternal War from having free reign crossing the Nexus.

Impossible that the priest tending the weather house would ignore what just happened.

Word always made it back to the Greylord who had it built. Gavin knew enough to be certain it wasn't his Lady's weather house.

A misstep.

Even as he had fulfilled the terms of his agreement with this new caravan, as soon as the Clan of the Kurios Benedictine din'Favorance returned to their carts, he discovered they felt the same way. A fight-capable messenger was fine, as was nobility. They'd even harbor a solid soul-spinner of the average sort, no matter which facet they served.

"But not a Greyblood!" Rizzymink fluttered all four tiny hands."*Not a crossing herald! We be snatch-grem here! Ai! Look!*"

Gavin looked, eyes black and pulsing subtly, following the obvious change in the overcast sky. A red-orange glow appeared at first, swiftly turning yellow and crawling along the bottom of the clouds. As if there might finally be a sunrise in the twilight of the Greylands.

Strange weather, indeed.

"*You have limited time to distance yourselves from me,*" he said, lifting his pack onto his shoulders and picking up his walking staff. "*Prepare and make haste.*"

They did, and Gavin continued alone, choosing a different direction from both the caravan and that golden glow. The Umbaldes promised they would not mention seeing him, and although he believed them — in that they would rather pretend nothing ever happened and shift blame wherever they could — it would make no difference if they were approached.

That glow on the horizon and what it represented would more than likely catch up to him whether the Grey Merchants or their mercs ratted him out for a profit or not. Not even destroying them as witnesses would help.

Gavin Walked away.

His humming mind and body tried to think of a way out before an agent would find him as the weight of the fear tried to slow him. The part of him scarred by his release from the Bane of the Wasp also prepared himself for another potential lifetime of captivity and interrogation. He would mourn the loss of the shards in his pack, the roots of his heritage, before he ever studied them.

No. Gavin gritted black teeth and shook his head in denial. *Not so easily will I give up.*

Stride and staff propelled him as he murmured a quickening spell, using the soul power of those he'd just consumed to cross a much greater distance in the first, tense day with seemingly endless horizon passing by. He wasn't sure how to get to the nearest ally point but knew he must cross this wasteland without getting caught. He could no longer follow the trail of the Umbaldes, who may yet be linked with the weather house showing a sunrise, of all things.

They will be devoured if they are.

Ghostly words repeated with the scenery, words he'd listened to as a child while writhing on a bare stone floor inside the room in which his father kept him confined during his seizures.

Hem shena ... Xrukel nigoth deru ...

Look closer ... You'll surely find the way ...

"My Lady," his whispered.

I will.

Far behind him, something like thunder rumbled with no flash of lightning. No storm of the Black Seas came to sweep over the wasteland. Perhaps something else was coming to consume him. Or to try. First, it must catch him. First, it must face his wrath, tempered into a single, focused ray of black hatred he would—

"*Deathwalker! Hold up!*"

186

Why?

"*I said slow down, Herald! Just stop!*"

That voice …

Who are you? … .how are you reaching through my aura at such speeds to call to me … ?

The voice offered no reason to stop; no proof of alliance, no identification except that she may be female. One he had heard before.

It could be a trick. A ruse.

"*More resistance from you,*" she griped, "*and we'll form a perfect beacon for Val'krynn to home in and appear, you stubborn son of a Zauyrian goat!*"

Her words struck him like twin Dwarven hammers. Gavin dispelled the excessive speed in the wake of her invoking the infamous Celestial mercenary as well as the insult hurled at him. His magic dissipated as a blowing, insectoid equine galloped up to him carrying its irritated rider.

Gavin turned cautiously all the same, holding his staff in both hands as he appraised the Caelif Steed as well as a face from his home world.

"You are Zauyrian?" he asked, recognizing her smaller form, still armored and well-equipped like a soldier, complete with helmet and gauntlets, all chitinous Bane Wasp armor painted white, grey, and deep blue markings with a thread of gold hinting at a rising sun.

"Not these markings, but yes."

That was the correct answer.

She kicked her mount to turn in place so she could offer her hand to give him a lift. Gavin eyed that possibility skeptically. She snorted. "*Just clasp it, Herald. I won't shatter, and I won't fall.*"

He did.

Her hand was tough and resilient. The smaller figure indeed had no trouble bracing herself, hauling Gavin up and onto the tall mount behind her, much stronger than she appeared.

The Herald balanced pinion behind her but was suddenly unsure where to put his hands. He glanced distractedly at the swiveling, red antennae of a beast large enough that his long legs did not drag on the ground.

"*Your name?*" Gavin asked. He still wanted confirmation.

She glanced back at him with a scarred, twisted smile on her pale brown face. "*My name is Houda. Cross that staff under your pack and hold on tight.*"

The alien gait took getting used to. Not only was the Caelif capable of a rolling lope or canter, like a horse with a pronounced spring in its hindquarters, but it could *jump* quite high. Houda's mount cleared cliffs no horse would have been able to navigate in less than an hour with great risk to its balance and legs.

"*Dizzy?*" Houda asked once they had settled out onto a different flat plain.

Gavin held onto her waist tightly out of sheer necessity. "*A bit.*"

"*One gets accustomed to it. Try not to tense up so much.*"

Gavin allowed a quiet moment to pass as he scanned the surroundings, assured he wasn't missing an imminent chase before he spoke again. "*Where are we going?*"

"*Somewhere safe for you,*" she replied, eyes forward, seeming to guide her steed with the lightest of touches and aura pulses. "*After we break our own trail.*"

That seemed difficult, given how open and exposed they were, but Gavin wrapped up his burgeoning aura as small and tight as he could within the halo of whatever power Houda used to feed her steed.

She sensed it, adding, "*That's good. Keeping doing what you're doing.*"

Regardless of his efforts, however, ominous streaks appeared in their periphery as they charged ahead. Suddenly, a bolt with the appearance of thick oil struck the dusty ground behind them, deft as a frog targeting a fly with its catapulting tongue.

The first one missed to their left, but a second was forming.

"*Can you strike with any form of light?*" she asked him.

"*Blue and cold,*" he answered.

"*Good enough. When we stop, give it all you've got on your left side. I'll take the right. Those things flank their targets after herding a while, and the final attacks hit at the same moment to meet in the middle.*"

"*Understood.*"

Each Deathwalker built their aura, and the oil strikes seemed to sense it. They leaned closer, pushing them, testing their speed and direction to lead the ultimate attack.

Houda swung her mount around at the last moment, narrowly avoiding dropping off a cliff, as twin streaks darted in and kissed in the middle just back from that ledge. Houda's mount hissed and shrieked in an aborted leap.

"*NOW!*" she cried.

Gavin released the excess power he had and more, attacking his left side in a blast of heatless, blue light. Houda fisted her right hand and struck with her arm in a solid punch, cracking the dead air itself and setting off a strike of truly hot, golden light as if called from her desert of origin.

While Gavin's attack sent the black mass reeling back, collapsing into writhing, disoriented coils upon the dust, Houda's power seared and evaporated the other half of the threatening spell entirely.

"*Good,*" she said again, hauling her mount around. With another sunblast from her armored fist, she put the remaining hunter out of its misery.

The blackness around them disintegrated, and the Caelif Steed sprang off the cliff to land far, far down with barely two bounces before Gavin could fully grasp what just happened.

"*What — ?*" he began, pausing when she reached back to squeeze his thigh with a disturbingly warm gauntlet.

"*Wait on it, Herald. We're close to the Citadel. You'll be safe there until our Lady calls you.*"

CHAPTER 7
NYX'S CITADEL, THE NEXUS. TIME UNKNOWN.

FROM A DISTANCE, THE CITADEL MAY AS WELL HAVE BEEN ONE MOUNTAIN AMONG many. Not until they drew closer did Gavin make out looming architecture which *bore* some grace beyond the worn bones of the Nexus. The entrance to his Greylord's stronghold was not immediately apparent nor could the Herald determine what made this place unique among the Grey Maiden's holdings.

Odd sensations crackled along his nerves and aura long before they entered the subtle shadow cast by a giant structure, and he wondered if they had passed through some illusion or unseen protection.

He would not find out.

As happened the last time his Lady's agents had retrieved him, Gavin simply blacked out.

The Herald of Miurag would come aware again when it was safe for him to do so, his consciousness at last dragged up from a deep well. He took no insult. The rules were different for him than Houda and for one very simple reason. Gavin would cross over again into the world of the living, still able to eat their food and drink their water.

Houda never would again.

"*Where is my pack?*" he asked, lying once again on a raised, stone platform.

"*Beside you on the floor,*" the Zauyrian Deathwalker answered. "*I haven't opened it.*"

With a sense of having been here before, Gavin sat up and rolled to reach something which would help him while the warrior of the Grey Maiden watched over him with intense, subtly glowing eyes. Gavin glanced around but did not sense any Shaegoth in the ascetic room, and he managed to snag his pack and set it before him on the reed-like pallet.

Sitting cross-legged, he began unpacking, counting the pneuma flint shards immediately.

Houda waited patiently while he did so. She'd removed her helmet and gauntlets; they sat on a small table nearby while she relaxed in the only chair in the room. Her posture and poise reminded him somewhat of Willven Isboern ready to negotiate at various tables at Manalar.

Her hair was as black as it might have been back in Cris-ri-phon's time, her skin that ashen-brown marked with artistic, ritual scars stained with charcoal. Her eyes were crystal blue with black encroaching from the sides, a shade of blue like his but not exact.

Satisfied that no shards had gone missing, Gavin cinched up his pack and set it on the far side from Houda, ready to focus on whatever conversation there was to be had.

He wasn't sure where to start.

"*Your occupation changed a bit,*" he said, eyes trailing her soldier's garb.

"*The Deathless made it necessary,*" Houda replied placidly.

"*Will you describe to me why that is so?*"

The first Deathwalker of the V'Gedra Court smiled at him. "*No questions why I came to help you? None of whether someone sent me, or if it was my initiative?*"

Gavin shook his head. "*No, I am merely grateful to Our Lady that you did. Yet I have seen you use a sun-weapon, something I thought unheard of here, and you seem expert in mounted combat when you were described as a quiet mystic in life. You say the Deathless made this change necessary. I want to know why.*"

"*In a hurry, are we?*"

"*Now, yes,*" he replied. "*I have been gone from my world for quite some time. I sense a need to return soon. Perhaps before winter sets in.*"

Houda tensed up even as she nodded. *"Winter. You know snow?"*

Gavin didn't see what that had to do with his request. *"Yes."*

She smiled a bit, her scars folding in ways they may rarely have when her body was outside the Nexus. *"I never have. I knew sand and heat."*

He watched her, and when she said nothing else, he tried a grunt of acknowledgement to bid her continue. It didn't help. She made him wait, standing up and collecting her helmet and gauntlets before striding confidently to the stone door.

"Find me in the birthing chamber," she said.

And left through a grey door, shutting behind her.

Birthing chamber?

Gavin breathed out his irritation, only now wondering if Deathwalkers could be jealously competitive for their Greylord's attention. He didn't see why not. Perhaps Houda had set to find him on her own initiative, as she had hinted, and sought only to delay him in his work while still claiming to have "saved" her Lady's Herald.

Oskar had been straight forward and obedient to his task, generous toward Gavin, even as he hinted at future — or past--encounters.

Houda, perhaps, had no such reason to be so forward with information. She had lived at various Courts, Human and Elven. Perhaps she still played those games in which Gavin knew he was at a disadvantage. Just listening to Sirana and her "reasons" for why the Dark Elves chose to do certain destructive and unfathomable things convinced him of that.

"Purka cessio," he muttered in his father's language, swinging his legs over the edge of the platform.

The Citadel held little in the way of decoration or wealth, nor was it densely inhabited. Not empty, however, nor abandoned.

Walking out into the hall when he was ready, taking his pack and staff with him, Gavin saw other souls here, passing him as they went about their business. Some of them had true physical bodies like a Deathwalker or a

Nexus-born. Others were eidolons, souls of other realms whose "bodies" manifested by sheer will to appear as dense material to interact with the environment.

Whatever form these eidolons chose in the Greylands — rarely appearing as when their mortal body had died — they could remain as they were for an extended existence within the Nexus if they desired, so long as they possessed a way to rejuvenate both their Vis and Vitas.

Should they lack the ability to do one or both, they would degrade and weaken, attracting capture by a stronger entity — to become part of the currency of souls in the largest cities — or become lost in the wilderness, one among the Slaugh. These hungry ghosts were doomed to haunt a shadowy crevice or join a "swarm" of plague, consuming in mindless greed all which was touched with life, be it native, traveler, or invader.

Gavin admitted, of all the places of the Greylands he had been thus far, these residents appeared the most familiar to him. He'd crossed a substantial distance of the world on which he was born; he had seen a range of peoples who looked rather like this.

All of them worked as well; repairing and strengthening parts of the structure which might have been derelict not too long ago, as opposed to attacked or destroyed by some focused force. This fortress had the sense of having been encountered or rediscovered and was in the process of being put to good use.

Ordinarily, Gavin would avoid such "crowds," especially those too familiar to him. Never had they welcomed his presence among them, and he would be a fool to expect fair treatment. He'd glimpsed curled lips, anxiously turned heads or bodies, or outright fearful, contemptuous expressions, filling most of his living memories. He had been better accepted among the Umbaldes.

The mood was different here. Gavin sensed no threat or resentment when a soul passed him; no wariness. Some of them bowed their heads in that basic dignity long denied him by his fellow Human. His lack of physical appeal meant little, if anything, to these residents.

Possible that they focus on something else.

Just as he was doing with them: the quality and wholeness of the soul, the power of the aura, the age of the eyes. Gavin still muted his magic but not completely; those who saw him knew he was a ritual caster of some skill. At least a priest of Nyx, or an acolyte, if not her Herald.

If not a Greyblood.

Gavin stopped when he reached the top of a wide, curved staircase in good repair, rebuilt recently. Although, the exact definition of "recent" could extend some centuries back depending on many factors. He opted not to think about this and walked calmly down the well-built stone. At the bottom he lifted his hand forward, stopping an eidolon carrying a brown clay pot with a light purple paste within.

She blinked wide, dark eyes at him. Her voice was much lower than he expected it to be for her size. *"Ushkya, Deathwalker?"*

"Can you direct me to the birthing chamber?" Gavin asked, hiding the fact that he did not know why it was called this or what he meant to do once he reached it.

"I can, Deathwalker."

After the briefest pause, Gavin nudged the spirit. *"Direct me."*

Bobbing her head once, she rattled off a series of turns beginning with the hall behind his left shoulder.

"It is carved far back and up into the mountain," she explained apologetically. *"But there is a private window and a balcony, unreachable in an illusory cliff-face but giving the watcher a vast view of the horizon."*

"Private? Private for whom, eidolon?"

"Infrequently Her Ladyship comes here, and we all answer to Her," the servant answered, causing Gavin's aura to pulse once in his surprise. She did not reveal if she noticed. *"Presently the chambers are in the stewardship of the Summoned Light. I believe she awaits you at your leisure, Herald."*

The Summoned Light. *Houda?* Gavin nodded. *"Repeat the directions again."*

He was reminded of the Ley Tower, listening. It would not do to get lost in his Lady's Citadel if it went this far back into the mountain. Nodding in thanks, he left the eidolon, walking steadily but without hurry, following directions precisely.

After many turns, he assumed the double-wide door was the correct one for the birthing chamber, like few of them on the way. He stood outside a moment, considering whether to knock. He sensed no wards at all, no protections beyond some sleeping glyphs. All was in good repair and functional, more as if the protections had been intentionally released.

So be it.

He pushed open one heavy door without knocking. As he leaned cautiously forward, he spoke aloud. *"Houda?"*

"Enter."

Gavin did so.

He stepped into a clean and open space, tiered and facing a broad, startling view of the horizon.

A bit more than a 'private window and balcony' …

Gavin froze at first, hardly daring to set down his staff lest it leave grit on the pale, smooth stone. He looked around.

Multiple rooms circled three-quarters the top tier above his head. None had doors, and all of them faced the view outside. Leading down from those chambers, shallow, semi-circular steps made of grey stone. The amphitheater was complete with an oval stage at the lowest point, right in front of the broad, transparent panel, the Greylands wilderness providing the only decoration.

A bed, or perhaps more a nest of padding and blankets, lay in the center of that stage, and sitting cross-legged upon it was Houda staring outside. The ancient Zauyrian was out of her armor and wore a familiar kind of robe, the hood down and short, dark hair bare.

"You have arrived," she said, sounding pleased.

"The directions were true," he replied, remaining where he was. He was covered in dust and had already tracked that in.

The elder Deathwalker chuckled and glanced over her shoulder at him. *"And what of when there were no directions for you to follow?"*

Gavin blinked, realizing the intent behind her first announcement. *"Then I look closer. I will find my way."*

"As all of us must. How about looking closer now?"

Gavin took a step farther into his Lady's private chambers. Then another. He left prints of grey dust and grit behind. It bothered him. For the first time in a hundred years, it crossed his mind whether a bath was necessary. An attempt to show courtesy.

One of those upper chambers must be a washroom, and he would not be surprised if this citadel protected a rare, permanent water source, and yet ...

Why?

"*Keep the pneuma flint close,*" Houda added, patting her hand toward one edge of the nest, as if suggesting he set it there.

Gavin shored up his confidence and finished his descent down the easy stairs. Resting his staff against the wall close to the giant window, he stepped to the softest place in the chambers, shrugging off his pack as he went. He set the container down as if it contained a mass of delicately shelled eggs and remained standing, gazing out at the expanse of the Greylands.

"*Sit with me,*" Houda said. "*Pay no mind to the marks of travel.*"

So much for uncertainty.

Gavin grunted and selected a place on her right side, sitting cross-legged but so there was a head-span of space between their knees. The elder Deathwalker didn't comment and in fact finally moved things along.

"*Our lewensbluen, yours and mine, shall decide the next era for the Davrin when they meet again,*" she began. "*It may be the last era for them, unless they somehow rise above their forebearers.*"

The Herald did not blink as he turned his head from the window to stare wordlessly at her. The sad smile touching the blade-marked, uneven lips would have been difficult to read for anyone concerned with beauty, but Gavin could read her aura well enough.

Houda was grieving.

Gavin frowned in deep thought, meditating on the meaning of the word by which she suggested a common experience.

Lewensbluen.

Roughly translated in the Dead Tongue as "life flower." He wasn't sure if any Greylord used the concept as Nyx did, but it referred to one of the few souls in a living body whom a Deathwalker may choose to cultivate on Miurag, even indirectly, for the lush and diverse contrast to the rest of Her servant's morbid duties.

Although it remained his choice, Gavin believed a life flower was essential for any Deathwalker not to lose sight of one's home world or what it meant to be alive. A *lewensbluen* was constant reminder that the flux of life and death upon Miurag was not his to control. If he were to *forget* life, to cease its observance in favor of control or some other temptation then, over time, he would become worse than Sarilis or the Deathless.

Perhaps worse than the Ascended.

"*I hope you will have time to prepare,*" she murmured, gazing at his pack of pneuma flint. "*Should your flower achieve her full bloom and mine finally find her peace, then the tasks remaining are …*"

She paused.

"*Numerous as stars?*" he guessed.

Houda's smile shifted as though she remembered a desert night sky. "*Perhaps as grand. Less the number and more the ways in which they align with each other, and the possible collisions in their pathways.*"

Stars move. They *could* collide. This did not surprise him anymore, but his mortal self would have been skeptical. He wasn't sure Sirana even knew.

Houda asked, "*Did you know I'd chosen Cris-ri-phon first? Someone more suitable to my expected lifespan.*"

Gavin grunted. "*I would not have presumed, though we knew you nursed and tutored him as a child, though he came to reject you when he met Innathi.*"

A nod. "*Would you like to hear more about that?*"

A grunt. "*I would, Summoned Light.*"

Houda grinned in a way that would have frightened the living. "*Close, and related.*"

"*How so?*"

"*You'll have to look closer, Herald. Will you?*"

The smaller woman again patted the bedding next to her, and Gavin wasn't certain about the invitation. Or did not want to be.

"*Truth lies in a touch which my words cannot match,*" she said, not without sympathy but he detected a tender chiding. "*I believe you have witnessed this?*"

Grudgingly he nodded. *"My ... lewensbluen is quite expert at it. I prefer to leave seduction and all its tenants, including touch, to those with a natural urge or talent."*

"A wise and admirable choice for respecting the living, Herald," she smiled patiently, *"I do not suggest your preference needs to change. But when invited, the sense of touch is a most powerful focus. Your greater experience in utilizing it shall better serve our Lady, though I see discomfort remains even now. It may cause you to lose opportunity now and then. Something our birth world may not be able to afford."*

Gavin scowled down at the nest rather than looking out the window. If he had his choice, he'd indulge in no contact at all. The occasional dream in the presence of his Lady was "touch" enough, something so awe-inspiring, capable of spearing him down at his base essence, holding him helpless as a paralyzed mouse.

It also crossed his mind that perhaps Houda was using leverage against him, and she did not necessarily speak for their Greylord in this supposed "requirement."

"You doubt my word?" she asked as if reading it right out of his grimoire.

"I have been in the Greylands a long time now," he murmured. *"I must work much harder to recall some memories of our birth world. For lack of a better word, I have 'lived' here now four times longer than I lived as the beaten houseboy in my mortal form. Either place, it is wise to consider untruths and selfish motives, all the more dangerous when my goals and direction seem to be coming from servants and not from my Lady."*

Houda smiled in satisfaction at that. *"Ah, I see. Perhaps you wish to confirm Her approval."*

"That would be preferable, yes, but you cannot give it."

Houda leaned back, straightening her spine as she turned to gaze out the window again. Perhaps she saw no way past his resistance because she began to speak instead. *"I was nearly twenty years old when Cris-ri-phon was born to his father, Begir-al-phon, the Third Sorcerer of the Zauyrian Realms. I was there when his mother died just after the birth. I helped her cross over safely to Musanlo's arms, to my ruler's eternal gratitude."*

Houda's voice relaxed, settling into the familiar cadence of storytelling.

"His elder son, Leur, was already a teenager learning magic and learning how

to rule a desert realm. He was not much younger than me, and despite our very different lessons and teachers, the two of us formed a friendship of sorts, beginning with mutual concern for his little brother." She smiled warmly. *"Leur's and his Sorcerer-father's respect for my craft and calling despite my rather homely appearance was my greatest fortune in my mortal life. Their trust removed many obstacles, the choices open to me given a farther reach than they might have been otherwise."*

Houda's smile turned wry. *"In truth, I think Zauyrian men trusted ugly women more than they did beautiful ones, even as they inevitably wed the beautiful. Cris was a beautiful boy as a result, and strange from the beginning, hearing a song none of us could hear.*

"The second-born possessed potential to learn death magic if he focused, and he easily grasped the arcane as his elder brother learned. He had a mind for medicine and healing care we thought could be cultivated." She shrugged. *"He had too many talents, perhaps, all in a handsome face. It was enough to draw the attention of the Dark Elf royalty just as he matured, when we had primed him to choose a path, Leur and I."* A grimace. *"Hers was a cursed gaze, as it turned out."*

Gavin listened as the story continued, how auras flared between Sorcerer's son and Heiress Innathi at Koorul, the intractable attraction, the furious coupling propelled by life magic brought to the fore in young Cris-ri-phon.

He listened to the harm it did to the younger Seer princess, Ishuna, when she attempted to interfere. He heard the exposed ignorance of the danger thanks to the ruling culture of the Elves at the time, which rejected or suppressed all mystics and divine-touched whose talents could not be traced to something arcane — based on the To'vah Tongue, as it turned out.

Houda and Leur had tried to help the situation, to mend and soothe the damage to the young mages, even in their own limited capacity to understand and act in direct competition to the desires of the Queen's Heir.

"I know much more now, of course," Houda said. *"I understand what went wrong, and why Cris and Ishuna were born as they were. I was too close to see in its entirety in my limited, mortal view. Innathi stole Cris from us, intent on using him as the Queen-Mother had taught her. We could do nothing to influence how he*

heard his song at that point, and he could not be my lewensbluen."

A pause. "I focused on the injured Davrin princess, Ishuna. She was different from her family for she also heard a song. I tried to help mend her, to cultivate what I could. Perhaps I only delayed the inevitable as Ishuna was even more damaged by the choices of her Mother the Valsharess than Cris was, and her life was meant to be much longer in her suffering. I could not stay and still worship the Grey Maiden. I chose Our Lady."

Gavin nodded in approval, but the ancient Deathwalker was staring at the horizon as if seeing those times play out in front of her. He looked but could see no visions himself.

"Too soon, it seemed, I died," she finished, "and crossed over for the final time. But my tasks related to V'Gedra did not end with taking my body into the Nexus, to exist with and serve the Grave Mother as I'd sworn on the pact and earned with my service to the living."

Gavin blinked as Houda, mentioning her body, removed the small belt of pouches from around her waist and tugged on small knots intended to keep her grey robes closed. He stiffened when she parted the simple fabric and shrugged it off her shoulders, baring herself from the waist up. He noted her body was not old as it would have been when she died in Leur's Realm, but as she might have looked with Cris-ri-phon just born.

"What are you doing?" he asked.

She didn't answer but removed a bluish shard with golden speckles from a pouch. Holding it and nudging the rest aside, she shifted to turn herself on the bed to face him, dark eyes intent and unblinking. Her greyish-brown skin was fully decorated, well beyond her face and arms. Ritual scars tattooed with charcoal, drawn in tight spirals and curves, angular chevrons and closed shapes, suggesting a disciplined and dedicated practice in years long past.

"I have not the words to speak the rest," she said, pressing the most colorful shard he had seen in the Greylands between her palms. "You want to know more, you must touch me, Herald. By Our Lady's bidding, I am to teach you what, after your tests, you are primed to learn."

Gavin eyed her warily, but then noticed something odd about her nakedness. She was Human as far as he could see, with one exception:

curled next to her lowest set of ribs was a subtly shifting mass the same shade as her skin but glossy, appearing harder as if formed of a shell. He spotted joints, many of them, and the suggested dexterity when one of them flexed intrigued him.

"Growth rising through the skin from your bones, perhaps?" he murmured as he studied her well below her breasts.

Without speaking, she transferred the glittering blue shard from her primary hands to the smaller, semi-insectoid hands which had been curled tight to her ribs, protected by that small flap of shell-like skin. The small limbs and hands — like the Umbaldes although not an exact match — seemed to know exactly what to do with the shard.

Gavin sat mesmerized as Houda's delicate hands turned the shard this way and that, pulling out mystical threads from the dense pneuma flint, colorful strands which could be ... used somehow. Woven, perhaps, like a spider web or a silken chrysalis.

Ordinary Human hands were not built for what this Deathwalker was doing with that shard.

He glanced at his pack containing his most precious finding in all his travels. When he looked back Houda nodded at the connection.

"*You consumed and destroyed the first shard you dug out,*" she said. "*Not without value as you now contain the knowledge and recorded it as well, but there is a way to study wisps of a previous life, to see their secrets more than once without disrupting their structure.*"

Gavin frowned, a possessive surge pulsing in his core. "*Do you mean to say you will inspect them all on my behalf?*"

Houda shook her head. "*Not my desire or Our Lady's Will. But you* must *touch me, Herald.*"

She pressed her earnestness by rolling up to her knees, using her empty primary hands to slip free of her robe, until she was nude upon the stage in this elegant chamber. Only the blue-gold shard in her secondary hands could distract from the uncomfortable fact she was wholly exposed.

He could see every mark and tattoo; he could "read" their subtle call to whom she served. Suddenly, Gavin wondered why he doubted the Zauyrian Deathwalker, as if she could be so self-serving as to trick him in jealousy.

She is indeed a dedicated servant.

Like him.

The more Gavin considered lifting his hands, of taking an action as simple as placing them upon her shoulders, the more he contemplated the distance he habitually kept from the living. He would claim a husk or a shell no longer needed, would kill it when necessary, in a manner not truly different from the intelligent races and the animals hunting each other for food. Like them, he did it to continue living.

More accurate: to continue learning.

Like those who must breed, who must hunt or those who must heal and nurture, Gavin must learn. He must deconstruct, understand, and even revive or repurpose the energy released with death. His calling had as many nuances — perhaps more — as the rules for the material bodies of the living. The greatest transition was not an end of any kind, but so mysterious and difficult to observe that he must look closer.

Look closer.

Houda spoke in a low, death-like voice. "*I am not propositioning you, Herald. Neither of us have the talent for it. I am, however, insisting you look through the false, fixed boundaries you have set, where you are constrained. Think of your lewensbluen, and what you have learned from her.*"

Interesting that Houda would bring that up now. Gavin was just considering what Sirana had told him.

"*Early on in Sirana's attempts to understand her psionic talent,*" he said, "*she told me she had a chance to focus most when in states of pain and pleasure. I have seen evidence of such. We both associate these things with touch. To lay a hand on another meant one or the other. It is what the living exists for.*"

"*But not solely of their realm,*" Houda added, shifting her marked body and lifting the blue shard a bit higher. "*Even your captors at the Black Sea used the same.*"

"*I have forgotten that pain already.*"

"*But not the helplessness. Not the separation from your focus. Touch serves dual purpose, always: to reconnect, or to sever. Your hands know this better than your mind, which does not balance an essential tool with your body. That is why you are*" *here with me.*"

Gavin sighed to himself. Houda made her case. In his brief time observing Sirana, he considered her many trials. She did not, he thought, enjoy the rough treatment of the Deathless or the Ma'ab, nor could she understand turning it about on that Witch Hunter in jail in the search for her sister. She would not seek it again but beyond merely enduring it, had used it to focus her talents. She had not submitted to overwhelming fear, had not avoided but confronted. She had learned.

She had this mastery of touch, and he did not.

This will not do.

As Nyx's Herald, he could treat no tool at his disposal like a writhing snake about to strike. Gavin's refusal to touch Houda now with greater understanding seemed as impractically dogmatic as the Manalari oaths of his youth. So loathing was the distant concept of despoiling themselves with a woman, of becoming distracted from their devotion. that an old habit transformed into a daily test of discipline against an imagined foe.

There may be some of that in his actions, but Gavin understood Houda was no foe. He was also aware he simply lacked the desire to touch. He was not curious with an impulse to be kept in check, just something too easily forgotten or not considered unless pushed.

Avoid, or confront.

Could he afford such arbitrary limits when his existence may be as long as an Elf or a To'vah? Even if *he* could, perhaps his Lady could not.

Nodding slowly, Gavin shifted around to face the naked woman. Houda smiled — not a pretty smile though not malicious — but she did not move closer, did not make it easier for him.

First, he leaned over and reached out, still sitting cross-legged, and brushed the tips of his fingers down her upper arms, feeling the ridges and texture of her scars and tattoos before drawing back his hands.

He was surprised at the result.

A pale, blue light briefly illuminated the markings he had touched, slithering through curves and angles like water poured into a spoked canyon before dissipating. He had felt the sample of her essence along his skin as well, eventually tasting it in his mouth. It was, perhaps, like what the Elves described when they "merged auras" during some of the better mating, though it was not pleasure Gavin received in the touch but ...

Knowledge.

If Gavin had been holding out even the slightest distrust in Houda's motives, that blue light dispelled it like the Sun chasing the shadows of the night. Yet he was hesitant to speculate beyond that first impression, the ephemeral *knowing* which he sensed about her.

He would have to touch her again. And confront what came.

Gavin climbed to his knees facing her, carefully easing forward to close some of the distance. The smaller woman kept her smile as she looked up, her tiny secondary arms holding her shard close even as it remained active in her fingers. Her primary arms remained at her sides and did not reach for him.

In the world of the living, it would almost appear she was a prostitute offering her misshapen breasts to the unskilled groping of a naïve, paying client. Even when he'd ever been in such a circumstance, he would have felt no curiosity to equal what he did now.

Gavin took firm hold of her bare shoulders, his palms covering and pressing down on new marks, receiving a stronger surge of knowledge about this Deathwalker. Unfamiliar intensity pulled an odd sound from him; at first he thought it was pain and distress — the reason to pull away as further proof why not to do it again — but Houda clasped hold of his forearms, slipping her hands up his loose sleeves and gripping him by the skin.

It will pass, she assured him. *I will not harm you. Know me. Know who I am.*

He did.

And he was astonished.

CHAPTER 8

"My Lady! My Lady, he's back. The Deathless crosses your lands once again!"

Had she the ability, Houda would be weeping tears of guilt in her helplessness. She should have tried *harder* to convince him when Cris had first arrived with Jester and those Infernal servants, but it was not to be. As in her living time, she had no influence over him once he'd become obsessed with the life circle of the Elves.

Once he tried to become *part* of it.

But she hadn't known what would happen. *I didn't know!*

"He is different than before," she cried. *"Even the first time!"*

The Maiden of Shrouds stood in this familiar chamber, empty eyes contemplating an empty view. The Greylord hardly moved before she nodded. Slowly. Her voice was restrained, heard in a frequency that would not harm her devoted servant.

"He repeats more quickly than most paths I have seen."

Houda was kneeling low in front of the window, trembling, uncertain what to say. She no longer knew this soul at all, what he became after leaving here, what he *sought*. What she sensed now frightened her as nothing in the land of the dead did.

Let him never find Ishuna.

The Deathwalker prayed instead that her Greylord could see a path through which he could rest.

Him and *Ishuna, please.*

"*Help us, My Lady. He harms so many natives each time he passes through! They say he is even aiding Abalok's slaves to revolt! His war could engulf us and take away our Citadel!*"

Nyx did not reply though she had heard the plea. Eventually she asked a question. "*Would you help to protect them from this fate, Houda?*"

Yes.

"*I-I am not strong enough, Grey Lady.*"

"*If you were?*"

Houda's voice caught in her throat. "*Y-yes. I would protect. How?*"

Nyx's cracked, moving mask peered down at her. "*Think of this traveler as a bringer of freezing floods. You have seen the toll taken by such a brief but violent passing.*"

The Deathwalker nodded, staring up at her Lady's face. Still, she could see her people caught up in a primordial flow that seized their soul and stopped its existence *completely* for only a moment but enough for that soul to splinter, to break down as it should not inside the Nexus. The threat held the barest scent and trickle of the oldest powers, those which should have neither dominion nor advantage in the Center.

The same power which had doomed Cris-ri-phon's world.

"*You cannot stop it,*" Nyx whispered, "*nor can you find the source in time; it is far beyond your reach. Instead, you might possess enough of its element to redirect it. You can channel it back to the Black Pillar and help prevent its spread off its spawn world.*"

Houda nodded, gesturing her acceptance even as fear intensified inside her. *I will possess some of the same element … ?*

Enough to understand where it must go to do the least harm. But what if she could not control it? What if it overwhelmed her?

"*Jester,*" Nyx said.

An altogether different chill spread up Houda's back as the shadow assassin appeared in a formal instant. "*Here, madam.*"

"*You have retrieved it?*"

"*Right here,*" said the slim, void-like entity behind his laughing mask, one arm peeling away from the torso. "*Still fresh as the day of its harvest!*"

The Archivist of Woe held out a lantern-like soul trap, the style frequently used by the raiders on the plains.

"*Empty it, please, and contain its essence.*"

The elder Shaegoth set the soul trap down on the stone, so quick and deft in retrieving what lay inside, Houda missed it as she blinked. With a chuckle, Jester allowed her to squint at a sliver of pneuma flint cradled in both shadowy palms.

That taste …

The essence of a newborn eidolon in its most malleable form. The shard was odd, though. It couldn't represent an entire soul; it was not nearly dense enough for its size.

"*A piece of an eidolon?*" she muttered to herself, "*either chopped or siphoned off.*"

"*Very good!*" the shadow chimed. "*Any guesses which part?*"

Houda jumped, only to realize the Shaegoth had drifted much closer to her as she had been distracted to give her that full, flavorful view. She flinched back without intending insult.

He loomed, his head tilting, writhing dreads swaying with the motion. His cross-shaped pupils expanded within burning blue eyes. "*Well?*"

A second glance.

"*A … a finger?*" she guessed.

The other servant did a little dance of glee. "*Perfection! Indeed, it is! And whoooo does it smell like, hmmm?*"

Houda glanced at her Mistress, who had neither moved nor spoken since summoning this creature. After a pause she leaned forward to "sniff" the grisly shard. For the wonderful, beautiful memories and feelings that stirred from drawing on its Vis, Houda might as well have her nose in a bouquet of roses at peak fragrance.

"*Ohh … !*" She folded her arms around herself, holding tight as intense nostalgia and homesickness overwhelmed her. Doubling over, she trembled, captured in a timeless moment.

Cool, dry desert wind blew along his skin at night. Silver light from two moons made it easy to travel and follow the stars. He experienced sheer ecstasy in a pink sunrise as the chill of winter was chased away, of drinking fresh water from a guarded well after a long horse ride. He remembered eating — anything from toasted seeds to the fresh flesh of cactus pads and raw, bloody lizard … to a royal Elven feast, benefiting from their centuries of cooking techniques.

"Come to me, my Consort-General. Take me as I most enjoy it."

Houda cried out and shook her head, drawing back from the Elven intensity as she could, as Cris could not.

"Easy, easy," said the Shaegoth, touching her brow with the tip of one finger. *"Come on back, now."*

Her mind cleared.

"Ohhh, my Lady …" Houda groaned, teeth gritted, unsure if the intensity could be likened to pain where she would, under normal circumstances, wish fervently for it to stop.

"You alone of my servants share the same birth pool as the originator of this shard," Nyx murmured. *"This shall put you in sync with the Deathless, shall enhance you rather than conflict. With practice, will, and devotion, you shall be able to sense when he is near. You shall have influence over the effects of his actions within the Nexus, as you've long wished you had on Miurag. What mortal memories have gone grey since you crossed over shall be vivid again. You shall understand what you see rather than fear it. You shall confront it on behalf of us all."*

Rocking on her knees, Houda nodded. *"Tell me what I must do to accept, my Lady."*

"Eat the shard, Houda."

She reached without hesitation, plucking the finger from Jester's open palms. Tilting her head back, she slipped it in, swallowing it whole like a small fish. The shard seemed to grow spurs the moment it slid down her throat, scraping her raw from the inside. As it worked inexorably down, her old scars reappeared; the whorls and spirals from her life walking the Red Desert marking her once-clear skin. Inside, the shard wounded her only so she might heal around it later.

To become one with it.

Her moans filled the chamber as her soul transformed for all time.

GAVIN WAS SLOW TO PIERCE THE VEIL OF MEMORIES AND DRAW BACK TO HIS OWN mind and awareness. Some part of him wanted to stay, but it would be pure self-indulgence if he did.

He also became aware that, at some point, he had shrugged out of his own robe to increase their direct contact. The garment had been caught by his belt; like her, he was nude from the waist up.

Houda clung to him, pressing scarred breasts and belly to his skin, her arms holding tight, and her head tucked under his chin as if she were a child seeking a parent's protection. Her cheek pressed to his chest, and he sensed her eyes were closed while the designs on her skin glowed in response to his aura.

She seemed a little weak.

Gavin reached back to peel her tense hands away from his spine, where the fingernails dug directly into the exposed bone laced with pneuma flint. He was much stronger than her despite their age of service, and he had to unravel their auras himself before gently laying her down on the bed.

Unconscious and separate, Houda would now be able to replenish her own Vitas with rest. Her tiny, secondary arms clutched the blue and gold shard tight to her middle, protecting her — and perhaps protecting him — from too much transference between them.

Gavin's thoughts remained in constant flux as he stood up to approach the window. He thought to set his robe aright and close it up, but he was too "hot" still. He would remain half-naked until the excess energy he'd drawn in bled off.

Before then, one corner of his mouth curled in an ironic smile.

The Grey Maiden had somehow come into possession of part of Cris-ri-phon's soul, a pure shard of the eidolon before he'd become a world-eater. Nyx used it to create a Godblood in Houda. This fundamental essence could not have come from his Lady directly; only a living God could have provided it.

Something Musanlo may not be happy with but cannot deny the reasoning for her existence.

209

Houda was the only soul Gavin could even imagine summoning the Sun Brother's Light here within the Nexus. The sunlight of his birth world.

The Summoned Light.

Little wonder Houda was the bastion and guardian of this citadel in the Grey Maiden's absence, or that she had stepped through the rift with Ada and Oskar at Manalar. Little wonder now why she had appeared as the warrior she was. To be trusted with such a jewel and service based in another realm was, Gavin knew, at least equal to his own as a Herald, and perhaps rarer.

Houda could not have described this in words to where he would have believed her. Touch in its pure form had been necessary; his Lady had wanted him to understand.

I believe I do.

Gavin had begun wandering up and down the stairs of the open chamber, feeling the necessity of Walking as he thought on a great many things. The decades crowded in upon him as he combed over them again, all of it leading him to where he stood now. He had been gone so long from Miurag, so many years, he now ... finally ... felt the urge to Walk across and return to it.

I must be there when Sirana seeks me.

Most of the pocket-rooms he passed as he walked along the top tier were empty. Some possessed stone pallets or chairs built from the walls, and simple, woven rugs in a few of them. One held a tub, empty though it was, answering his meandering thought from earlier about the outside dust and grit still clinging to him.

Gavin stopped abruptly outside one small room. He had been unable to see inside it the majority of the time he'd been here, but what he witnessed now stunned him, scattering all this thoughts but one.

The Shaegoth holding him down on the operating table as the Chirurgeon R'ril-gya had cut into his abdomen, meaning to extract dangerous offspring, whole and alive.

Three, glossy black chrysalises hung together in this one room, fixed to the ceiling with tough, hardened excretions natural for the species. Each pod was as large as an average man's torso, the semi-translucent quality of the protected pupae suggesting it was still stretching downward, growing even in this transitive form.

Gavin swallowed, trusting his gut — without humor — that these were the young his Lady had wanted from him.

"Your journey has yet to see its full potential, my Herald."

He might have stumbled against the wall, his knees giving out, had he been mortal and feeling the powerful response to Nyx's eternal whisper. Grappling with his sudden trembling, Gavin turned to his Maiden standing with him atop the amphitheater, her form that of Houda's naked body, her voice coming from the mouth of another.

He bowed just after he glimpsed her endless, black eyes. *"Mother of Shrouds,"* he said.

Nyx was quiet and still for a time; choosing her moment she stepped past him, using Houda's fingertips to lightly brush his head, and entered the chrysalis room.

Gavin lifted his gaze and watched while she visited each cocoon with all the care of a mother tending to her infants. She lifted her hand to caress each one, blowing gently on them as if they were shell-less eggs underneath the water needing more air and current to keep them fresh. Pale blue light in a mist form coated the cocoons before seeping in, feeding them.

She smiled, and it wasn't Houda at all. He knew this mask-like beauty, no matter the flesh or the scars covering it in this moment. Her joy in their existence and the pleasure of nurture made every moment of agony for him in carrying them worth it.

Then the realization struck him like a thunderbolt.

"The wasp girl," he whispered.

"They will emerge long after you must return, Herald," she whispered. *"You know this."*

"I am ready, Prophetess."

"Good. You lack only a boon for your gift to me. Do you wish to accept?"

Gavin slowly stood up straight before answering. *"I do wish, my Lady."*

Houda's body stopped caressing one chrysalis and turned to him. Nyx smiled again. "*Granted.*"

Surreal moments were common in the Nexus; the word had lost its meaning during this Walk.

She who had been a constant presence in his boyhood and young manhood; she who had aided and guided in his transitions despite all fear, yet whom he'd not seen sign at all for more than a century. He not only heard her voice again but stood in her presence in his true body, far beyond a dream or a trance or a mere glimpse as a rift opened …

This was a first, and Gavin sank down to one knee, heady from sheer awe. When the long-dead and naked Zauyrian Deathwalker gestured with her arm outspread toward the stage of the amphitheater and suggested, "You will want to strip down fully," he didn't hesitate.

Gavin shed his belt, boots, and robes, placing them near his pack of pneuma flint shards, kneeling on the nest while he waited without any real trepidation. Just what was normal for any soul in the presence of one who had witnessed the births of deities.

He chose not to look behind him as Nyx approached; it would not do for his eyes to play tricks on him. He closed them and basked in a presence he had known since youngest childhood.

"*I am not always this way, Greyblood,*" Nyx warned him through Houda's lips. "*The Ice Lord speaks Truth in what he told you.*"

"*As you must be, my Lady,*" Gavin spoke low, nearly an incantation, "*so am I, and forever will I be.*"

Houda's body kneeled behind him, placing both her hands upon his shoulders. Gavin shuddered on a gasp of shock as his Greylord's essence suffused his very skeleton like a horseman seizing bridle and reins. She *had* him. If she wished, she could make him dance for her until the Citadel eroded away or make him stand guard in one place for ten thousand years without the will to move on his own. As when he reanimated and controlled a corpse, so could *she* command his whole being for any petty entertainment or minor duty.

But she did not.

Because she did not have to.

"*Lie upon your back,*" she whispered. "*And receive your boon.*"

Houda's body shifted back as he did so, yielding room for the tall Deathwalker to position himself. Nyx circled to the side and again he met her endless gaze; her grace seemed to flow over him with such potency that Gavin did not really notice as Houda straddled him, settling her buttocks upon his lower abdomen. He didn't notice the softer weight until her hands — all four of them — caressed his darkened, partially exposed ribcage.

"*Augh!*" he cried, as he had not when when R'rilgya had put her scalpel to him.

Pain.

As he would expect of any fundamental change. The dense bone of his lower-most ribs softened in a moment of intense, minutely localized heat, and as soon as Nyx released the pressure, she reformed it, not unlike magma cooling into rock to form a new landscape.

But one pass wasn't enough; she had to do it again.

And again.

Gavin gripped the blankets tightly with his hands, surprised at the need to do so. He was not falling, and no amount of pressure applied elsewhere would truly alleviate the disruption to his core.

Slowly, he recognized he was staring at feminine breasts and the markings upon them, focusing on them as he slowly uncurled his long fingers and accepted her. Her and her boon. Writhing or still — and he would do plenty of both in the coming moments — acceptance was his only choice.

The only path through the next eternity.

His black teeth were gritted and exposed, but she still caressed him, shifting her weight on his stomach, leaned forward and back as she worked on him.

For a very long time her presence anchored him, reached deeply into him, and yet her exploration drove his mind into a rare, primal state where his intellect meant *nothing*. His awareness, unfocused, saw all at once. He made the primal sounds to match, but whether anyone else could hear him didn't matter.

He submitted to the transition as it turned to ecstasy, a young mortal's dream come true.

"*You can let go now.*"

Her mouth was near his ear as he returned. She leaned over him, stiff nipples brushing his chest as one hand cradled his head to keep it from flopping to one side. Impossibly, sweat dotted his forehead.

"*Let go, my Herald.*"

Gavin shuddered, his long arms far out to the sides and away from his Lady. He had already let go of the blankets.

What ... ?

Several instants passed before he realized he was indeed clasping her. A pair of small, secondary limbs, black as his bones, clutched Houda's dusky-brown ones like grappling beetles. The inhuman hands with which Houda had been able to weave soul stuff without destroying it; he now possessed a similar pair.

"*Oh ...*" he exhaled with even greater awe. "*My gratitude, my Lady.*"

Houda's malformed lips smiled in genuine pleasure, and she leaned up. With a touch of regret, he released her hands, at which point the naked woman stood up over him, stepping to one side and padding lightly to the window. Gavin had a streak of dampness along his navel.

"*You must Walk now,*" she said, looking out. "*Rejoin your lewensbluen on her journey. Eat the fruit, lest you forget.*"

"*Yes, my Lady.*"

Gavin rolled out of bed and stood up, preparing to don his dusty clothes. Though his ribs ached, and his middle burned, never had he known such contentment rising from any pallet.

His patience renewed for another lifetime.

CHAPTER 9

3101 S.E., THE LEY TOWER OF THE LONELY ONES

THE HERALD WALKED THROUGH DEEPENING SNOW IN THE DEAD OF NIGHT, SENS-
ing the western spoke of intersecting Ley Lines leading toward the tower.
His feet, shod with oddly textured boots with decent waterproofing, were
not bothered by the cold.

Grey robes, complete with cowl covering his head and obscuring his
face, were like those he wore when he left. He carried his walking staff as
simple aid for balance, and a pack containing no food but everything he
would need to grow in the next few decades.

After a long climb, he paused and looked out all around him. Even
in the dark, an amorphous shape drifted up from the tower's valley, in
some ways darker than the sky. Not stone, mountain, or cloud, but potent
magic warning others away. Whether a premonition with a mystic's eye or
merely vague unease as a mage or mundane, the deterrence would work
on sentients who didn't already know something was there.

Go around. This land festers.

He refused the suggestion, trudging through the snow and ice.

"Lovely weather this evening."

Gavin stopped, searching for the aura to go with the voice. *Masked.*
He answered aloud. "If winter is to your liking."

"If it wasn't, I'd not have taken a long rest so far north."

The Ice Lord stepped from behind a broad trunk, the snow barely shifting beneath him. "Welcome back, Herald."

"Lord Rousse."

"Bold of you to have left now, of all times."

"And I've returned."

A cool, Infernal smile as bared arms crossed over an equally naked chest. "Fortunate for you, I have been busy."

Gavin shrugged, his expression unchanged. "No cloak of your own, Lord?"

"I haven't needed one in centuries. Besides, we're quite alone." He tilted his head. 'Hm. You seem worn but ... restored. How long has it been for you?"

"I am not certain."

"At this point, I suppose it doesn't matter." Charm seeped into the smile, ivory horns dipping in the direction of the Ley Tower. "But the time has come to renegotiate on behalf of your Maiden."

"Agreed." Gavin bowed his head with neither resistance nor confusion. "This year, Lord Rousse. I have some work to do first."

Featherless, red wings lifted like a bird looking to the sky. "And why should I wait, Herald?"

"Because the Davrin stand at a crossroads not yet passed."

"Ah." Fangs on full display. "Have you insights? Through my grand-daughter, perhaps?"

Gavin shook his head. "Not without entering the Deepearth myself. I'm certain you can sense more. They are your children."

Indrath's smile tightened a little. "Alas. Even if the Abyss did nothing to obscure my visions all this time, the underground has long been like a sealed tomb." A chuckle. "Complete with a guard dog to chase out uninvited guests."

The Deathwalker grunted, and the Ice Lord's eyes gleamed.

"What is in your pack, Herald?" he asked. "The aura is most intriguing."

His hand tightened on the shoulder strap. "Records from the Nexus."

"Records?" His interest intensified. "Concerning what or whom?"

Gavin frowned. "The Ascended, for certain. Perhaps the Deathless."

"Ah." The Ice Lord straightened. "His origins?"

"Unlikely. His involvement with the exodus at best."

The smile broadened. "I see. Where the Deathless is concerned, I may have more to offer in our future negotiations, Herald. Would you likewise be open to trading the knowledge found in what you carry?"

If Gavin had been wrong about Houda coveting his find, he saw the contrast at once in the Infernal Elf before him. "I cannot say."

"You 'cannot'? *Heh*. Fair response in your position. Should you need some enhancement in reading them, I may have tools I could loan you."

The suggestion tugged at a long-buried sense of humor. His mouth quirked with amusement. "Noted, Lord Rousse. We have time yet, and I have work to do before the year is out."

"Hm. Very well."

Winter's chill did not hide the Ice Lord's temptation as Gavin turned his back, for his aura pulsed at last. It smelled of Hellrime, a cold so strong that it sublimated the soul rather than burn it.

Whatever action Indrath had been about to take did not come to fruition before the two noticed their observer sitting on a limb of the nearest strong tree.

"You," said the devil.

The masked Shaegoth perked up. "Me?"

The barbed tip of a red tail flashed briefly from underneath the Ice Lord's sarong. "What are you doing here?"

"I'm only here to see our new diplomat make it home safely." Jester lifted a spindly hand to the frozen, grinning mouth as if passing a secret. "It's still a rough neighborhood, you know."

Gavin witnessed Indrath's demeanor change, a critical moment he felt compelled to grasp after Sirana's valuable insights. This was not fear of the Shaegoth, nor intimidation. Nothing so direct.

It's dread.

Dread for something Gavin could not see, something beyond the Shaegoth.

Oskar had spoken it in his library.

"*I am not privy to where our Lady sends him, even with all these records. You might ask him but don't expect a serious answer.*"

"*Why not?*"

"*He jests.*"

"*Jests.*"

"*One of the few Shaegoth that does. Although, I would be remiss not to mention one doesn't* want *the Archivist of Woe to show up on one's home world. As his title suggests, it's a bad omen for those living there.*"

The Ice Lord dipped his chin toward Gavin, his ivory horns collecting crystalline flakes of ice drifting in the air. "I shall leave you to your studies, Herald. We shall talk again."

"Very well," he said, having nothing more to say.

"Oh!" Jester waved his hand before the devil could leave. "Congratulations, Lord Father, I hear it's a girl!"

Indrath froze, his aura flaring an otherworldly green as he turned around, so intense Gavin made room for the two should they come to blows.

"You shall *not* speak of this, Archivist," he hissed.

Shadowy shoulders slumped. "Aw. I was hoping you kept a tiny painting in a locket, ready to whip out in pride! With such parents, I'm sure she's lovely."

Indrath's nostril curled, exposing one fang. His blank, ivory eyes turned crimson.

Jester sighed. "Rest easy, Daddy. I will wait until she comes out to society. It's only proper."

The Ice Lord stared at the Archivist of Woe, his thoughts locked behind any number of barriers. With a hand wave, he opened a portal, stepping through, vanishing without another word.

Gavin stood in the snow, pondering many things, when Jester chuckled.

"There you go," he said with great cheer. "Fair swap for what you so freely offered him. You *really* need to get an intermediary next time you talk to the Hells, at least until you learn some tricks. You're pretty far out from the monastery."

"Noted," the Herald replied. "And thank you."

The Shaegoth beamed behind the mask. "You're most welcome!"

"Will you be staying?"

A shake of a dreadlocked head. "Uh-uh. Have places to be. But I'll check in from time to time."

With that, the Archivist of Woe vanished, leaving Gavin truly alone upon the mountainside. He continued his way through the snow. Among the many voices in his head, the Ice Lord remained audible.

"The underground has long been like a sealed tomb. Complete with a guard dog to chase out uninvited guests."

Sirana. A life flower blooming in a tomb.

A suitable image, in hindsight.

The Deathwalker must eat some fruit soon, but he'd not Walk again until he confirmed whether his *lewensbluen* survived her crossroads. If she did, they may have more they can talk about than he realized.

In whatever language she chooses.

The idea held appeal, but he held no expectation. Not of her or anyone except himself.

As you must be, my Lady, so am I.

Forever, so will I be.

HARROWED'S BREATH

A TALE OF MIURAG
BY A.S. ETASKI

CHAPTER 1

3100 S.E., YONG CH'HAI, CAPITAL OF YUNG-AN

DESHI BREATHED IN, THEN OUT, HIS HEART STILL IN HIS CHEST.

In.

Out.

The night was peaceful but not quiet, small frogs and crickets a soothing drone underneath the snaps of twigs and the sway of branches. Occasionally, an animal would cry, grunt, hoot, or howl, and unknown foot falls disturbed the grass while whispers rustled the leaves.

In his homeland, even the days of ending summer were long, the nights much shorter. The spirits had limited time to play their tricks unseen, to bargain or offer their wisdom to those brave enough to seek them.

His brothers Nianzu and Peng-lok slept in the barn outside the capital port city. They needed a good rest before returning to Augran. The landlord did not know the two Guildsmen travelled with a revenant.

"To know is bad fortune," Nianzu had repeated, reassuring Deshi as much as himself. "We mean no harm. We only want privacy this final night."

Always a risk to sneak what we want.

If the ordinary farmer were to see Deshi, he would believe in a moment he saw a spirit of vengeance. In Yung-An, such surprises and strange tales flowed like the streams from all parts of their land. No matter how many warlords or self-proclaimed emperors tried to rule the rugged peninsula stretching to the top of the world, this land north and west of the Great Lake had never fully been tamed.

The Yungian people worshipped and blamed the spirits every day as part of living. Their sorcerous sightings were frequent enough to keep the people's minds open to them, cultivating a long history filled with rich stories. Unlike many of the pale peoples to the south and east, his people lived among the wonder of the gods from cradle to grave, in equal parts joy and fear.

A wise man once said joy often stands beside fear. It is only that fear makes the uglier face or has the louder voice.

Deshi had witnessed, far closer than he had ever wished, how the pale men among both Ma'ab and Manalari saw the spirits every day, too. Fear had thundered over joy for centuries now. Both had reveled in it, drawing on their hostilities to please their gods with the loudest calls, as if they could frighten away fate itself.

It led only to war.

"*Breathe in the native breath. Take it in deep, harrowed soul, and do not let it slip away. This is your anchor now.*"

Lady Death herself had spoken to him. These words, he remembered. He had drunk deep of life's breath through Janshi; some part of his soul had healed and became the Harrowed. Granted his vengeance for his murder, Deshi had helped shift the balance of the conflict. The fighting had ceased sooner than the Guild of Augran had dared hope, and Manalar would have a chance to notice joy standing beside them again.

Where it has always been.

He breathed in, slowly. *Death and life.*

He breathed out. *Fear and joy. Do not stop seeing one only because the other craves more attention.*

Alas, this night, his fear shouted above the joy of crickets and frogs.

Now what?

A good question. If the Grey Maiden's Herald had known more, he had been unwilling to speak clearly. All Sho'shien had confirmed was an unknowable existence stretching in front of Deshi. It *could* be never-ending.

Dying was easy, in hindsight. Only one direction to go. The simple need to live now frightened Deshi as nothing he had experienced.

Six years inside the Guild, and he had been required to leave it. His time as a Guildsman had ended when Janshi helped him transition from his mortal life. At least he believed his former leaders would fulfill the "death clause" in his contract. They would notify his surviving family beyond his brothers, and they would pay a sum agreed upon.

Which felt strange as Deshi breathed, unceasing. He was grateful, and yet ... *Perhaps I should have asked for my vengeance to kill me a second time.*

Perhaps he *should* have simply let go of everything, as the Grey Lady had suggested.

Too late now.

The life auras of the stirring pigs below lessened in intensity, not because they were dying but because the sun would rise soon. The grunts of sows and squeals of piglets overlapped as several got up to wander out of their pen through the smaller door cut in the side.

So far, Deshi had avoided upsetting the dogs locked outside, but now chances were good an early riser from the house would come into the barn to release the cows and horses and to invite their guests for breakfast, and that one would let the dogs in. Farm dogs were both smart enough to detect spirits and stupid enough to inevitably try to chase it beyond its master's fence.

Deshi nudged Peng-lok, who woke instantly, focusing dark eyes on him. He used Guild sign. ★Dawn. Final day.★

Peng-lok nodded and breathed in deeply, sitting up and shaking Nianzu, who was more reluctant to open his eyes. Though still dark inside the barn, any opening or crack or gap would be exposed as the daylight grew stronger.

"Ugh, still dizzy ..." Nianzu complained when Peng-lok shook him harder with a hiss to wake up.

"Sorry," Deshi muttered. "Your breath will brighten after you eat."

"*Mm.* You know this?"

"I do."

"From man, animal, or spirit?"

Deshi paused. "From woman."

Nianzu roused himself at last with a slow roll upward and a huge yawn, asking no more as he dug for something to chew on. Peng-lok was pulling on his trousers but paused to inspect the jagged scar in his thigh, left behind from the Herald's extraction of the Malok barb.

"Does it hurt still?" Deshi asked.

"It arrives and leaves again. I think it will fade in time. ... it's lumpy." Peng-lok was probing it with three fingers. "Wolf said he felt no pain after the Godblood healed him. He could fight and lift heavy objects after only a short rest."

"Fortunate for him," Nianzu said, digging into a pouch of dried meat. "His lips were white as his face as Sho'shien extracted the barb." Chewing on his mouthful, he rubbed his eyes. "Do you regret refusing the Godblood's healing?"

Peng-lok considered that, then shook his head, finally pulling on his pants. "I do not. It was foreign prayer-magic, its strength dependent on devotion to one god." He shrugged. "It may not have healed me the same, if at all. I know the Guild's magic, and I have praised the spirits all of my life. I am grateful I can still be Guild. It is enough."

Still a Guildsman. Still alive. At least Peng-lok had not lost either of those with nothing else to gain.

Unlike me and Groa.

The three got up to stretch, preparing to leave the barn. Deshi had accepted a hooded cloak from his brothers, if not a new pair of boots, and retained his blessed dagger from the Herald. He would move into the woods and wait for them as the elder two spoke with the landlord and negotiated for supplies.

The three would meet each other one last time, then go their separate ways. The grieving Guildsmen could be sure their dead brother had made it back to the wild lands of his ancestors, and the Harrowed spirit would be grateful for the farewell for as long as he existed.

One day Deshi might be just as he was now but Peng-lok and Nianzu could be centuries dead. *How does a living ghost continue without going mad from loneliness?*

One of many secrets he would learn among the spirits to whom he'd been reborn.

DESHI TRAVELED MUCH FASTER ALONE. NIGHT OR DAY, HE NEVER HAD TO REST; he outran any dog who set upon him and frightened any traveler he did not want to slow him down. He felt the air, always, yet his fingers and toes never complained of being wet, of cool mud sucking at his heels, or of sunbaked rock and dried-out pricker balls hidden in the grass prodding the tough soles of his feet. As he made his way north and west, Deshi might discover if he was immune to deep cold, taking his trance on the great sheets of ice at World's End.

The Harrowed wanted to touch the great bodies of water cradling the whole of his people for all their history. He had already dipped his feet and both hands in the Great Lake as he bowed to the wealthiest of Yung-An's largest city; this was the first of three.

Next was the Sea of Fish touching the smaller but equally important city of Ang-Ling, which provided all the saltwater fishing and performed all reasonable trade with the varied settlements along to coast in both directions, west toward the great sheets of ice at World's End, to the east leading ever closer to the pale barbarians of Dargevold.

Following this, he would cross the farms, pastures, and steppes to reach the barren and ice-covered tip of the peninsula, where the seals coated the rocks and hunted under the ice, evading the giant white bears forever tracking them in circles.

Three of four points of ancestral waters.

The last and most difficult waters to touch were those of the Sea of Storms to the south of World's End, beyond the tallest, craggiest mountains of the continent.

The Lonely Ones.

Once outside of Ang-Ling and traveling the central paths, the chain of jagged peaks would never truly be out of sight. They longed for company, providing eternal escort for every Yungian traveling the peninsula, protecting the land from the worst storms coming off the western ocean. Between the Lonely Ones and the sun, a constant supply of the cleanest water trickled down, feeding the fertile land in summer.

Outside of those mountains, no one truly became lost in Yung-An.

Within them, many souls had vanished, never to be heard from again.

CHAPTER 2

3100 S.E., ANG-LING, YUNG-AN PENINSULA.

"*Fadai feng*," DESHI MUTTERED IN AWE, STANDING UPON HILLS WHICH WOULD lead him to the sea's edge.

Am I here already? Can it be?

He remembered falling into a trance as he ran, his thoughts light and swift as the wind, a meditation which sent the world into a blur. He looked up at the stars, sure of his direction and the road he had taken, even having gone off it at the first whiff of salt air.

Then he saw the dark statue outside the coastal city's landlocked gate.

Lung-Yu.

The Dragon who was said to guard the sea around this port: a long, winding creature, his scales half-pale and half-black as if representing the moons and the night sky at once. Small horns and elegant crests lined his entire length, gills flared off his jaw, and a powerful set of arms gripped the stone base up front with no legs in the back, the whole body wound until the tip touched the ground. Deshi imagined some magician giving the smallest seahorse the blood of the giant serpents along with all the powers of the ocean storms.

Definitely Ang-Ling.

His run had been faster than a horseman trading fresh mounts one after another between Yung-An's two largest cities. A messenger expected just over three, more likely four days if he did not want to kill the horses or himself, yet it had taken Deshi not even two days without stopping.

I can outlast any man I once knew. Any natural animal I have ever seen.

Even the riders and falconers of the Yungian Steppes would be hard-pressed to escape him if he chose to follow. They had to stop; to drink, to eat, to sleep. The void in the bushes.

The Harrowed did none of those things anymore. With Nyx's boon, Deshi's massive country, the single largest and longest-lasting culture anybody knew, had just shrunk to a one-month trek at a non-stop sprint.

Unless I lose myself in the Lonely Ones.

He wasn't sure how much of Nianzu's breath he had used in getting here. Even though he was not hungry yet, he did not want to be in a deep wilderness between villages when he *became* hungry. Deshi did not really know what would happen if he simply failed to find sustenance.

Would he suffocate like being buried in dirt? Would he fade away so easily for a Greylord's messenger? Would he do something he regretted, grow desperate and uncontrolled in his need? Would he hurt someone to slake his thirst, as Mathias had done to him? Would he kill by accident, neither wanting nor knowing when to stop as he sucked their life away … ?

No. That shall not be.

Deshi swallowed more by habit than necessity, quelling the troubling thoughts. The teachings of every instructor he had had, in the Guild and before, would have told him to plan where possible, be in the present until then, and try not to fall into that pit of avoidance and self-sabotage.

The Harrowed need not run up to his very limits the first month of his existence; he need not even discover that his first year! If he did meet this limit so soon, it would only shame his teachers, including the Dragon Spirit of Yong-wen, that Deshi had been so thoughtless.

"*Hei,*" he breathed out with a nod, calming his anxiety as he pulled the hood of his cloak up to cover himself. He would try to drink life's breath here, his first test among strangers to find what methods worked best.

Just another night spirit seeking a bargain.

229

The People of the Peninsula were used to that.

THE FAMED CITY OF FISHERMEN WAS QUIETER BY MOONLIGHT THAN DESHI WAS accustomed to. Even if none but the smallest boats ever fished by magic lanterns, other work, drink, and stories should have continued well into the night, every night, in most cities of any size.

Perhaps they do, but only near the water.

Most Yungians out of hearing of the waves were truly at rest, such that Deshi could bypass the main gate and walk with a flash of blue fire through an overgrown piece of iron fence.

The first tavern he discovered to be open was a biji bar favored by unmarried fishermen not planning to sail at dawn. The place was dim inside for they had stopped feeding the central fire as patrons had stepped out. Something about its smell and abundant shadows made Deshi smile, and he stepped inside.

The first word he heard was not Yungian.

"*Dargevold,*" a white-whiskered grandfather insisted to another two decades or more his junior, pointing his calloused, knobby finger.

"You've never been there, laofu," the younger replied with gentle skepticism, taking a sip of biji.

The grandfather grumbled, narrowing his eyes. "I have, and do not doubt me, xao'ren. More than white devils with beards of fire there to protect the glaciers."

A grin of amusement. "Do tell, laofu."

"Wolfs and hunter cats who take the form of men! Bare-breasted women with wings of blood! If Ang-Ling is the Bounty of the North Sea, those crags are the scavengers feeding on their own young up there! This servant tried to protect his Lord, but ..."

"Laofu, it is late. Time for sleep."

"I promise on my Greatest of Grandfathers, xao'ren — !"

Deshi did not stare at them, but the conversation brought to mind

230

the intelligence which had only reached him once joining the Guild in Augran.

Dargevold.

It was Noiri, and the translation in Augran-Common was "Dragon's Hold," with speculation the root language for the pale man's Common had come from that area as well. This translation alone was the reason any Yungian wealthy enough had ever sailed that far up the coast. Always they followed rumors of a great Dragon's hoard of riches and the bearded Dragon-warriors who supposedly knew where it was.

According to the stories which made it back in their twisted form, most kinsmen seemed to doubt it was worth the expense and danger of "trading" that far up the coast. Some never came back, and the Guild had reports of slavers not at all picky about the appearance of their captives persisting in the much drier tundra to the East, even not counting the threat of the Ma'ab Empire at Ennikar.

"No more biji tonight, honored friend," said the tender behind the bar, startling Deshi out of his thoughts, "though there is stew remaining if you are hungry."

The Harrowed raised his fist to his chest before laying it open and flat in a sign of peace. His eyes scanned the counter and the walls, where small, stone idols of numerous spirits rested. They had been made with care in marble and jade, representing many forms from fish to fox to owl.

An owl statuette larger than most.

The harbinger of death. A good sign.

Deshi said, "I require neither, qienbe zhu. If you have, instead, an open corner for this servant to sit out of the wind this night … ?"

The biji master began to nod an affirmative but paused, squinting dark, narrow eyes accented with deep crow's feet. His mouth tightened at the corners. "May we see you without your hood, peng-yo?"

The old storyteller and his probable relation had stopped talking to pay attention. One more bleary-eyed drunk held his head close to the wood of his small table, nearly asleep. Deshi signed acceptance but moved first to the small batch of carrying candles near the central fire, lighting it before coming to the bar where only the proprietor would clearly see his face.

The Harrowed quelled the impulse to run. He was ready should he need it, but this was a place of stories and personal accounts of magic. He had some coin to use, sparingly, but it wasn't his first offer. His face alone could also be worthy barter for some, if wisely propositioned.

Deshi lowered his hood and placed the candle to his left so it would illuminate three parts of his face. He signed in respect, indicating the owl statue in the same motion. "This servant of night has little time before sunrise, qienbe zhu. Will you barter?"

The biji master flinched but glanced toward his quiet patrons before fixing his eyes on the paler face of the young Yungian. He squinted as if he wasn't sure what he saw then shivered. "Jingshen Siwang … your eyes. Does this humble master see a ring of gold trapped within the deepest of blue ice?"

"He does," Deshi answered, not blinking as the candlelight flickered over his face. As the Guild had taught him, he let the sense of mystery do the work for him.

The old storyteller behind him had gone very still; the xao'ren whispered comfort and courage as he reached to squeeze his arm.

"Does Siwang come for one of us tonight?" the barkeep dared to ask, calling all his courage to keep eye contact between them.

It impressed Deshi and he smiled. "She does *not* send me for one of you," he answered honestly. "I am only passing through."

"Why does a servant of the Compassionate Lady need the unworthy shelter of men?" the grandfather boldly spoke from, causing the snoozing drunk to grunt and shift as his head tried not to drop past his stoneware mug.

"Perhaps she tests their awareness and nothing more," Deshi murmured, quiet and calm and watching the proprietor, who held that equal mix of joy and fear which he had never seen anywhere else but home.

"Surely, good men strive to make their life worthy of its gift," the barkeep said with a grin. He bowed and slapped a meaty palm on his own counter. "Of course you may stay beneath the wretched roof Hong, biji master. May your patience prove eternal, rongyu'shen."

He cleared his throat as his two wakeful patrons shifted and straightened up in their chairs. "May this humble merchant ask but a story or two in exchange? How did you come here, and how do we call you?"

Deshi smiled, answering the unspoken gesture if the other two might come and join in the talk. Fear had stepped just behind its brighter twin for now, though it would always be waiting for a misstep from a careless ghost.

"You may call me Dawn-Seeker, and I have just come from a great battle far across the Great Lake," Deshi said. "The Compassionate Lady has a message which at last reached the hearts of the night-fearing people of the Sun Temple. Hia-Yo now shines less harshly in the hot land."

"Why would we care of the bakgwei from so far away?" the younger man asked.

His grandfather elbowed him in the ribs so hard that he grunted. "Apologize, Ping," he growled. "You do not choose the story. The story finds you when you are ready to listen. Do not shame me before a benevolent servant!"

"I apologize, Dawn-Seeker," the younger man said with appropriate earnestness, rubbing the sore spot. "Please, we listen." Ping coughed as soon as Deshi accepted the apology, glancing at the master of the place. "May I have more biji just for this, Hong?"

"Last service was half chime ago."

"I know, but, an honored guest —"

Deshi contemplated what he would say next as they got this sorted out.

"May I make you an offering, night spirit?" Hong asked as Ping looked on, hopeful.

"Um." Deshi twisted his fingers. "I cannot partake. No disrespect, Master Hong."

The younger man leaned in. "*I* will take your offering in his honor, H-Ho-*ow!*"

"Sit back, xao'ren!" the white whiskered man barked with elbow at the ready for another plunge.

"Indeed," Hong confirmed. "Last service is passed."

"That I doubt, honored master," Ping chuckled. "If there's but *one* fallen warrior or another taken by the sea in his tale ..."

"*Hmph!*"

The Harrowed waited a few beats as the men exchanged looks, then announced, "Indeed. Hia-Yo has a new warrior of honor among the Temple People of Manalar. Take interest if you hear of the *Capitan* Willven Isboern."

Hong frowned. "Odd name, even for a southerner."

Deshi smiled. "Willven Isboern is from the Lonely Ones, to the west. But he is wise beyond his years and has won over the Manalari people. He is the new guardian of their sacred spring. His stories may spread across the Lake, as it is *he* who welcomed back the Compassionate Lady on behalf of the men of Paxia. I am but the first messenger; others may follow me from all corners of the continent."

Hong grunted and nodded. "This may change trade through Yong-ch'hai and Yong-wen in Augran."

"Oh, it will, honored friends. Manalar may one day become open to pilgrimage as no Yungian alive has witnessed, and this is through the effort and blessing of our own Dragon Spirit of Yong-wen. He has allied with the *Capitan* not only to turn aside the dark wave of Ma'ab rampaging outside of their grey tundra, but to expel the violent Bishops of the Sun Temple and return Lady Death to a place of honor beside the Living Sun."

"Have you *seen* him?" Ping asked, his eyes widening as his interest spiked. "The Dragon Spirit of Yong-wen?"

"I have *spoken* with him. I received his blessing as a messenger between Hia-Yo and our Compassionate Lady. He is one reason I am here."

Ping's breath quickened. "What does he look like? Does he carry the singing swords?"

Deshi blinked as he caught a whiff. His smile became a grin.

The Harrowed would field these curious questions for some time, but none of his Human companions noticed the lateness of the hour. They even fed the central fire and poured the drink to listen longer to the Harrowed's joyful words, tempered only by knowledge that the Ma'ab army had not returned to their homeland for good.

"To the Compassionate Lady," Hong said, pouring more drink, "and those fallen warriors who finally know her name."

DESHI WATCHED THE PINK OF SUNRISE OUTSIDE THE SMALL, SHADED WINDOW OF Hong's meager guest room, the hint of light already making the ocean sparkle.

Ping's breath mingled with Nianzu's fading inside him as Deshi steadied himself against the wall. He felt better. Very good, in fact. Revitalized, even as he reflected on this first breath infused with fermented drink. It did not affect him as the drink itself had Ping, but the Harrowed was in no mood to move quickly just then, much less run.

The late-night story of the battle at Manalar — with selectively chosen details — had aroused the imaginations of all three men, but Ping ended up being the one to offer more when both older men could stay awake no longer.

Deshi remembered a nervous but excited bow when Ping followed him in the hall, young and bold enough to risk a brush with death.

"You look young, but you must be older than you seem," Ping whispered, his face flushed from alcohol. "Do you still take your pleasure from humble mortals?"

Oh.

"Hm. If offered," Deshi replied, not commenting on the rest.

"I would offfer, Dawn-Ssseeker, if you would ..." A soft burb. "Accept."

He was slurring. Deshi hesitated.

Had he succeeded in his task? How much was a mortal to know in order to consent to share his breath? Could an intoxicated giver understand a simple mystic's answer?

"I might," the Harrowed answered. "But I am not a hungry ghost such as I fought at Manalar, Ping. I do not need your body or your blood."

The young man, no more than a few years older than him, was intrigued. "What do you need, honored one?"

Deshi found himself unable to say it, especially as he noticed the rise in the other man's trousers. He took Ping's wrist instead, feeling the heat difference between them.

"Come with me. I will show you."

Ping had grinned and sloppily kissed him after they'd laid down on Hong's guest straw bed, eager as Deshi had brought his mouth near enough. Deshi held his patience and kissed back but had also started feeding on his breath right then, sucking hard to pull out that first lungful.

It was a bit harsher than he intended.

"Ung-wh-wha — ?" Ping stuttered, pulling away.

"Shhh, just breathe out, gift-giver. Take a breath. Like this."

After that they'd gotten in sync, and the trance overtook both of them, and eventually Deshi had forgotten about the hard cock pressed against his thigh, slowly going soft. Ping drifted to true sleep during the feeding, never fully woken up, and he probably wouldn't before Deshi needed to leave.

It hadn't been unpleasant for Ping, Deshi didn't think; he was snoring softly now and occasionally sighed or grunted or twitched, perhaps having strange but pleasant dreams. Deshi would make sure the other man had food, water, and a little more biji before he left to bow to his ancestors in the Sea of Fish.

The Harrowed was curious what the mortal might remember when he woke up, but he couldn't stay.

CHAPTER 3

3100 S.E., THE YUNG-AN WILDERNESS

THE HARROWED MOVED NORTH AND WEST FROM ANG-LING ALONG THE COAST subduing his aura and the blue flames to draw fewer eyes among the early risers. Before the sun had fully cleared the horizon, the Lonely Ones arose barely visible on his left. He did not have the strength of heart to repeat his story or his news of joy to every village or town he glimpsed, so he favored the fields and forests and avoided the roads for the next several days and nights.

Like the Herald, Deshi had to stop and sit still for some hours until the world faded behind him. His breath and his mind centered before he would wake and skip all Human rituals of eating, drinking, or eliminating waste before being on the move again.

He did not crave fire or warmth but sometimes missed the light, even as he dared not attract the attention of mortal or spirit with a campfire. Neither the growing heat of the day nor the deeply cool nights drove him to seek shelter greater than something to break the directness of a particular strong wind or a storm.

Swift shifts in the air caused his mood to change just as fast, startling him as he might hear words spoken from before in the howling space within.

Ping and Nianzu. Janshi with Janhuren. Yunze, and her sun-haired forest

237

sister.

Lastly, the veiled Manalari ...

With them would come the emotions tied to those breaths. He could *feel* them.

Deshi could not simply stand inside the windstorm, not without the possibility of the blue fire flaring to life, lighting up his body and showing his bones beneath his skin. With no Ma'ab targets here to suffer his wrath, and no Deathwalker to defend from the Grey Maiden's enemies, the Harrowed had to keep his balance.

Until I discover my true purpose.

He must believe he would find it. The voices of his life's breath spoke that he was not truly alone forever.

If I care to listen.

With minimal rise of his spirit energy and avoiding injury, Deshi went weeks without feeding again. With speed and unceasing touch of his bare feet, the wilderness changed, as his education told him it would, though this was his first time seeing it. The landscape transformed from rolling hills and forests to fields ever sparser, until it opened to the ranges and steppes.

Perhaps a week's run before I see the ice fields at the edge of the world.

The Lonely Ones changed with the landscape as well. Green and gold dotted with summer flowers in red, yellow, violet, and blue welcomed him at the start. Now the yellow grasses turned more like the dun of the wild horse, the foothills dappled with squat, dark shrubs as barren, rocky mountaintops watched over them.

Soon Deshi found nomadic settlements of the horse riders and falconers on the steppes of Yung-An, the far-west mirror to the Kurgan riders of the east. Among these he knew he must feed again soon.

Much different than a permanent city of fisherman and merchants eager for news and with plenty of surplus in trade, the mobile tribes of the northern half of the peninsula had less to give and worked harder for it.

They were said to be far more suspicious of those who might try to take what they had earned from a cooler, harsher home, but the Harrowed had no choice. He was even less likely to find people at the land's end, and the "Dawn Seeker" already knew he had no taste for animals, assuming he could even capture and hold something large enough to sustain him for it to do any good.

Probably be injured in trying and not even feed enough to heal.

Deshi took his time to watch the nomads, remaining downwind of their horses and hiding well enough from their giant hunting birds. He could see their auras well in advance and was never taken off guard, night or day. Half the men would ride out with their animals to hunt for game, large or small. That half could be gone for days at a time, but the other half never left their families unprotected, and they would take turns.

The women's routines included watering the animals by the river, of fishing, of weaving and leatherworking, of cooking over open fires and in smoldering pits. He noticed their long, long walks out to gather medicines, roots, berries, and other resources.

He doubted he could approach the Steppe Yungians and snare their curiosity with only words and his strange eye color as he had in Ang-Ling. He must offer a gift of more tangible worth first, then the words. Even with a barely common language between them, the Steppe people knew much less about what existed far to the South of them.

With even less reason than Ping to care.

Was it even a good idea to reveal himself to all of them at once, to try and earn the venerable awe of half a tribe of hunters and gatherers? Assuming Deshi managed that, what reason would they have to let him near their families for any reason, to lie down next to a daughter or a wife or a sister? He didn't know. He might not even have the right tribute to soothe their masculine pride.

Deshi might have to negotiate with a man again to drink his breath if he tried that way, but he was running out of time to be patient, and it held more danger than approaching late-night gossipers in a biji bar of a wealthy city. He could be injured, true, but he wasn't afraid of the other men because, ultimately, they couldn't stop him. He'd be more likely to hurt the attacker, which wasn't what he wanted.

The tribal women seemed to share most everything about the work, even caring for children. Approaching one small group of women would be easiest if Deshi acted more like a fox than a lone wolf. Opportunists succeeded for a reason, and the Guild had taught him nothing if not to watch for the right opportunity.

Deshi sighed. He had enjoyed giving "good news" to those hungry to hear some, but that wouldn't work here and neither would the coins. Needs were simpler; more like his own and yet not.

We both need sustenance and cannot wait for traders to bring it to us, yet I require a living, thinking person to hold still like a plant while I pluck off a handful of their berries before walking away with thanks.

The Harrowed spent more time watching the women than the men, sensing opportunity late in his first day. Although his hunger gradually rose up in his chest with each breath he took, he managed to observe three days undetected.

He spied a woman older than him, one who did not seem to have a husband to care for. Whenever any rider or group of riders returned, she did not look up expectantly; she did not go to meet them, seeming sad. She had a daughter close to marriageable age, certainly old enough to help with the work but just as often chatting with a relative. If he counted back the age of the daughter, then the woman had birthed her around his own age.

Deshi focused on this possible widow, his mind turning toward the spirit of the fox. She had dark, well-weathered skin, and wore the long, leather dress of her tribe. Her black hair, very lightly streaked with white, was combed well to show her capable and caring enough to groom herself, even as she plaited and bound it to keep it out of her face on the windy Steppes.

A necklace special to her was always around her neck, a pendant of opaque blue stone, set into a wrap of tarnished metal attached to a strong, leather cord. She rubbed her thumb across the smooth stone often, whenever she lifted her head from her work to think of something — or someone — for a moment in her day. She would also touch her lips or stroke her breasts or her thighs through her dress on occasion, after checking to be sure she wasn't being watched by the other women.

Deshi recognized loneliness in her; it called to him.

Perhaps, this time, he could be the gift-giver.

On the fourth day, the widow left on one of the long walks with five others, and he trailed them unseen late into the morning. Opportunity would come in knowing the women stayed within shouting distance of each other but not in a cluster as they searched for nuts, roots, berries, and medicine.

In time, the widow separated from the other women, her gaze mostly on the ground but looking up every so often.

Now.

Deshi found his luck in a heavily laden bush of olfen berries ahead of her apparent path. Stripping the largest from the bush, he collected the tangible offering in his ragged cloak and folded it up, then removed his blessed grave dagger, stashing it beneath a few heavy stones. His thin shirt and pants looked worn but were serviceable enough. Deshi didn't want to scare her senseless so she shouted for the others.

Though I shall inevitably scare her a little …

When the Steppe's Widow turned her back to her basket, Deshi crept up and poured the food into it. She heard it and spun around, her mouth open on a shout.

"*Jia'ren, jia'ren,*" he soothed, both a compliment and a greeting, holding out an open hand. "I shall not harm you, good mother."

He had no trouble appearing the lusty spirit smitten by a striking mortal woman; it was a common theme in many Yungian stories. She paused, showing comprehension of his compliment, reconsidering the scream. Cautiously, she glanced down into her basket, saw the huge number of berries which had been added to it.

He waited, breathless, to see if she'd accept.

"*Y-yaung'pen't?*" she asked, pointing to them.

Her accent was thick, but he thought he understood. Nodding, he spread his hand, suggesting she try one.

She shook her head, indicating him. "*Mei-nin. Nin.*"

Him?

"I can't eat mortal food," he said honestly, and she struggled with his dialect. He hoped he sounded more mystical than someone who'd been living in Augran for the last six years. He repeated it once more, slowly, pantomiming as if eating a berry, then covered his middle as if in pain. "Cannot eat berry. Poison."

"*Hmph*," she grunted with an amusing frown, already pulling her courage around her like a fur blanket shielding her against the winter.

He smiled again. "*Jia'ren.*"

She scoffed and tossed her chin upward, crossing her arms as he crouched low and unthreatening by her basket. ★"Mei.★ *Ao.*"

He shook his head no. "*Mei. Jia.*"

"*Ao!*" she insisted, but not too loudly so as not to draw the attention of her sisters.

Deshi resisted chuckling. "To a spirit like me, you are very young, *jia*. What is your name?"

She planted her feet, staring at him, studying his strange eyes especially, and his apparent age. Deshi didn't think he was wrong that he would have been similar in age to her husband when she conceived her daughter.

"Jun," she answered.

"You are beautiful, Jun."

She spoke in her unfamiliar lilt. "What is it you do want, spirit?"

"You don't want to know my name?"

"No! No name. Be that bad luck."

Deshi quelled the urge to laugh. That was what a married woman would say to a younger man to whom she considered giving her attention.

Jun probably isn't her real name, either.

"What is it you do want?" she asked again.

"I want a kiss for the berries, Jun."

She narrowed dark, slanted eyes. "Did I ask for berries?"

He looked mournful, just a bit pathetic. "I am lonely, Jun. Keep the gift no matter your answer, but you asked 'what is it I do want.' I want your kiss."

"Hmm." She considered, listening to him mimic her speech with respect. Then Jun tightened her mouth and tapped her lips with a finger. He made it obvious he was watching her mouth in hunger; it wasn't hard, he caught whiffs of her breath on occasion.

"What kind of spirit you be?" she asked cautiously, looking for some sign. He was glad he was not carrying any weapon.

"Wind spirit," he answered. "I have blown down from the Lonely Ones. A mortal must give me air to return to them, or I am trapped here."

"Go I with you? I will not!" she stated firmly, with heavy emphasis on the last word.

He nodded in agreement. "I return alone with only a memory of your kiss."

She clutched her blue stone, smoothing it over with her thumb by long habit. "Not you will haunt tribe!"

"I do not want to haunt your tribe, Jun, but I have chosen you. You protect them even now with your strength. You are beautiful, Jun."

Loneliness proved stronger than her fear. The way she looked over her shoulder to where her tribe sisters would gather, Deshi knew the answer was yes.

"Come with," she gestured, picking up her basket and leading him farther away over the next windy hill. "Tricky spirit, telling me what it is I want to hear!"

Deshi blinked. "You don't believe me?"

Jun snorted, looking back at him with a startlingly beautiful smile. "No! Trick, yes? But your words and your face, and your berries, I like. Give I will to you your kiss."

The Steppe woman's embrace was a strong one, and he was relieved as he practically fell into the grass with her, clutching the first warm, living person since leaving Ang-Ling.

Thank the gods …

The first kiss was a cold one; she wasn't impressed with his body temperature. But he sucked in a short breath, kissed her again and extended it, made her desperate to take a breath, drawing it in as she did.

"Oh!" she gasped.

He drew in another and let his hands wander where she fast encouraged them to go. He squeezed her generous bottom, stroked her back through her dress, and continued kissing her, keeping her short of breath. She started gasping, moaning softly as she pulled him into multiple kisses easily matching his hunger, and Deshi felt himself heating up from the inside out with her generosity.

"Jun."

Soon his hands warmed from her feeding him her berry-sized pants of breath that his hands could go beneath her dress as she lifted it up. To her, it would feel to her like the fingers of a living man stroking her thighs, teasing oh-so-close to her *yinchun*. Jun quivered, gasping again almost in shock before breathing out in his face.

She whispered, "Yes, wind spirit ... *shi'chumo* ... *banlu!*"

Deshi sincerely wished he could please her that way.

That is one thing I will never do again.

But he still had a working tongue and very capable fingers.

Deshi raised his face and met her eyes. "I cannot," he murmured. "I need the air from your kisses, Jun. But I will give you the touching you want, if you will help me."

She studied his strange eyes, convinced he *was* from another world. As he waited for her to understand, she reached for his crotch. It took all his courage not to pull away, to disperse the shame no longer his as it swept through.

Comprehension dawned on her face, and she formed her mouth into an "O."

"You do not need a wind-baby with no husband, yes?" he jested, kissing her neck affectionately while stroking her slick, fragrant folds.

He received a short coo before she tested him in return. He allowed her to test, as she needed to, even knowing she would only find him flaccid.

"I-I ... um ..." she stammered, her earlier confidence shaken. "Kiss? Truly, just kiss? No more?"

Of course, she'd assumed he meant a euphemism for something more when he'd been playing his "spirit trick" on her ... and she'd been willing to give all of it regardless. Deshi leaned over her mouth as she spoke. and he breathed in, letting the bliss show on his face he'd tried to hide from Nianzu.

Beautiful. It is so beautiful ...

"Nothing more, Jun. I will touch, I will taste you. Tell me what feels good, I will do it for more kisses."

He slipped a finger into her to prove it, to test her in return. She was fairly tight — a lonely mother indeed — and her eyes rolled up. She arched up slightly when he added a second.

"Oh … oh, spirit …"

The steppe woman sucked a deep breath, releasing it deliberately, slowly, her eyes fixed his own lust as he kept his gaze on her lips. She smiled, beginning to understand.

She released his unresponsive manhood and relaxed, moving her body closer to him, lowering her hand between her thighs to cover his.

To show him how to touch her.

"Take me high as wind, spirit," she agreed, grinning again. "Will give you the *best* breath."

Jun's slow climb was ecstasy in every gasp. Though he offered, she did not want him to "leave her" to use his mouth instead. She was content to cling to him as they pleasured her, until her *yinchun* was running like a river down her thighs. Hot, sweating, he shared her warmth.

"Ah! … .Ah! … ."

Her cries resembled those of the local birds as she edged close to her peak, and she filled her lungs to their capacity just before grimacing and quivering in silence, holding that breath as the wonderful sensations burst through their barriers.

"*Ahhh … .!*" she exhaled, short at first, her body shuddering at this first drop before coasting down. "Ohhh … *.ssshhhiii … .!*"

Deshi lay stunned by the life breath released in that moment of ecstasy, more potent than any he'd taken in thus far. He drank deeply, feeling that release, that pleasure, helpless to do anything else. His eyes rolled back as he forgot anything outside of infinity, blind for a few moments, but soon gazing at Jun's flushed face and sparkling eyes in full sunlight.

Her life aura was overwhelming. He was shaking, and she stroked his face with the hand which had a moment ago been clutching to him deep enough to leave fingernail marks.

"You glow blue, spirit," she whispered in awe.

Deshi blinked, lifting his hand completely coated in her woman's juices.

She was right; his spirit energy was showing whether he willed it or not.

"*Hei*," he whispered. "You are bright with life, Jun."

She giggled in afterglow, taking his hand and just barely licking the tip of his finger, mixed with her fluid and blue fire. The contact seemed to shock her, as if she had touched metal after rolling in a wool blanket on a dry winter day.

Deshi was about to apologize but she looked intrigued.

"Hmm. Think do I remember how … to live." She looked mischievous. "Again? Or you are 'full of wind'?"

"Again," he agreed at once, not caring whether he needed more or not. "Will your sisters miss you?"

She sucked on her lower lip, thinking. She was eager. "Will be faster. Need touch again."

She pushed his hand back down between her legs, her leather dress bunched messily about her hips. She squeaked in anticipation as his fire crackled, as her flesh yielded again to his probe. He sank inside her, drawn in by her willing body.

This time he had just as much to give as she did.

Jun breathed out, slow and trembling and letting him enjoy it, her eyes wide and glazed. "Faster. Touch of sky-strike … !"

"Yes, Jun."

She opened her legs to him. "Harder. More!"

"Yesss … *noyji* … kiss me, Jun."

Under the big sky that day, neither of them were lonely.

CHAPTER 4

3100 S.E., YUNG-AN, THE BEAR SEA

WHILE WITHIN JUN'S SIGHT, DESHI HEADED IN THE DIRECTION OF THE LONELY Ones for her sake.

"I will not come back to haunt you," he promised her.

On the edge of the last hill, he glimpsed her rubbing her blue pendant with both thumbs but then, almost defiantly, she slipped the necklace beneath her dress out of sight and picked up her basket to rejoin her sisters.

Rest lightly, Jun.

He circled back for his grave dagger but then, after four days in this valley, returned to the quickest pilgrimage any Yungian had ever taken.

Traveling through the foothills and along the steppes, Deshi passed herds of antelope and giant deer feasting on the growing season's bounty. The sun set and the stars revealed themselves while the Harrowed never slowed.

As the first of the Sister Moons rose, the dark silhouette of the Lonely Ones dropped away from the horizon, as if the massive rise of rocks had simply crumbled into the ocean. Moonlight graced the exposed land in a blue-tinged blanket of night and the wind was much stronger now. Deshi could hear Jun's song of mourning and feel the loss of her husband.

"Wo'hui shengxin ... wo'hui shengxin ... shaoshang caichan weili ..."

He sensed but the barest of patterns after he drank from mortals, most easily recognizing the loss of loved ones. He could not be so sure when he drank from the spirits.

I wonder, could I be lifting that heavy feeling, freeing it through the air I breathe in? Do I merely share it for a time? Do I ... strengthen it ... ? Will it become my weight as well?

If the Herald of Lady Death ultimately served the dead, did Deshi then serve the living *through* their dead?

The comparison appealed to him if he were to belong to this world forever, but without asking a mortal later if that weight was gone from their hearts or if it was heavier, or only temporarily lifted, he might not know for some time.

THE HARROWED THOUGHT HE WOULD HAVE MET THE FANTASTIC SHEETS OF ICE before now but witnessed firsthand just how powerful the sun was even in a place this cold.

Bare rock with tiny, yellow flowers growing in between them, pools which had been liquid during the day dappled between them, just icing over tonight. Even avoiding recklessness, Deshi's feet should have more cuts, but they quickly closed up as he approached World's End.

He stood in the dead of night when he reached it, the second Moon setting to leave the sky its darkest before dawn, with the stars their brightest. Wind whistled at the top of the great peninsula, buffeting him, and Deshi discovered he would not have to slide along the ice to dip his feet into this third body of ancestral waters.

He only had to avoid the seals and their mating colonies.

The enormous, blubbering beasts were so numerous that, by the time Deshi found a decent patch of bare rock between two dozing herds, the sun had peeked out and found him once again. His light blue aura might have seemed strange to those grunting in the beginnings of concern, but Deshi made no noise at all as he passed through jagged boulders on his way to the water.

Ultimately, the seals ignored him. He had only to wait for one of the white, churning waves to come meet him. He braced himself, refusing to fall down when it struck him in the chest.

I am here, ancestors. Hear my prayer for your continued guidance as you watch over us, to be shown the wisdom of the stars above. One more ocean at the Sea of Storms, and I shall complete the circle made for our People ...

Deshi's feet and legs numbed as the water slapped at him three times; he had let his aura dim so he could sense it better, even without acute discomfort. The experience was a continued oddity he had yet to cease giving though: he could "feel," in that he could sense texture and temperature and moisture, but with a disconnect. Such abrupt changes no longer affected his mood or caused him unease or distress.

Only the air of Miurag in its multitude of forms can do that.

That was his anchor now.

The messenger squinted his eyes, focusing on something pale out in the water; pale, but becoming brighter with the sun. With patience, he saw it was a floating ice block — massive — carrying one of the giant white bears of this region. The bear looked scrawny and hungry, peering longingly at the seals on the beach but it would require quite a swim and a surge of energy that perhaps it did not have. Meanwhile the seals had plenty of time to respond.

The bear dove in anyway, and Deshi understood.

There is nowhere else to go.

All around him was the ocean, and he could not swim nearly as well as the white bear. The only land was behind him, and he would have to turn back soon.

There are no people living here.

As quickly as the Lonely Ones had abandoned him at the start of the Ice Plain, just as abruptly they met him again with open arms. They seemed glad to see him, clinging eagerly to his sight and slowing his progress along the rocky southern coast.

Deshi had to climb and clutch them in return to make his way, trying to reach the Sea of Storms without too many gashes in his flesh causing too much hunger.

This would be the toughest part of his pilgrimage. He may not find any people at all, and this coast could potentially lead him back to Willven Isboern's birth country.

I might be lucky to reach the middle point before turning inland to beg sustenance in the north.

He must keep his promise to Jun as well and not return to ask her again, no matter how hungry he might be by then.

I assumed it would be easy to keep.

Fear made him less certain.

Thick vegetation soon filled all the crevices of rock, and Deshi grew concerned how long this part of the journey would take him. Everything else had been so quick; he must be careful his frustration did not get the best of him.

He listened to the migrant birds building nests along the shore. More than once, they dove at him to chase him away from their nests. Fortunately for them, he only had interest in avoiding their sharp beaks.

He moved on.

The third day, Deshi felt a strange sense of urgency, yet it wasn't hunger for the breath of the living. His aura flashed once without his truly willing it, mimicking the luminescent insects of twilight around Manalar, though Deshi could not know just who or what he was attempting to signal. He did not know if it was a warning.

If it is a warning, who is it for?

Still, his bones had shown through blue flame and translucent skin, backlit and opaque. His teeth were sharp and bared like that of a wolf, his voice whispering and echoing like the shadow spirits of legend, vengeful as when he had seized upon Mathias at the Temple's wall.

Why is this happening?

Were Ma'ab nearby, somehow? Had Mathias somehow returned from his damnation? Deshi both *wanted* that and *did not want* to face that rage again so soon.

Faster. Find it.

Deshi wasn't sure he *could* go faster in this treacherous place, though the blue flames saw him passing through more and more obstacles as he climbed and descended the mountains throughout the day.

He couldn't pass *through* whole mountains, which may have made things easier, but in its way, he found his own trance within the Lonely Ones as grey mist rose up to dampen the coast. Rain threatened and it grew impossibly dark as night came.

Deshi made the effort to douse the blue glow of his form so other auras would be clearer to him.

With the Moons covered by thick, swollen clouds, being as close to blind as he could be in the stifling mountain forest, for the first time in his pilgrimage, Deshi found what he was looking for. He knew it the moment he glimpsed the pale aura above him through the ever-widening tree trunks.

There.

Excited, he slipped and shushed through brush and low branches, his own blue aura strengthening again as his form became incorporeal, closing the distance between him and the white glow. He heard voices, speaking with the whispered tongue of the Nexus, hinting of the deepest shadows. Yet neither were familiar to him.

"*Harnemue faelgeraphusss,*" crooned a voice which he could not tell at once if male or female.

"*Anashi kubleewt, vin'gre,*" came a reply, this one clearly female.

He hurried, aware he may be stumbling into a situation on which he could have no effect, but he must make himself known. If he possessed any instinct anymore, neither truly dead nor fully alive, it was that he must answer this mystic's call.

The two spoke on a small rock ledge. Deshi climbed up, ready to draw the gaze of a massive and frightening beast.

One he truly believed would only be found in the Lonely Ones of Yung-An.

The body of a giant cat lay low to the ground as if blocking its den. A long tail tipped with a hairy tassel, the hide short-haired enough to seem sleek despite its dull, muted color. Deshi noticed the naked breasts at once, he couldn't help it, but from the way she sat on her belly, elbows propping her up, he spied forepaws closer to hands like his than that of a feline, lightly decorated with a pair of ornate, golden bracers.

The mystical beast also possessed an irregular set of wings, semi-translucent and blue grey in color, with the apparent structural strength of a moth. Surely such delicate things could not lift a heavy body into flight.

"*Shrah* ... ? Who Now Approaches My Gate?"

Deshi jumped before he could focus on the second figure, baffled that he suddenly *understood* the beast. The speech sounded like Augran Common to his ears, but he couldn't figure how that could be.

"Answer Now."

His eyes seemed compulsively drawn to a delicate, feminine mask — not unlike his Lady's except the eyes were ice blue instead of empty— fixed in the center of a heavy, tusked skull. The enormous mouth of the skull opened, and he glimpsed blue light like his own while two black eye sockets stared at him on either side of the mask.

Ancestors guide me. Let me make you proud.

Deshi came forward and crouched down, steady on three points and fully visible, glowing brightly. The pose was humble enough but also a position from which he could spring up or forward or backward very easily. "I am the Harrowed of Miurag. Who has summoned me here? I heard a call."

"See? *Told* you," said a slight woman with a strange accent, although she was most certainly speaking a form of Common. "Am in correct place."

"Not Correct If You Cannot Complete My Task," the beast replied.

"This was nearest gate!" she replied, exasperated.

"And The Gate Is *Mine*."

The woman sighed with renewed patience. She wore a dull, brown dress of simple homespun which fell just short of her bare feet. In the mix of shadows and glowing auras, Deshi could not see her face as clearly as the mystical beast nor was she as spectacular to look at.

Her skin was extremely pale, though she possessed a profile unlike any Paxian or Noiri he had ever met, as if she came from a land even farther away than Manalar. Beyond that, while this woman struck him as Human, she had pointed ears somewhat like an Elf, and snow-white hair which belied her young age.

"Who are you, my lady?" he asked.

The woman craned her neck to look up at him with inhuman eyes. They were larger, angled upward a bit like his but far more than merely human. She smiled as if she'd known he was coming all along, her eyes void-black with sparkling flecks of pale blue. "I am the Ancient Child. Can you help me?"

Deshi moved closer, his aura brightening until he could see the shadows of his bones inside his hands and feet as he moved. A slight halo of gold surrounded his vision as he looked directly at the Sphinx, but it faded as he gazed at the small woman who was young and old at once.

"*Hu-xia*, mystic sister," he said with a bow. "You ask in need of help, I will help you."

She chuckled, turning fully to face him. She held the innocent charm of a child when she smiled at him, even as the rest of her was grown. "Thank you, Harrowed of Miurag."

The great beast shifted, gravel crunching and enormous talons scraping the stone, reclaiming Deshi's attention. The tasseled tail whipped side-to-side then curved up and over like a scorpion as the edges of the creature's wings vibrated enough to create a barely audible drone.

"Tread Lightly," the beast said, its dual sets of blue and black eyes fixed on him. "Do You Claim To Take On Her Task, He Who Helps?"

"What does this task get her?" Deshi asked, far behind on what was happening.

The heavy jaw lifted briefly in a contemptuous rise, as if the tusks might spear the swollen, grey clouds above. "I Forgive Her Trespass Through My Gate."

The Ancient Child sighed softly, looking apologetic. "Afraid I did stumble, Harrowed. Thought the Gate was unguarded."

"It Was, Until You Stepped Upon This Plane."

"Why not I see you on the Nexus side?" she asked curiously.

"Because This Is Where I Am."

The Nexus side.

Deshi considered the dun-grey fur on the body and the boney, eyeless head, wondering if this was a creature such as the Roh'ghast coming through a portal like at Manalar? A Gate, they said. His eyes landed on the bare breasts again out of habit but did not linger.

"Um. Has the Ancient Child been sent by a Greylord?" he asked, and the giant head swung toward him again.

"Yes. What Does It Matter?"

"You do not know of the Greylords in the Nexus?"

"I Know. We Are Amongst The Lonely Ones, Yungian. Greylords Have No Claim Here."

So the creature knew exactly where she resided but she was not from here.

"What claim have you on the Lonely Ones of Yung-An?" Deshi asked.

The voice boomed like the threatening clouds above. "The Gate Is Mine To Guard, He Who Helps. None May Say Otherwise."

This part of the discussion sounded final, and Deshi frowned.

"Out of her typical territory?" he asked the Ancient Child, his tone encouraging.

The white-haired maiden spent a moment admiring the creature as she pondered. "Not truly, no. Enough magic given, and Sphinx can go anywhere which pleases it. Much choice out of the Nexus. Once Sphinx chooses, it is chosen."

The Greylands beast deeply expanded her chest in pride, releasing a rumble partway between a purr and a growl. "Indeed, This Is True."

"Trespass must be satisfied," the Ancient Child assured him, "or I cannot go with you."

Go with me?

Deshi shook his head, setting that aside for the moment.

"What is the task that would satisfy you?" he asked Sphinx. "You offered that I could claim it on her behalf."

"You Must Accept, Or Not, To Be Given Said Task."

Again the Harrowed looked toward the pale white woman, this time with a raised eyebrow. "Does she change the rules? Or make them up?"

The Ancient Child grinned in amusement, as if she'd forgotten the danger. "Perhaps long ago. Is fixed habit. Look not for sense."

"And you could not perform the task?"

"Sphinx has not yet given it."

Oh.

Deshi wished for an instant he hadn't been in such a hurry but the very next chastised himself.

I heard her. She called me.

"I accept her task to forgive her trespass regardless, Sphinx. If I fail, she is still allowed to leave, unharried and unharmed."

Sphinx considered with a slow, wide tilt of her head. "If You Fail, You Remain, The Ancient Child Walks. I May Eat You."

Deshi morbidly wondered how he would taste to a beast like this, being what he was? "If I succeed, Sphinx, we both leave your Gate unharried and unharmed."

"*Shrah!* Agreed."

The Harrowed straightened up fully and bowed in the manner of his people, slow and respectful. "Speak your task, Sphinx."

"The Task Is A Riddle And A Gift."

"Uhm. Two tasks?"

"There Are Two Of You."

The strange woman giggled softly and did not seem to be heavily concerned. Why should she be? Deshi had just negotiated her release regardless of what happened.

"I like riddles," the Ancient Child commented. "Hope it is new to me."

"Can she assist?" Deshi asked.

"She Cannot Answer."

"Done!" the white woman agreed promptly, even eagerly. "Let us hear the riddle, Sphinx."

Deshi watched as the creature nodded and settled down onto her belly, folding back those wings not quite like a dragonfly's. Sphinx got quite comfortable before saying anything more. Deshi took the signal to sit as well, taking a slow, centering breath while the Ancient Child hugged her legs in anticipation.

Sphinx began as if telling a story. "Two Princesses Eat Dinner Together. They Both Drink Iced Tea. One Princess Drinks Very Fast, She Drinks Five In The Time It Takes The Other To Drink One. The Princess Who Drinks One Dies While The Other Survives. All The Drinks Were Poisoned."

The pale traveler frowned. "Horrible story."

"Oh? Is My Riddle New Or Old To You, Ancient Child?"

"Both," she answered. "The method new. The story ..." She appeared saddened. "Far too old."

The Greylands beast chuckled and looked at Deshi. "The Answer To My Riddle, Harrowed, Now. Why Did The Princess Who Drank More Iced Tea Survive?"

For a moment, he sat back in Yong-wen with his trainers. They warned him, time and again, if he tried to chase after the answer, he would miss something part of the whole picture. He relaxed his mind and considered the scenario, letting the answer come to him.

"The poison was in the ice," Deshi answered.

Sphinx purred, fixing that dainty mask on him for several long moments. "Correct, Harrowed."

"What?" The Ancient Child blinked at him with her star-black eyes. "You simply *know* this thing?"

Deshi shrugged, both relieved the riddle had been so easy and figuring the youthful woman had not been a killer in her time. "It's a good idea for the right target. Assuming you have observed their dining habits."

"Still a Guildsman," the Sphinx cooed.

"Still horrible story," the Ancient Child repeated.

Deshi's face would have flushed if it were still possible. He sat for a moment, wary of responding to that last comment from Sphinx.

How did she know?

He had already met several spirits who could read thoughts and memories. Perhaps that was how Sphinx chose her riddles, based on a memory?

But it was also logical; the Nexus traveler could have come to the same conclusion, given enough time, except that she hadn't really wanted to think about it.

He cleared his throat. He was half-way to freeing both himself and the new Deathwalker. "You have your Riddle, Sphinx. What about the Gift?"

Another nod. "Obtain For Me An Unbroken Seagull Egg Dipped In Salt Water."

Deshi blinked. Slowly. "Hungry?"

"Before Sunrise."

"Define sunrise. It's so cloudy."

"When The Grey Clouds Match On Both Sides Of My Gate."

Deshi frowned at Sphinx, looking behind the Sphinx into the den, assuming that was where the Gate was. He couldn't see anything but stone. "That's not truly fair. I can't objectively confirm that."

"I can," the Ancient Child offered gently, still sitting on the tiny ledge high on a Yungian mountain. "You have a quarter of the night left, Harrowed."

This took a moment to sink in.

Mule balls!

The Harrowed sprang up and started running back the way he had come, toward the nests he had passed on his way here.

"See you soon!" called the pale mystic behind him.

SPHINX WAS BENDING THE TOP OF A TREE OVER AS SHE PERCHED LOOKING DOWN at him. Her front hands gripped the limb while her rear paws clawed into the bark. She was still in line-of-sight of her Gate, when Deshi returned in the dimmest of the grey dawn, his skin marked by a number of beak stabbings which didn't hurt as much as the gulls had wanted them to.

"I would love to know how you landed up there," Deshi said.

"Another Riddle For Another Time, Perhaps," Sphinx said, and though neither the mask nor the skeletal jaw could smile, the Harrowed heard one in the tone. "Is It Unbroken? Not A Single Crack?"

Balanced on the rocky slope on the balls of his feet, Deshi lifted the egg up in both hands. "To be dipped in salt water, you said."

"Hurry, Harrowed!" he heard the pale woman call through the trees. "Sphinx distracts you!"

The Greylands beast purred. "Try Not To Break Your Chin As Well As The Egg."

Deshi was soon crawling down toward the waves. As he got closer, he realized this would be the final tribute to his ancestors; he would touch all four bodies of water on all four sides of his country.

My ancestors strengthen me.

The waves of the Storm Sea coast were brutal indeed. He could only be thankful a full squall hadn't yet brewed this grey and dreary dawn. He did not break his chin when the first wave consumed him, but he did swallow some salt water and slip from his single handhold on the rocks. The waves grabbed his legs and heaved backward, trying to draw him out into the surf. His body was raked across several lengths of beaten, pitted rocks.

Hia-Yo!

Deshi nearly crushed the egg in his fist; he instantly feared drowning. The salt water had him retching beyond control as he clutched one last handhold but was soon covered by a second wave. His ears filled and water roared dully; he lifted the egg above his head, holding it in a cage pressing his fingers together but allowing the egg to shift where the water pushed it without leaving his hand.

I can't breathe … ! I need air!

Jun's gifted light dimmed in the surf without air!

His limbs seized up and strained to their limit to hold him to the rock wall as the wave retreated, trying once more to pull him down with it. Gasping one precious breath, he scrambled as fast as he could to crawl just beyond the reach of the next.

He coughed, expelled more salt and water, and inhaled deeply.

"Harrowed! It's almost dawn!"

Deshi glanced at the egg in the cage of his right hand. *Still whole.*

His aura flared as he hauled himself straight up the cliff in ways his Guild brothers could not manage even with spells. The fingers of his left hand were broken by the brutal twists of the ocean's attack but still worked. His legs pushed him up in bounding rises which should have required a levitation spell or two. He bled still from pecking, abrasions, and gashes, his ankle twisted at one point which would have put any other man down for weeks, yet he kept going, his body unfailing when he needed it.

Once he'd hauled himself over the edge, Deshi hustled back into the thick vegetation, somewhat protected from the now-falling rain. He wasn't shivering, though the deep ocean was frigidly cold. Sphinx was still on the tree above, but he ran straight for the Gate and the white-haired woman. The creature of puzzles turned and glided back toward her Gate, drifting above him without a single sound or a single stroke of her ill-formed wings.

Sphinx landed first on her hind legs just ahead of him before those strange, inhuman hands touched the rock. She looked ahead and back again, comparing the grey of each side as Deshi literally fell to one knee before her and lifted the egg cradled in his own two palms. He glanced at the pale oval to be sure.

"Not a single crack," he croaked.

Out of the corner of his eye saw the Ancient Child smiling and clasping her hands in joy. He didn't have to ask or to wait to be told, because she knew.

He'd made it in time.

"Mmm. Well Done."

Sphinx lowered her great head, bringing that strange mask down level with his gold-rimmed eyes. Deshi focused on the solid blue gaze in the mask itself rather than the black, empty sockets to either side of it. The huge, tusked jaw opened, revealing that otherworldly glow once again, and jutted out like a shelf.

Deshi presumed she was asking him to place the egg there, so he did. It rolled in and disappeared as Sphinx closed her mouth; he heard no crunch of shell at all, and the beast did not chew, swallowing it whole.

"My Task Is Complete," said Sphinx. "Trespass Is Forgiven. Be Wary, Shunraeki, Should You Come This Way Again."

"Thank you!" The Ancient Child quickly rose to her feet and held out her hands to Deshi. She wanted to leave, and he believed they should. *Right now.*

With broken bones and red wounds vivid against his greyish-brown skin, the Harrowed encouraged the smaller traveler to climb onto his back and cling there.

"Let us get you safe and far from here," he said.

CHAPTER 5

3100 S.E., THE LONELY ONES, COAST OF THE SEA OF STORMS

THE SMALL WOMAN'S AURA SHONE BRIGHT WHITE AS SHE SPOKE OF HAPPY THINGS, somehow making the Lonely Ones less forbidding as the rain eventually stopped and the clouds began to thin. This decidedly Human woman with Elven ears was beautiful, mature, and persistently optimistic. She enjoyed his company for what it was and asked no intrusive questions.

She made him forget they both looked so strange.

"I am sorry I cannot help you heal, Deshi," she said once again.

"It is alright, Shunraeki."

"I can make a poultice, perhaps. Maybe use your shirt to wrap those wounds?"

He smiled, simply happy to have her company as he completed his trek. "It won't really help but thank you."

Their conversation became easier in Common. She was a fast learner, as if she only needed the exposure to adjust her speech. As if she had done it many times before. Would he be doing that exactly over the centuries? Learning the "new" ways of speech from those younger than him?

"May I ask, lady," he began, when they stopped for a time. "Were you of spirit kin even before you died? Or only after?"

Her smile was slow and pleasant, her eyes drifting as the blue specks began to coalesce in the center. "I don't understand. My father was Human,

I remember him. But there are many spirits, Deshi, and we are all kin in a way. Even Humans are spirits, you know? We all have a Name."

Humans are spirits, too?

Once beyond that distraction, Deshi noted that she did not answer his question. He may not know if those were Elven ears or some other creature.

So be it.

He studied one of the cuts in his flesh. The barest itching sensation arose as it worked to close. He would heal faster if he was allowed to drink life's breath, but he still felt Jun's generosity giving him strength. With enough time, he would heal even if he did not find a living spirit immediately.

"Where is it you must go to next?" he asked when the Ancient Child had been staring off into the distance for several minutes.

"Hm?" she blinked. "Oh. I must go to Manalar. Do you know the way?"

Deshi felt his middle tighten in remembered misery. "May I ask why? The war is ... over."

Worry pinched her eyebrows. "Am I too late?"

"For what?"

"For the new God Warrior? I heard ... I mean ..." She ran fingers through brilliant white hair. "Oh, what was his name?"

The young man felt the impulse to swallow despite himself. "Willven Isboern?"

"Yes!" she cried, hands clapping. "Yes, that is he! The Brother's Warrior, Isboern. He's not dead, is he?"

"Um. Not when I last saw him."

"Then I must meet him. Alive." She looked around the temperate forest as touches of blue spread in the sky above them. "But ... It has been a long time. I need you to show me the way, Harrowed." She blinked at him. "Please?"

A numbness encroached as if he had dived once again into the sea to drown. To go back so soon? When Sho'shien, Janshi, and the Dragon Spirit are all gone.

"I ... could," he began.

"But will you?"

He breathed.

"What's wrong, Deshi?"

"Manalar is my ... death place," he said. "I died there during the war." He paused as Shunraeki stared at him, wide-eyed. "The most recent war."

"Oh! I ..." The small woman placed a hand over her heart. "I am glad to know that. My ... my, uh, father has died there as well. Several times."

Deshi did a double take. "What? Several ... ?"

Ridiculously, she smiled. "Don't ask how many! That city, I swear, draws the strangest events!"

On a deep exhale, the Harrowed finally asked. "Who is your father, Shunraeki?"

Whose daughter have I saved from getting eaten by a Sphinx?

Her warm smile remained though it carried a hint of mourning Deshi found all too familiar. "Cris-ri-phon, son of Begir-al-phon, once of the Third Zauyrian Realm of the Red Desert, where I was born."

The Red Desert ... ?

She was a native to Miurag and had come back? How?

And why?

He grumbled, "We could stand farther away from the Red Desert only by returning to World's End."

"But I'm *not* going to the Desert," she insisted. "I must go to Manalar."

"Just to see Isboern?"

Shunraeki shook her head adamantly, her hair shining as true sunlight pierced through the thick trees. Some of it touched her pale skin, which then began to darken.

"*Hsst!*" Deshi sucked in, caught by surprise. *Like Sho'shien ...*

"What?" She looked around for danger. "What is it?"

"Step ... uh, step with me over here, please?"

Deshi took her arm gently, guiding her into a rare, full sun patch in the damp forest. Shunraeki's dark spots spread at once, until all her visible skin turned pitch black, though her hair remained snow-white. Her Davrin Elf blood could not be more apparent to him.

And yet …

If Deshi's heart could still pumped, he would have heard its beat in his ears right then. Her mystical eyes finally grew defined, the sclera black while her pupils illuminated an icy blue.

Like Sho'shien, crossed over from the Nexus.

"Are you a Deathwalker of legend?" the Harrowed asked. "The guides who once came out of the Desert Realms?"

The Ancient Child smiled with open joy, clasping her hands. "I am! Yes!"

Within the briefest private moment, Deshi relented. "Then I will take you to Manalar. I will make certain you arrive safely."

She bounced on her feet. "Thank you, Deshi! I need your help!"

He smiled ruefully. "May I ask what the purpose is besides meeting the Captain?"

"Of course, Harrowed." She nodded with a charming formality she must have learned from another Elf. "My purpose is …" She paused, choosing the words. "To do what I can to help these lands when the Deathless returns again."

The Deathless.

And now, his daughter. Might she help put him to rest?

With a deep breath, Deshi bowed to her. "I understand, my lady."

As last.

"And I am honored to escort you."

"Thank you, Harrowed! Whew!" She hugged him, her relief wrapping him up like a warm blanket. "Oh, I knew you were a brave soul when you answered my call!" Stepping back, she smiled at him with a Deathwalker's eyes. "Could we discuss protection as well? Perhaps as my bodyguard for a time? Until I get used to the world where I am now."

He smiled back, for a moment feeling weightless. "Of course, we may discuss it."

Thank you, Most Compassionate Lady.

Have you picked up the Tales of Miurag anthologies: The Desert and The Deepearth? at https://etaski.com/tales-of-miurag/ Read about secrets lost in the ancient Queens of V'Gedra, and the entanglements of Valsharess with the Black Dragon.

Join my Patreon to read the next anthology early: The Dragonchild at https://www.patreon.com/c/etaski. It takes a village to raise a To'vah-krav. Six tales all linked to Mourn, the half-blood who has our Davrin heroine's back!

Visit Etaski's series lore at World Anvil! at https://miurag.etaski.com

I also have fantasy maps, timelines, and a glossary! Read extra tidbits about the characters and places in the story.

ACKNOWLEDGMENTS

My most humble thanks to my friends supporting me:

Eris Adderly, Axelotl, Dark Pulse, NecrosisBob, Pastor of Muppets, RainbowNight, Tone, and Vox Verina. Much love and gratitude, today and tomorrow, with my Hubs.

Special appreciation for Doc Kangey, the anchoring presence working behind the scenes. Check out our hard work and lore yet to come at Etaski.com & Miurag.Etaski.com

THANK YOU! My Top Patrons who support all my efforts to see extra stories written to flesh the world out further!

Korfitz, Chris R., NotSoWeird, Pastor of Muppets, SirCumference, Axelotl, Jesse C., Does, John K., Julie S., Paul B., Carla H., Briana R., Josanna, Ryan D., RainbowNight, Lesley PLAY, Leonard, Kalculyszero, Zenor , Kelly D., Raymond T., Johnathon Matlock, Daolord, Bradley L., Roy Meyer, Brian P., Tessa, TheQuietOne, and Elizabeth Cossette.

ABOUT THE AUTHOR

Etaski has entertained herself with fantasy stories since the first day she sat on a school bus looking out the window. When hand-written letters were disappearing, she scribbled no less than five pages to be worth the postage. Her early stories were written by hand, and she had a writer's callus and three embarrassing novels before graduating high school.

She studied science, archaeology, history, and theater. Frank discussion of sexuality was rare growing up, so she wrote fantasies, theories, and observations within stories for deeper contemplation or just be entertained.

History speaks little on sexuality, yet biology demonstrates how it sways basic choices. Drama reveals our strongest bonds but may fade to black at its most intimate. In the Sister Seekers, the sex and the story are inseparable, and their discoveries will change the journey of Miurag without cutting away.

Etaski's Website: etaski.com
Etaski's Book Page: etaski.com/sister-seekers
Etaski's Series Lore: miurag.etaski.com
Etaski on Patreon: www.patreon.com/etaski
Etaski on GoodReads: www.goodreads.com/etaski
Etaski on BookBub: www.bookbub.com/authors/a-s-etaski
Etaski on Facebook: www.facebook.com/asetaski
Etaski on Mastodon: mastodon.online/@etaski

www.ingramcontent.com/pod-product-compliance
Lightning Source LLC
Chambersburg PA
CBHW052023020726
47501CB00004B/1218